ROSALIE'S APPLE TREE

ROSALIE'S APPLE TREE

ANN GARCIA

River Blossoms Press
Bay City MI
riverblossoms.com

ISBN 978-1-7372735-3-0 (paperback)
ISBN 978-1-7372735-4-7 (ebook)
Library of Congress Control Number
2023908719

for my parents, who showed me how to fly
&
for those who told me to keep going

"Even if I knew that tomorrow the world would go to pieces, I would still plant my apple tree."

— MARTIN LUTHER

Prologue
Three Years Ago

If you have a heart, which you must, you'll grant me this wish. My one desire. Please love my men like the mother and wife I'd always hoped to be.

Rosalie Ambrosia Keller

Part One
Reunion
May of This Year

ONE

KATRINA

The whole idea was ridiculous, yet there she was—sitting at a table along the back wall of Greene's Steak House—about to have a dinner date with a man who hadn't seen her in fifteen years. A man who lived nearly two hours from her home, which was too far away. A man who'd buried a wife three years ago, which was too sad. A man who had a child, which was too uncertain. A man who most likely had baggage, which was...

Baggage. It was this that scared her most. Baggage led to hurt and she couldn't deal with any more hurt. Her own baggage had been enough. She'd dealt with it. She'd moved on. She was happy. Secure. *Free*.

And she wasn't prepared to tell him why she'd come. Even worse, she wasn't prepared for any sort of relationship, especially a long-distance one. All she knew was that lust was driving her mad.

The dreams were to blame. Dreams of his five o'clock

shadow nearly brushing the back of her thigh. Of his long-lashed eyes drinking in the length of her legs. Of his lips nearly grazing her neck. Near, but never touching.

Oh yes. His lips. There was something about Aaron Keller's lips that made her want to open wide and let him taste. Heart pattering, she bit the inside of her cheek to stifle such thoughts. Aaron hadn't seen her in fifteen years and what she was doing was crazy.

Wasn't it?

She'd achieved everything: a Ph.D., her own home, a kick-ass dog. Life was predictable. *Safe.* And at age thirty-five, venturing over her emotional walls was the stupidest thing she could do. It was a risk. And she was *not* a risk-taker.

She shouldn't have come.

Dreams were just dreams. They didn't actually *mean* anything, but the damn things had become a constant distraction. She needed them to stop, and an in-person visit seemed the only way to make that happen.

So there she was, sitting in Greene's, maintaining composure while fear of all the unknowns danced with lusts and anticipations that had been building for who knows how long. As she'd learned to do by age six, she took a slow breath to calm the confusion of feelings she was reigning in.

After repeating the exercise several times, her pulse slowed.

It was foolish to hold hope this could end well. After all, life had taught her that men were neither trustworthy nor necessary. Well, men were necessary for one thing, of course, but for nothing else.

She wasn't the woman who *needed* a man; she was Dr. Katrina Lopez, the woman who remained alone.

She was happy to be...alone.

Wasn't she?

It had been eleven years since she and Connor split. And

because she didn't trust men, it had been eleven years since she'd had sex. Not because she didn't have opportunities. And she wasn't a prude. Hell no. Vibrators were her salvation. She hadn't had sex for one simple reason. She was scared —always scared of the inevitable hurt that followed attachment—and this frightened part of her was strong. It had lived in her nervous system since she could remember, constantly ready to wreak havoc whenever her brain sensed danger or abandonment or judgment or whatever it decided was an attack.

This was why she didn't *need*.

This was why she didn't *want*.

This was why she tucked herself away in an independent life.

But the dreams, damn them—they were beautiful and sexy and everything she didn't want because they would lead to hurt.

The dreams were the only reason she was sitting there, waiting for the man she'd once turned down for a date because she'd been in love with Connor, the second man to destroy her belief in the fairy tale that marriage was supposed to be.

"May I get you anything, Miss?"

She tore her gaze from the door, asked the waiter to bring a Bloody Mary—because a Bloody Mary sounded good right then—and waited.

She had nothing to fear. It was Aaron. He knew her. Kind of. Maybe.

Not really.

Playground chases and pulled pigtails did *not* qualify as anything more than acquaintance. Never mind he used to play with her hair during story time in second grade. Never mind he always smiled at her during passing time in high school. Never mind he asked her for a date. Twice. Never mind the mind-blowing dreams. And never mind her white-hot desire to strip him down to nothing so she could have her way with his—

Oh man. More memories of yesterday. It was just about twenty-four hours ago that she'd finally done it. She'd pushed through her rioting nerves to ring the doorbell of his massive traditional two-story home. And when he answered? He stood there—in the door way—with nipples showing through the near-dripping white fabric plastered to his spectacular v-shaped torso. Nipples. That memory alone had made her wet all day. To top it off, his dark-blonde crew cut was cut sharp, just like his five-o'clock shadow. He was masculinity at its best.

But the memory that melted her most was how his long-lashed bright blues looked into her with an intensity that stirred lifelong yearnings and an age of dreams. His gaze had always given her a sweet moment of calm amid the storm that was her life as a child. And yesterday, his gaze birthed lustful sensations that threaded through her belly and into her loins where they tugged tight her desires just like in the dreams that had been haunting her—day and night—for over a year.

AARON

Since he'd started dating again, life taught Aaron that women fell into one of three categories: 1) zero sexual chemistry, 2) resentment that his three-year-old, Isaac, always came first, or 3) refusal to accept a child with Down syndrome altogether. Category 1 had never been an issue in regard to Katrina, but Categories 2 and 3 were risks that had Aaron bundled in tension.

Every morning, when he lifted Isaac from his crib, Aaron's chest did a tensing and releasing thing. Something about the morning routine reminded Aaron that Isaac would eventually be an adult with no brothers or sisters to love him or care for him, a probability that squeezed Aaron's chest to the point of discomfort. He knew it was ridiculous to predict a grim future for Isaac because many people with Down syndrome grew up to live quite independent lives, but what if Isaac's delays were big ones? What if he needed lifelong supervision? Who would protect him? Who would be sure his needs were met? And, worst of all, what would happen to Isaac after Aaron died, too?

But the moment he tucked Isaac's tiny body against his chest for a morning cuddle, Aaron reminded himself that Isaac was only three and there was still time. Aaron had trained his mind to reroute from its destructive path in order to make the tension release, which was proof he'd come a long way toward recovery since Isaac was born.

Isaac, the long-awaited gift left behind by Rose, Aaron's first and only wife, was top priority, and it was vital for Aaron to remember this fact. In moments, he would be facing a possibility he'd neither hoped for nor imagined—a possibility named Katrina Lopez. Aaron's determination reminded him he'd have to say goodbye to this possibility if she proved herself to belong to Categories 2 or 3. And for Aaron, saying goodbye to Katrina Lopez was unfathomable.

When she'd shown up at his house—unannounced—just twenty-four hours ago, he thickened with a sexual energy he'd never known. It was a foreign sort of attraction, heavy with a protectiveness that filled him like it used to when they were kids and she looked up at him with a gaze too fervent for the little girl she was at the time. Hers was an intense gaze that always urged him to pull her close and hold tight.

But he never did.

As he'd stood in his doorframe, unable to formulate anything sensible to say, he savored the sight of his long-lost crush standing on his porch. She never used to wear eyeglasses, but now dark frames accentuated the rings encircling her irises that still hadn't decided whether they wanted to be green or brown. Gentle waves of dark brown hair rested next to the dip in her snug olive V-neck sweater, and she still had his two favorite things—wrapped in tight black jeans and standing atop black heels, they were the epitome of sexy-professional-casual.

Yes, a few minutes on his doorstep was all it took for Katrina Lopez to command his attention around the clock. She'd even danced for him in last night's dreams, which intensified everything he'd always imagined about being with her.

Dreams. They were a cruel unreality most of the time, weren't they? An entity that enjoyed messing with the man inside himself. The man broken by loss and mental illness. The man he wouldn't allow to take a seat at Katrina's table.

Isaac, who was home with Grandma, was the reason for this date. Aaron swore he'd never enter a relationship with a toxic woman, so he prayed Katrina would prove herself to be safe because Isaac was top priority.

As Aaron stood next to the podium where the hostess was busy with another Greene's patron, he repeated his mantra: *Isaac is my priority.* He drew a breath as he scanned the interior of Greene's. After a handful of unsteady heartbeats, he found Katrina sitting at a table along the back wall of the restaurant, so he left the hostess and thanked heaven for this opportunity.

Katrina held his gaze as he approached.

As he always had as a little boy, Aaron felt her. She was intensity, and her gaze was a plea. Something inside her was longing, and he wished to set it free.

Each step closer became heavier with a hope he was afraid to embrace. It was a hope he didn't want to mistake as his future.

KATRINA

Gentle self-confidence in a light blue dress shirt, top button undone, and sleeves rolled to the elbow, Aaron Keller was making his way across the room. Finally. Their first date had arrived.

Katrina's head was a little light, but she forced herself to hold his gaze as he and his tanned arms approached the table. She rose from her seat with the confidence to be expected of a woman in heels. Nobody would've known she was battling a light head, racing heart, and urges to ogle his arms. And pelvis.

She offered a handshake, but he pulled her into his chest, gave her the hug she'd craved since forever, and whispered into her ear, "We're old friends. No need for formality."

His words shot down to her center as her face nuzzled his neck and her body pressed into him a little too much maybe. Oh man. He felt perfect and smelled fine. Sweet and woodsy. All man. And he wasn't letting go, so she held on tight.

Yeah, he could keep holding her forever.

Forever would be alright.

"It's great to see you again, Katrina." She took this as a cue to release him even though he held onto her a little longer.

She stepped back to find those long eyelashes, but she couldn't resist a glimpse of his chest where nipples were hiding behind the crisp cotton. Couldn't she just—

"Shall we?"

Her gaze snapped to his face, which was smiling widely as he motioned to their seats.

The waiter arrived with her drink, took Aaron's drink order, and reviewed the evening's special with them, but she didn't care. She had to get her head together.

"So, you're in town for a conference. What sort of conference is it?" His eyes were soft, sincere, much more relaxed than they had been yesterday.

She drew a long breath and hoped for the best. "It's an assessment conference. I teach psychology at Great Lakes Community College where I'm one of the campus leaders in assessment. Today, I presented on classroom assessment techniques."

"Did your presentation go well?"

"It went very well. Thank you for asking." Not sounding stupid was helping her nerves settle down a bit. "And how was your day?"

He smiled. "Less intellectual than yours. I did yard work."

Her body was relaxing, so she took a sip of her drink, welcoming the bite. "Really? I envy you. I would've loved to be outside today. It was a perfect day and I was stuck in a conference center."

He chuckled. "You envy I was doing yard work?"

"Yes, I love yard work. I have a century-old farmhouse that sits on four acres, which I tend myself. I work outside any minute I can spare on days like today, and, if the weather is nice, I plan to prep my vegetable garden next Saturday."

His eyes widened. "You take care of four acres on your own?"

"Absolutely." She took another sip of her drink while reminding herself that most men wouldn't believe such a truth about a rather polished woman. Taking care of four acres alone was physical and challenging. "I love to work with the earth. It helps me connect with nature. Gives me peace. On the rare occasions I need a man's help, I call my neighbor, Jeff, or my brother, who lives nearby."

He gave her a nod. "I see."

"Well good." She flared her eyes for emphasis because this part of her was precious. Working outside—in sun or rain—

released internal knots tightened by everyday stressors. It helped lower her emotional walls, which stood rather high—but not as high as they used to. In terms of nurturing her emotional health, only one thing was more effective than working outside. And it wasn't sex.

He watched her with what seemed to be playful unstated things dancing on his lips, so she bit her lip to see how he'd respond. When he looked at her mouth, she winked.

He leaned forward. "I'm curious what gives you peace during the winter months."

She leaned forward, pleased with his flirtatious eyes. "My primary winter hobbies include dancing, reading, and walking with my German Shepherd, Jake."

He leaned back and watched her again.

That five o'clock shadow looked tempting. Would he like to brush it against the back of her knee sometime? Because she would like that.

Very much.

Oh man. She pressed her arousal into her seat while she grabbed her drink. "Let's go back to the yard work for a minute. Your yard is gorgeous. Do you tend it all by yourself or do you have a service, too?"

"Thank you. I do it myself. Gives me an escape. I guess that's something we have in common. Enjoying the outdoors."

The waiter delivered Aaron's pop and asked if they were ready to order. Eyes committed to Katrina, Aaron informed the waiter they'd need a little while yet, which was fine with her. His focus on her felt glorious.

She set down her glass. "So, what do you like to do when you aren't busy with yard work?"

"Basketball. Lift. Run. During the winter, I go sledding—snowmobiling—if I get a chance. Most of my time is dedicated to work and my son, Isaac."

Yes. Isaac. His name was in the obituary she'd found after convincing herself she could handle looking Aaron up. An uncomfortable combination of relief and sorrow plagued her for weeks following the discovery that Aaron was a widower.

But the child—the obituary didn't reveal anything beyond his name. Out of respect for privacy, she hadn't snooped birth records. Did Aaron have a sullen teen? Regardless of age, was this only child spoiled? Had there been other women creating a nasty step-mother vibe in the years since Isaac's mother died? Was he kind? Spiteful? Happy? Depressed? These were sick thoughts, but they were real. Fears. Of *baggage*.

Yes, Katrina was a contradiction. Forever afraid of the very thing that made her who she was.

AARON

"I'm aware your wife passed away. I saw her obituary when I looked you up." Katrina's eyes were warm and comforting. "Rosalie was her name, wasn't it? I'm sorry for your loss."

"Thank you." Darkness shifted inside him, so Aaron took a long drink to buy himself time because he didn't want to talk about Rose. He set his glass on the table. "I don't see a ring. You ever marry?"

She shook her head like the idea was repulsive. "I was engaged for a while, but things fell apart. I guess I'm one of those rare 35-year-old females who have never been married and have no children. They should bronze me." Her eyes widened with enlightenment. "Or maybe I could join the circus as a sideshow."

A laugh escaped him in spite of the odd mixture of relief and disappointment fingering its way into his gut. She never married, which meant he lost time. "May I ask why the engagement fell apart?"

"Seriously?"

Unsure whether he really wanted to know the answer to his question, he nodded.

She let out a long breath. "Connor and I started dating during freshman year at Michigan State. We were very serious by junior year and got engaged during senior year. I moved to University of Wisconsin for graduate school. He remained at State for med school. As time went on, I began to feel it wasn't going to work."

Disappointment growing, Aaron waited while she took a break for a drink. It sounded like she broke it off with Connor, which was a good thing. Pushing away a med student meant she was independent enough to walk away from future money.

Her gaze returned to his. "He was going to be a terrific physician. A cardiologist. I wanted a man who would love me and, someday, our children more than he loved his career, but it was clear to me that his career would always be more important. He couldn't deny it. We said goodbye on good terms."

A friendly parting that left her single all these years? What a waste.

The waiter couldn't have arrived at a better time. Given neither of them had looked at the menu, she suggested they keep it simple and order the special. He didn't argue with that. She was decisive and she ate steak—his kind of woman.

"Aaron, do you remember asking me out when we ran into each other that one day?"

Shit. How could he forget? Her refusal was so immediate. So sweet. So *uninterested*. He knew he never had a chance. Not then. But now...

He slid his hand to the center of the table in request for hers, which was delicate compared to his. He liked delicate. No. He liked *her*. Her soft skin under his thumb was like a shot of whiskey, making his insides all warm and quiet, so he stroked and savored it. "To be truthful, I remember it like yesterday."

"Well." Her voice was meek. "Now you know why I said no to your request. I was with Connor at the time."

His hand released hers because his darkness took a turn, giving him a flicker of emotional pain deep inside. Until three years ago, he'd been mentally healthy. And fifteen years ago, he was a different man. Katrina's rejection was nothing more than a disappointment. Nothing to lose sleep over. Nothing to hurt over. Nothing of significance. She was just an incredibly beautiful woman who said no to a date. It didn't matter how much he felt for her because she felt nothing back. She said no and that was that. He got over it. No biggie. In fact, if he'd known she was dating another guy, he'd have respected her for turning him down because it was the right thing to do. But now...

Mental disorder is irrational. It doesn't make sense. All it does is hurt.

His darkness took this news of Connor and, in an instant, turned it against Aaron. It infused his mind with regretful ideas like...if this date happened fifteen years ago...if he'd held her hand ages ago...if he'd have given her that hug long ago...if he'd married her...everything would be different. Better. No loss. No heartache. No demon inside his head.

But that would've meant no Rose.

And no Isaac.

These ideas sickened him—tightening his throat and pulling tension to his eyes—right in front of Katrina.

She grabbed her drink. "So, I already mentioned I have a dog. Do you and Isaac have any pets?" She plucked an olive from the cocktail spear and popped it into her mouth in what appeared to be an attempt to lighten the mood.

He smiled in spite of his darkness. He smiled for *her*. "No pets. Too much work."

"Yes, they are a lot of work. My Jake keeps me on my toes, but I wouldn't have it any other way. So when you have the time, you enjoy yard work, sledding, basketball, running, and working out. Where does the rest of your time go?"

He sighed, unable to match the bounce she was bringing to the conversation. The mere thought of where all his time went exhausted him. Being a single father of a son with special needs was a full-time job all its own. There was always something to take care of. Diapers. Medicine. Bathing. Dressing. Meals. Messes. Preschool. Bedtime. If it weren't for curbside grocery pick-up and an innate drive to clean his house as he used it, Aaron wouldn't have time to rest. His only respite during the week was Tuesday evenings when Isaac spent the night with Rose's parents so Aaron could play basketball with his buddies.

But Katrina didn't need to know any of that. Not *yet*, anyway. "I'm a physical therapist. I own a few clinics in the area. Running the business and maintaining a patient load for myself keep me busy. Weekends are the only days I have a chance to relax."

She beamed. "Well, I'm really happy you're spending some of your precious weekend with me."

But the pleasure he found in her words was cut short when his peripheral vision caught a large figure moving toward their table. Foreboding hit him, so he took a proper look. A man that could be mistaken for himself was making a beeline for Katrina. He had short blonde hair, fierce blue eyes, and muscles defined behind a white polo shirt, but Katrina had no clue because her eyes were closed for some reason.

It took all Aaron had to remain still when this interloper leaned on the table and placed his right hand on Katrina's shoulder.

KATRINA

"Hey, Kat, I've been looking for you all afternoon." Cam Stevens was leaning on the table, his free hand massaging Katrina's shoulder. "When you're done here, why don't you join us?" He gestured to a group of college faculty she hadn't noticed sitting together on the opposite side of the restaurant.

Oh no. Out of her control, her heart pumped blistering fuel for her response, as it did every time her brain perceived a threat—whether real, imagined, reasonable, or irrational. Every part of her was ready for a fight, but she had to keep her temper. She had to keep her wits. She glared at Stevens. "You better get your hand off me."

He released her shoulder and stepped back.

She stood and gestured for Aaron to stand as well. "Cam Stevens, this is a very old friend of mine, Aaron Keller." Her words cut the air as they flew. "Aaron, this is Cam who, unfortunately for me, is a colleague. He tends to run around and I bet he has a girlfriend back home while he's here brazenly interrupting us."

Her glare pierced Stevens who was standing there, hands on hips, sending daggers right back at her.

She dropped into her chair and busied herself with the celery in her drink. Stevens. Damn him.

She sensed the men shaking hands.

After a curt, "I apologize for the interruption," Stevens walked away.

She sensed Aaron taking his seat, but she didn't look because a tear had forced itself out of her eye. Why did this have to happen? Her luck, of course. She dodged Stevens all day only for him to show up and fuck up her first date with Aaron? Shit. Anything to make life difficult.

She wiped the tear and forced herself to look. "I'm sorry

about that. I don't think he'll ever do that again. At least not to me."

Aaron stared at her, his face blank.

Her heart drummed a directive, pressing her to explain. "He's a philandering colleague who's been trying to get into my pants for the past few years. It's never going to happen. I'm thinking this little episode tonight might have gotten through to him. You know, because I was kind of mean to him—no...I was a lot mean to him. And I'm mortified."

Shit.

Shit.

Shit.

Aaron was still staring at her with no expression.

What were the chances? Of all things that could've gone wrong, why did it have to be Stevens? Beautiful and talented Stevens—the only man who'd succeeded in kindling what Connor left untended. Stevens—her perfect match except for his major flaw. The man couldn't wait for sex, and Dr. Lopez wouldn't have sex without trust. Sorry, Stevens. You lost.

But Aaron wasn't speaking. He was still staring—at her—expressionless. She must've sounded like such a bitch. Surely, he'd walk out on her, a thought that made her heart drum louder.

Tears would soon fall in earnest, but she managed to speak. "Okay, Aaron, if the date is over, I understand." She looked at her hands wringing in her lap. "Please say something."

Her breathing stopped.

Please stay. After so many years of wondering, please stay.

It couldn't end like this. Not over Stevens. Not. Over. Stevens.

"I like a woman who stands up for herself."

Oh god. She looked up and found encouraging eyes. "But I was so mean to him."

Aaron folded his arms on the table and leveled his eyes with hers. "He was acting like an asshole, so you treated him like one. Well done."

"An asshole, huh?" Her hands stopped wringing. "You don't know how long I've been discouraging him. And he kept pursuing and pursuing." A shaky laugh escaped her. "I hope that was the grand finale."

Aaron shook his head. "I can't believe those words came out of your mouth. Very well done."

"Neither can I," she lied. She'd always been a direct and truthful person. So much so that some people considered her to be antisocial. But she wasn't antisocial. Quiet? Yes. Introverted? Yes. But not antisocial. Being direct and truthful was a protective mechanism. She didn't skate around topics that could ultimately hurt her if people weren't clear on her stance. She wouldn't let anyone take advantage of her. She wouldn't let anyone misunderstand her—if she could help it. She wouldn't let anyone hurt her. So, she stated harsh truths even when people didn't want to hear them. She was *honest*.

In an attempt to lighten the mood, she held up her glass and quipped, "Clearly, this Mary isn't a virgin."

He laughed.

"Seriously, Aaron, I'm a pretty tough pill for most to swallow. I tend to be quite assertive, especially when I'm confronted like that. I feared you might walk out on me."

He placed his hand in the center of the table in another request for hers. "Now that wouldn't be gentlemanly. Would it?"

His words sent her belly into a somersault. "I know you're the gentleman. You always were." She gave her hand and he massaged it, tracing her fingers one at a time, orchestrating a symphony of feelings that swirled and flipped inside her.

Yes, this was the way it was supposed to be. The two of them together.

This explained the dreams. All doubt was erased.

"So, you danced in college?"

She swallowed the last of her wine as the waiter cleared their dishes. The meal was delicious and she was riding high on the fact that their conversation had flown without any turbulence whatsoever. He was as beautiful on the inside as she'd always imagined. A kindred spirit.

"Yeah," she replied. "I danced in the company at MSU all four years. And I made the company at UW, so I danced there for two years before my schedule got too busy. My position at GLCC allows me to use the studio, so I dance several times a week these days. Music kind of lives inside me and someday I'd like to learn piano. I have melodies in my head I'd like to play. Someday."

Aaron finished his pop. "How long have you been dancing?"

"Since I was five."

He cleared his throat. "What type of dance do you do?"

Odd. His gaze was rather intense for such a simple question. If she didn't know better, she'd say it was on fire. It was kind of making her feel naked. She'd have loved to show him some skin, right then and there, but they hadn't yet discussed his stance on one of the only risks she enjoyed: exhibitionism.

Anyway, if he'd seen the dance she did for him last night, he'd know. Did he dream that little dream, too? She stifled the smile triggered by her secrets. "Contemporary dance is my favorite. Feels like flying."

"Contemporary." He spoke the word as if it had significance, which was a good sign. Maybe he enjoyed the arts, too. "I got curious this morning," he continued, "so I looked you up. Found your bio on GLCC's website. You're an expert in special education. Is that right, Dr. Lopez?"

She laughed. "Well, I'm not an expert, but I earned a specialist's degree in educational psychology prior to entering the Ph.D. program in clinical psych."

Aaron lifted an eyebrow.

Of course, he wasn't fooled. And it felt nice to share her accomplishments with him. When they were little, nobody would've predicted she'd someday be a doctor. "Well, I guess you could say I have expertise in special education."

He nodded. "Which means you know a lot about children with disabilities, right?"

"Yes. I studied educational psychology because I didn't have the best start in life, which played out in a not-so-good way during elementary school. I wanted to know how to help kids succeed. Then I decided to pursue the clinical degree in order to have more options in terms of career. I'm very happy teaching, but I can work for a hospital, open my own practice, or practice in the schools. Options are important. They give me security."

He smiled. "I'm impressed. You've done well for yourself."

"As have you." She smiled back.

The waiter arrived with the check, so she nabbed her card from her clutch and handed it to him. As he walked away, she returned her focus to Aaron only to find that all symptoms of his smile were gone.

"You aren't playing nice. I should've paid."

His words weren't playful. The fact that he seemed dead serious coaxed out fear she'd tucked away since the Stevens episode a little while ago.

She'd paid on auto-pilot.

She always paid because she was always out...alone.

But what kind of guy gets upset over a woman paying anyway?

He was not a stereotypical jerk.

Was he?

He had to be kidding, so she cocked her head in an effort to make light of his comment. "*You* should have paid? According to whose rules?"

But his smile was nowhere to be found and it became clear. In *his* opinion, she fucked up.

"Well, I guess I should thank Dr. Lopez for dinner."

The chill in his voice pricked her. Maybe the confidence she'd been feeling over the past hour had been a mistake? Maybe it was the wine?

No. It was her. Brazen, frightened, strong, contradictory Dr. Katrina Lopez who was too independent for her own good, like always. She stared at her clutch as she moved it into her lap, loathing the hammer inside her chest as it drilled a reminder that she needed to protect herself. He was liable to reject her, and she needed to be strong.

She forced a smile and looked up. "You're welcome, Mr. Keller."

But his focus on her was gone. He was busy typing something into his cell phone, which she hadn't seen in his possession all night. He pulled out the phone after she paid the check? What the hell?

The waiter brought the receipt, so she settled it without delay, her stomach turning the entire time. Aaron still had his phone out when he offered a hand to help her from her seat, so she was having trouble discerning whether he was playing the role of gentleman or actually being one.

They made their way through the parking lot in silence, her

heart throbbing with each step because he didn't like that she paid.

"This is me." He pointed to the shiny black pickup truck parked next to her SUV. "I'm glad you stopped by. I enjoyed tonight."

She didn't believe his smile. She couldn't believe unless he proved this wasn't the end even though she had no idea why she desired a future. "So did I." Her voice sounded too small.

He pulled keys from his pocket. "I hope you'll stop by next time you're in town so we can catch up again."

Oh no. She knew it. Her heartbeat ratcheted up several notches. This wasn't how it was supposed to go. She shouldn't have taken the check. But what kind of jerk turns cold after a woman pays? This wasn't right. She was spiraling downward, fast, while her head floated high above in a balloon of disbelief. "I won't be in town for a while, Aaron, but I definitely will."

"Sounds good." He pulled her into his chest, but she couldn't enjoy his embrace. "You've done well for yourself. Have a safe drive home tomorrow, okay?" After an extra squeeze, he let go.

She couldn't blink without dropping tears, so she stared wide-eyed at his chest to hold them in while her heart pounded her. Grit, Katrina. Don't falter. Be strong.

Her constricted throat was painful. "I will. Good night."

Katrina's Dreams

Last Year

Awakening

A Little Over A Year Ago

Her hands rest on the worn wooden rail of the footbridge. While a stream flows into the woods, she feels him.

She closes her eyes to focus on his warmth.

Her heart swells.

It's been so long since she's felt this. So many years.

Yearning fills her emptiness.

She trembles with need, so she commands her arm to reach for him—to touch—but her hand remains on the rail against her will.

She can't move.

Her throat is tight, locked, preventing speech. Her heart thumps as she battles her muscles. In vain. She can't turn to find his eyes or hug him. She can't tell him she's missed him or do anything but be aware he's next to her while she stands there, frozen.

Tears find their way down her cheeks, and she feels it. *He knows.*

His warmth leaves her side and places itself behind her,

enveloping her back...neck...arms...hands. Long-known protective warmth.

Now strong hands rest next to hers on the worn wooden rail. Aaron's hands. Just a sliver away. One on each side.

His body grazes her backside, teasing her. She'd give anything to lose herself in his chest.

But she can't move.

And she doesn't know why he's here.

She doesn't know how they ended up in this place.

She doesn't even know where this place is.

But she knows one thing for certain.

She longs to stay like this. Forever.

No.

She kept her eyes closed in an effort to retrieve the dream, but it was no use. He was gone.

Heart still pounding, she slid her hand down her pelvis and pressed into her desire.

He'd left her full, wanting more.

She rolled to her side and wiped tears on her pillow as memories of pulled pigtails and playground chases swept through her.

Feelings bubbled deep inside where she'd kept them locked tight. As she wiped another tear, she counted the years.

Fourteen.

The memory stabbed her. Aaron's faltering smile and gracious acceptance. Her disbelief she'd said those words.

A book closed because of Connor. A book shelved because of *her*.

Fourteen years.

She managed to place her mind on the bridge, but his warmth was nowhere to be found. Oh, why must dreams die?

She rolled to her belly to give herself a good stretch when a chuckle sneaked out of her. The pulled pigtails. He did that a lot, didn't he?

Memories of youthful imaginings evoked her smile. Memories of what might have been.

REMEMBERING
A Year Ago

All is shades of black and white except the bright blues watching her.

Gaze fixed on his, she places her palms on the park bench and presses down, forcing her shoulders back and breasts out. She smiles when his eyes blaze in reply. She'd give a wink, but he's not looking at her face. No. Those bright blues are drinking in the length of her legs.

Anticipation swirls inside her.

His sturdy jawline is dressed in a sharp five o'clock shadow, which is calling to her, so she uncrosses her bare legs and stands, a movement he mirrors from the park bench across from hers.

His gaze tracing a line from her ankle to breast, he approaches, igniting her heart in the most fantastic way. As he draws closer, his gaze locks on her collarbone.

Her breath comes faster.

Want rushes through her when his chest brushes hers. The shadow still calls, so she tries to pull it to her neck, but she's locked, frozen.

Damn it. Not again.

Lust pleads for his lips to seize her, but they don't. They don't even graze.

They *hover*.

His breath caresses the skin below her ear, torturing her with awareness that Aaron Keller's lips are a heartbreaking sliver from her neck.

And she can't touch him.

She shoved sweaty covers aside and sat, her breath quick from the encounter.

Vision still alive in her imagination, she savored his eyes. She'd forgotten the allure; gentle and protective with long lashes begging for intimacy. Oh yes. Butterflies twirled and flipped inside as they had years ago when fantasies of Aaron Keller were her favorite occupation.

Shit.

Fantasies of a man she couldn't have were the last thing she needed. But...

That sexy five o'clock shadow. Sensations of his barely-there lips haunted her neck in the most delicious way, sending a rush of blood to her favorite place.

It was ridiculous. There was no reason to be thinking about Aaron Keller. He was a closed book collecting dust on a shelf.

But if she could have her way, she'd pull the book, dust it off, and dive in.

She gave her long hair a tug. Stop it. He was married. She couldn't go there. Ever.

But what if...

Maybe they'd...

Jake groaned, letting her know his morning stretch was imminent, so she slid out of bed and stole over to the sheer curtains where morning sun penetrated the weave to caress her nakedness. She smiled as she tugged them aside. A sexy dream of Aaron was the perfect way to start a beautiful day. Dreams of Stevens were nothing compared—

That was it.

Stevens. It was around a year ago she'd caught him in the act. Her heart sank because *he* must've triggered the dream.

Damn.

Well...she'd take any dreams of Aaron she could get.

After all, he might have loved her if she'd...

Refusing to let sorrow for lost chances dampen a glorious morning, she went into her closet and got ready for a run with the only male besides Aaron who'd never let her down.

Jake trotted alongside as she went downstairs and out into crisp country air.

Part Two
Separation
May of This Year

Two

AARON

"You're home earlier than expected." Sarah, Aaron's mother, was working a crossword puzzle at his kitchen island when he walked in. "Did everything go alright?"

Aaron tossed his keys on the counter. It was 8:30 p.m. and, for the first Saturday night in ages, his energy was through the roof. Katrina had brought him to life, and it felt fantastic. Unable to make himself sit, he paced the tile floor behind his mother. "It went better than alright. Is Isaac sleeping?"

She nodded. "I put him down at 8:00. He went out like a light."

"Good."

He typed *Katrina Lopez Charlotte Michigan* into a search on his cell phone. As it was for Katrina, Charlotte had been his hometown. In fact, he'd lived there until his mid-twenties when he and Rose built a beautiful house in a small city named Auburn in the Great Lakes Bay Region of the state. Auburn, about two hours north of Charlotte, was closer to Rose's parents, who lived only ten minutes away and helped finance his first physical therapy clinic.

Keller Rehabilitation had grown from one to three clinics within its first five years, but not because Aaron wanted a large practice. No. He'd always hoped to own a single clinic with just enough staff to provide direct treatment to his patients while supporting a comfortable living for his family, but when Rose died, and Isaac's needs became evident, a larger practice made financial sense. Isaac needed security and the only way Aaron knew to give security was to make more money.

A throat cleared. "Are you going to tell me about your date?"

He looked up from his phone and found his mother's grey eyes, wary as ever, appraising him. When Aaron had started his new life in Auburn, his parents also moved north in order to live by their only child and his wife. They adored Rose. Who didn't?

His mother had been worse since Rose died. She'd always been a bit of a worrier, but Aaron's mental...*thing* put her over the edge. Worried about everything, she was. Not that he could blame her. Rose was like a daughter, and watching her son sink into the depths of mental disorder following such a significant loss was a blow she could hardly bear. She loved Aaron deeply —even more so since he'd become a widowed father at the age of 32.

So Aaron did the only thing that made sense. He snatched her into a big bear hug to lighten the mood. "She. Was. Perfect."

"Put. Me. Down."

Of course, she wouldn't enjoy it. She never enjoyed anything spontaneous since Rose died. But given her age, she wasn't overreacting, so he set her down.

With a half-smile, she steadied herself against the cupboard. "That's good. But was does *perfect* mean?"

"Perfect means that if she'd said yes when I asked her out fifteen years ago, this..." He gestured to the kitchen surrounding them. "...may not be my life."

Her half-smile disappeared. "Please tell me you've been drinking."

He shrugged. "Nothing but pop."

"But don't you love your life?" And now she was about to cry.

Damn it. When his darkness took over three years ago, Aaron developed some understanding of the depth of pain felt by people with conditions such as clinical depression and severe anxiety. Until then, he'd never been able to comprehend the sick feelings those issues create. And while he now had some understanding, he also had enough wisdom to realize that everyone's experience was different and needed to be respected as unique.

After all, just about everyone jokes that they have obsessive-compulsive disorder. They like things orderly, clean. They count things. They want things to be even and balanced. But nobody talks about obsessions that plagued *him*. He wasn't plagued by thoughts of germs or improperly folded fitted bedsheets. No. His obsessions were dark and deadly and a terri-fying thing to admit to himself, let alone discuss with someone else.

His parents knew all of it. He'd needed them to know because it was tearing him apart when his baby boy needed him most, but disclosing the truth to his mother sparked a fire of anxiety that must've smoldered beneath the nurturing exterior she'd shown Aaron since he was a boy. She needed him to be tolerant, especially when she was on his last nerve. She was hurting inside. He knew it. But he didn't know how to help.

Aaron took a deep breath and then clarified in order to lighten her worry. "I do love my life. I only meant…" Feeling unsteady, he took a seat on one of the barstools at the island.

She took a seat next to him. "What did you mean?"

Nah. He couldn't sit, so he resumed pacing. "Mom, I just spent three hours with the most amazing woman. I've been dead inside for so long, and she put me on a high." He stopped pacing to enjoy the memory of their first hug, which didn't last as long as he would've liked. A ridiculous grin claimed his face.

She stared at him for a long moment, her expression dead, and then shook her head. "You sure you didn't have anything to drink? You're not yourself."

"No. We had dinner at Greene's. She likes her steak medium. She loves classic rock. She enjoys action flicks and is into the arts."

"But why did you say that this…" She gestured to the kitchen surrounding them. "…may not be your life. You and Rosie built this beautiful home. And you have Isaac. I thought you agreed he is a *gift*. You're not making any sense."

Isaac's disability was a challenge. Becoming a first-time father while his wife was dying of brain cancer was one thing, but Isaac's Down syndrome was another thing altogether. Their only child, after all those years of trying, had special needs. The challenge never frightened him. He stepped up even though he didn't have a clue about childcare. He stepped up when the love of his life couldn't, and, in the process, he became more of a man than he'd ever imagined he could be.

But he also became the man he feared, and to be his old self —the man without the darkness—was an unspoken wish. An alternate past with Katrina would have meant a different present.

"Because." He got a glass out of the cupboard and poured himself some water. "If Katrina had said yes to a date fifteen years ago, I never would have gone out with Rose." But upon hearing himself say the words, his world stood still.

His gaze, which was directed at the glass of clear liquid in his hand, registered nothing but the memory of Rose's pretty green eyes.

He'd loved her.

He always would.

And Isaac, too.

But...

After three years of darkness and wondering and waiting.

Beautiful Dr. Lopez. Well-spoken. Interesting. Down-to-earth. Feisty. So different from Rose. She was a spunky little turn-on with a sharp tongue. Damn. The way she told off that guy. She was a strong woman.

"You mean this woman is *the one*?"

The sarcasm in her tone pissed him off. She was an absolute buzz-kill, so he threw the truth at her. "Katrina's always been *the one*."

But his words sounded as if they'd been spoken through a long tube. As if reality had bent and all was not quite what it had been a few short hours before. Aaron was floating in a new world. A world of possibilities and missed chances. A world where Katrina Lopez visited his dreams. Where she was in his life.

She scowled. "I think you've had a big night. You need some rest."

Determined to maintain the high his mother was killing, he headed to the basement stairs. "There's no way I'm falling asleep anytime soon. I'm going for a run."

She followed. "Aaron. Settle down. Please. I can't leave you in this state. You're not yourself."

He headed through the media room and closed himself in the bathroom next to his home gym. "Then stay," he called through the door. After changing into shorts and a t-shirt, he entered the gym and sat on the bench next to the treadmill in order to put on his running shoes.

She took a seat next to him. "Honey, I've never seen you like this. You're scaring me."

He hopped onto the treadmill and started running. She'd never seen him like this because he'd never felt like this. He loved Rose. He always would. But Katrina was first.

Flashes of elementary school hit him. The playground. Her pigtails. And the smile he rarely saw. The smile that was still so beautiful. Foolishness had stopped him from asking her out time and time again. She should've been his long ago.

Exercise had his heart working a little, so he looked at her and attempted to explain between breaths. "You've never seen me like this because I've never felt like this before. Not even with Rose."

She snapped, "Not even with Rose?" She pursed her lips. "Please tell me you did not propose to this woman."

Damn it. He stopped running, got off the treadmill, and sat next to his mother in hopes of explaining. "She came for a reason. For me and for Isaac. Don't ruin this for me."

The worry in her eyes was genuine, albeit unnecessary. She loved Aaron beyond anything and he loved her for it even though it stressed him out. She sighed. "Okay, honey, I'll back off. But can you just explain what you mean? What do you mean that she came for a reason? For Isaac?"

"She's intelligent, funny, beautiful, and independent. That's what's in it for me. But Isaac also needs her. She would understand him."

She shook her head. "I still don't get it, honey, but as long as you're this happy, I'll leave it alone. For now. Please promise you'll take your time to get to know her better and see where this goes. When will you see her again?"

Aaron jumped up. "I was hoping you wouldn't mind helping me out by taking care of Isaac next Saturday while I surprise her. I want you and Isaac to meet her, too."

Her nod was timid. "I think I can make that work. But are you sure you aren't moving too fast?"

He hopped onto the treadmill and resumed running. "I've known Katrina since I was five years old. I'm not moving fast enough." He smiled down at his mother in an attempt to reassure her all would be fine.

"I love you honey. Please take care." And without smiling, she blew him a kiss and left.

KATRINA

Why was she so devastated? So lost? It was as if someone died. What was *wrong* with her?

Katrina's mind knew the whole idea was one huge risk, but her brain tore up her insides nonetheless. She'd climbed over her emotional walls and plummeted into her black hole of loss —the one she fell into when her father died.

It was beyond comprehension. Aaron was only a childhood schoolmate. Deluding herself into thinking he'd want to have *anything* to do with her, let alone sex, was laughable. Yet she'd been crying all night as if she'd lost everything that mattered in life.

Ridiculous.

She didn't *need* a man.

She didn't *want* a man.

Her life was intact—just as it had been forty-eight hours ago. Before the visit. Before the date.

Thankful her presentation was yesterday, she ditched the last day of the conference. During her ninety-minute drive from the conference center in Saginaw to her home in Charlotte, she reflected on details of their date, which had been the perfect dream and nightmare at the same time. And, as always, the nightmare part would last a lot longer than the dream part did.

When she arrived at the kennel late-morning, it took fifteen minutes (courtesy of puffy bloodshot eyes) to convince the concerned kennel manager that she was okay to drive Jake home safely. Upon reunion, she gave Jake a much-needed hug. Or maybe he gave one to her. Either way, his soft fur felt like home. "Oh, buddy, I missed you so."

Jake licked her ear, but for the first time ever, his kiss didn't help her smile.

"Do you want to go see Grandma?"

He perked up and gave a bark.

"To Grandma's house we go." She led Jake out to the SUV and attempted to master her tears during the drive to her mother's 1950's brick ranch, the house Katrina called home until she was eighteen. Marina Lopez never moved after the divorce, always saying that dreadful memories were nothing to run from. A difficult past was to be embraced in order to make a better tomorrow.

The screen door nipped Katrina's ankle as she made her way into the modest entry off the living room and shouted, "Hey, Mom! I'm here!"

"I'll be right there!" Marina's voice came from the basement, so Katrina stood in the living room, numb, with Jake at her feet, and waited.

"My God, what's wrong?" Marina set a basket full of clean laundry on the recliner and rushed over to embrace her daughter.

"Oh mom." Katrina fell to pieces in her arms.

Marina guided Katrina to the sofa, set a box of tissues on her lap, and wrapped her arms around her again.

"It's Aaron." Katrina looked at her mother through a film of tears. "I went to see him while I was at the conference this weekend, but I'm not handling the outcome very well."

Marina's face was blank.

"We had dinner. And that was it. He didn't ask for my number. He didn't ask to see me again—except for the next time I happen to be in town. Those dreams couldn't have meant anything."

Marina grabbed a tissue and wiped Katrina's cheeks. "I'm glad you went." Her eyes offered reassurance while she squeezed Katrina's hand. "You needed to. But what makes you think the dreams couldn't have meant anything? Did you ask him about them?"

"Of course not. He'd think I'm crazy. Who in their right mind would visit a man because of having dreams about him?"

Marina shrugged. "Maybe the dreams meant something you don't yet understand. Do you regret going to see him?"

Katrina smiled for a second in spite of her pain. "Not one bit." Her body shuddered. "Mom, I know there was a connection. I felt it. So strong. But it all went to shit." More tears.

"What makes you think that?" Marina got up to fold towels, so Katrina got up to help.

"I took the check and paid it before he had a chance to do anything about it. I guess I came off as brash. He turned cold after that. Up until then, everything was perfect."

"Well, emasculating a man on the first date is never a good move, but he should be mature enough by his age to handle it. Don't be too hard on yourself." She looked at Katrina with gentle eyes. "If he's so weak as to push you away for buying him dinner, he's not worth your time, sweetie. And if he's meant for you like you feel he is, he'll reach out to you. Only time will tell. In the meantime, pray for guidance and peace."

Katrina stopped folding and pulled her thoughtful mother into a hug. "I will. Thank you, Mom."

Of course her mother was right. If Katrina and Aaron were meant to be, it would've worked. Aaron was not worth her time. She grabbed a couple more tissues and blew her nose.

"Do you want to stay for lunch?"

Katrina shook her head. "Thanks for the offer, but I'm going to head home. No appetite and I'm dead tired from all this crying. A long, hot bath and movies with Jake sound best."

"Sounds like a good plan."

"Mom, thanks for loving me." Katrina's smile was small, but genuine, as she pulled her mother into a long parting hug.

"That's what moms are for, sweetie. And don't worry. It'll work out as it should. It always does."

Her eyes fly open in the darkness.

He's home.

Please don't be mad. Please don't be mad. Please don't be mad.

The kitchen door slams, jolting her tiny frame and provoking the horrid hammer that lives in her heart—the hammer that pounds a familiar message through her body: *Hide, Katrina, hide.*

She ducks under the covers and clutches her pillow as the hammer pounds blood through vessels that pulse in her ears.

Please stop pounding. She needs to hear.

She holds her breath.

Her chest aches against the steady, driving rhythm that's telling her she's not safe.

Please don't yell. Please don't yell. Please don't yell. Oh, God, please make it so he doesn't yell.

The rhythm continues.

She exhales, straining to hear.

Plates clink.

Something crashes.

The refrigerator door slams.

Please don't yell.

Breaths come too fast as tears make their way down her face, but she doesn't dare make a sound. She needs to hear in order to know where he is.

Mommy's bedroom door creaks.

"I need to eat, woman." His words slur. "Get out of bed!"

Her clenched eyelids leak more tears. Please don't hit her. Please don't hit her. Please don't yell.

"I have to work in the morning, Joseph! Get out!"

Her veins burn, telling her to run away.

Run fast.

Leave.

But she has to hide.

She chokes on words in her throat, longing to scream *Mommy, be okay*!

"There's nothing to eat. Get out of bed. Now!"

Her stomach drops out when Mommy whimpers. Please don't hit her, Daddy.

"Damn you, you bastard. It's 3 AM. You want a meal? Get your ass home for supper!"

Please don't hit her again. Her throat clenches when Mommy sobs under another blow.

Her veins.

Run, Katrina, run.

"You blame me, Marina? You. Blame. Me?"

His voice is too calm.

More tears. Snot runs down her lip as she tries to tame her

breathing so she can hear. She doesn't dare sniffle for fear of not hearing.

Please leave, Daddy. Leave. Please, Daddy, leave!

"We'll see who's to blame, Marina. Come."

"No! You leave her out of this!"

Her body electrifies.

Next thing she knows, she's curled up under her desk, pillow and blanket clutched in her arms. The hammer is pounding, pounding, pounding.

Her bedroom light turns on.

The electricity inside her causes her head to float somewhere above her body—a body encaged in ribs that are sure to give way to the hammer.

She's about to die.

She forces herself to look.

Daddy's knees bend. His eyes find hers.

Through the blur, she sees tears running down his face.

"Who's right, Katrina? Daddy's right, isn't he Katrina? Katrina, who's right?"

Her body heaves under sobs. "I d-don't know D-Daddy! I-I l-love you, D-Daddy! I d-don't kn-know."

"Joseph! Leave her alone!"

Daddy's face turns cold. He stands up.

She clenches her eyes and buries her face in her pillow. Please leave, Daddy!

"Stay. Out. Of. This. Woman!" Daddy stumbles out of the bedroom.

She forces her rigid body to move and peek around the edge of the desk. He has Mommy back in the hallway just outside the bedroom door. Another shot of electricity—

Shut the door. Turn off the light. Get back under the desk.

She will die from the pounding of the hammer as she listens.

Knocks.

Thuds.

Whimpers.

Marina's whimpers echoed in Katrina's ears as the hammer struck her ribs, pounding and pounding, reminding her she wasn't safe.

Cold pricked her skin and a whine reached her ears.

Her eyes flew open.

It was only a nightmare.

Jake whined again.

Katrina's naked skin was ice in the wet bedsheets on which she lay. A storm was brewing and she'd need to close the windows so Jake wouldn't freak out.

Marina's whimpers still echoed in her mind.

She pulled the blanket over her legs and rolled to her back to look at her bedroom ceiling. Shadows of tree limbs and sheer curtains danced above her, so she watched them until the whimpers faded away.

A tear emerged from the corner of her eye and slid to her hairline, which would've tickled were it not for sadness over this black remembrance of what it felt like to be that little girl.

Wind cut through the room, so she rushed to close the windows and jumped back into bed, snuggling under the covers on the opposite side, away from the nightmare.

"Jake, go back to sleep." She listened to him groan, paw his bed, and settle down. "Good boy."

When she closed her eyes, her father's drunkenness stared at her.

Fuck.

She should've expected this. Losing Aaron triggered it this

time around, didn't it? Symptom relapse. Fear and fucked up feelings and fucked up dreams, but this nightmare?

Happy thoughts, Katrina, happy thoughts.

Her mother was safe and healthy.

She was not a helpless five-year-old. And—

Well that happy thought was dead forever wasn't it?

Aaron had to be dead to her now.

It was the only way to move on.

"'It is easier to build strong children than to repair broken men.' Frederick Douglass. Who would like to share their thoughts about this quote, which you will find on the cover of your course pack?"

Katrina was addressing students in the only summer course she was teaching—Child Development. It was the first day of class and, as expected, all thirty students remained silent.

She leaned against her table at the front of the room and took a sip of iced tea. "To those who may be a bit uncertain, know that you are in Dr. Katrina Lopez's class, Child Development. If you happen to be in the wrong place, feel free to leave right now."

All students remained seated.

She surveyed the eyes fixed on her and started a slow trek among their seats. "I'm going to leave the room and will be gone for ten minutes. I want you to get to know each other a bit. Relax, talk, and feel free to make fun of me. When I return, I expect two things. On the left side of the board, make a list of the things you need me to do so you have a successful experience in this class. On the right side of the board, make a list of thoughts about this quote. Any thoughts are welcome. When I come back, we'll have a conversation about your ideas."

She left the silent room and listened in the hallway, outside the door.

A few moments later, the ice broke.

Down the hall, she took a seat next to a window in order to absorb some morning rays; they soaked into her as if trying to fill the void that refused happiness deep inside.

Against her better judgment, she allowed herself to connect with the memory of their first hug. Aaron's arms held her so tight. So long.

Her warmth intensified, threatening something like happiness and hope, so she forced back the tear that pressed into her eye. She had to focus on the present. He didn't want her, and it was ridiculous for her to believe she wanted him.

She didn't *want* him.

If it hadn't been for the dreams, she wouldn't have given him a thought over the past year, let alone a visit. She wanted the dreams to stop, which was the primary reason for her visit. She also wanted to get an answer, which she did.

Yes, she was still attracted to him.

Yes, they got along great.

Yes, it was a wonderful time.

But that was it. They were old acquaintances catching up over dinner and there was no reason to grieve. The visit was likely to put an end to the dreams, and the sensual torment would stop. She'd go on with her life just like she'd done after Connor.

Connor, who'd been her first lover, best friend, and fiancée, was the last man she'd allowed inside the part of her that hurt most—in the place where Katrina hid deep down inside.

Katrina was the girl who craved love. Who craved connection. Who craved sex and heat and heart. Who craved acceptance.

Dr. Lopez was the strong woman Katrina built from the

inside. It took all her strength to walk away from Connor, but she did it. And she established this career, a home, and a life without him. Dr. Lopez would not let any man hurt Katrina again.

Katrina was *safe*.

But Katrina was craving like never before.

She went to the bathroom. While washing her hands for no reason, she examined her eyes in the mirror. They were still a little puffy, but much better than yesterday, at least, so the students weren't likely to notice. She applied another coat of lip gloss and fluffed her hair because feeling pretty always helped a little.

When she entered her chatter-filled classroom, which was much comfier than it had been ten minutes prior, she found a board filled with ideas. "It looks like you put some thought into this activity. Thank you. I want you to know that you can ask me anything. I will not always have an answer, but I know where to find them. Well, I know where to find them most of the time anyway. Challenge me. Try to stump me. I promise I will challenge you in return. And that's how we'll grow together this semester. Let's see what you need from me."

She reviewed their list of needs, which was sensible. Using their ideas as the foundation, she engaged the students in conversation about the structure of her class, the importance of each thing they listed as needs, and how she would meet those needs.

After the first fifty minutes, many laughs and ideas had been exchanged and she already knew several students' names from memory. A short break later, she turned the conversation in the direction of critical thinking. "Why do you think I started our class the way I did today? Why did I ask you to write your ideas on the board when I was out of the room?"

Jaz, short for Jazmine, an outspoken female with spiky

purple hair who elected to sit in the middle of the room, ventured the first response. "So we get to know each other."

"Yes, Jaz, but why did I do it in the manner I did it? I could have had us each stand and state something about ourselves. That would have helped us get to know each other, too. Think. Why did I do what I did?"

She waited.

A male student who had not said anything to this point raised his hand in the front row. "So we could talk safely."

He was bright. "Remind me of your name."

"Elijah Bennett."

"Okay, Elijah, explain what you mean."

Elijah shifted back in his seat and cocked his head with a confidence that matched the fiery crew cut on his head. "You don't know who wrote what on that board. If you didn't like one of the ideas we wrote, you couldn't blame me or any one of us for it."

She walked among the students. "What do you think, everyone? Do you think Elijah is on the right track?"

Jaz leaned forward in her seat. "I think he's right. You wanted us to feel comfortable talking to each other. Talking to you. It worked."

"You know what makes me really happy right now?" She walked back to the front of the class. "You're thinking. And you're correct. So, let's see what you had to say about Fredrick Douglass's quote, 'It is easier to build strong children than to repair broken men.'"

She reviewed the comments written on the board:

It's impossible to repair broken men
How do you build strong children?
Easy to make mistakes raising kids
Don't agree—It's tough to raise kids
Can we fix damage done during childhood?

"These are great ideas. I appreciate your thoughts and we will address most of them as we travel through course content this semester. By the end of this course, you should have a good understanding of how to build strong children, what challenges parents face while raising children, and how to nurture resilience."

She gestured toward the quote, which she had projected onto the screen. "For me, this quote means many things. One of the things it makes me think of is safety." She noticed Elijah look at his desk. "I think several of you were on the same path as Elijah, but he was the only one brave enough to speak up."

She spoke slowly to give the students time to process her words—words she'd developed during her lifetime of fear: "If a person feels safe, they are more likely to open up...If a person opens up, the world is more likely to see the beauty that lies within...If the world sees the beauty that lies within, the person is more likely to realize their full potential...If the person realizes their full potential, they are more likely to be happy...If a person is happy, they are more likely to be resilient in times of stress...If a person is resilient in times of stress, they are less likely to break in the first place. Why? Because the person felt safe to begin with.

"This happens to be my personal philosophy. What do you think? Is a sense of safety a building block upon which psychological strength builds?"

Some students raised their hands, but her question was rhetorical. "There is no saying my philosophy is correct. I appreciate some of you want to share your thoughts on this, but right now I want you to think.

"As we go through this semester, I want you to use critical thinking, and the research we discuss in this course, to determine your own scientifically-based answer to the question. That said, close your eyes and think about the following. Do you feel safe in my class right now? Do you feel safe to speak up? Do you feel safe to disagree with me? Do you feel safe to ask questions?

"If you answered yes to all of these, maybe I've created a safe classroom environment for you."

An hour later, after a review of the five major perspectives in psychology, her students filed out of the room. Class was invigorating, but her energy faded fast because her negative feelings were twisted tight—she was numb and confused.

Maybe the nightmare about her drunken father *wasn't* PTSD symptom relapse and had nothing to do with losing Aaron.

Maybe the nightmare was simply the mechanism her subconscious used to prepare for this lesson. She always discussed safety on the first day of class because fear was the reason she became a psychologist to begin with.

Maybe she needed to stop thinking her feelings were the result of a failed date.

Maybe she needed to stop thinking she failed at *anything*.

She'd *never* been a failure.

She plopped in her chair and stared at the materials she didn't want to pack because she didn't want to leave the class-room. It had been the perfect escape.

"Um, Dr. Lopez?"

The voice belonged to Manuel Martinez who was standing in the doorway. He hadn't spoken during class, but she remembered his name because he was the only person in class who looked more Hispanic than she. His dark skin, rough and tattooed, juxtaposed the soft brown eyes that appraised her. "Yes, Manuel?"

He approached her desk, eyes too serious for a smile. "That stuff you said, you know, about safety. That was smart." He pressed his fist to his chest. "I got a good feeling about this.

Your class, you know?" He gave a casual two-finger salute. "See you next time."

A little warmth settled in her belly, making a home next to the void. Maybe she wasn't as numb as she thought. She found a little smile, wore her wet eyes with pride, and saluted back. "Next time."

***

"Hey, Gen." Katrina approached the table where her perky friend, Genevieve, an instructor of English, was sitting in the middle of the GLCC commons for their usual Monday lunch.

"Hey girl, how are you today?"

Katrina pulled Gen into a tight embrace. "I'm alright. How's Baby?"

Gen pulled out of the hug and held Katrina at arm's length. "What's wrong?"

Katrina gave the inside of her cheek a hard bite to keep her response in check. Of course Gen knew something was wrong because Katrina's eyes were too honest. Silencing her feelings was difficult on a good day, and she was spent from the whirl-wind of grief that had nagged her since Saturday night. She didn't have the energy to pretend all was fine, so she gave her head a subtle shake. "I don't want to talk about it. Not today."

Eyes understanding, Gen rubbed a hand over her belly. "Everything's progressing as it should be. Max is excited to become a big brother. He's been pretending teddy bear is his 'widdow brudder or sister.' Right now, his favorite thing is to prop Teddy on Baby's bedroom floor and put puzzles together."

Max was the bright preschooler Katrina had tested as a favor to Gen when the physician recommended evaluation for giftedness. With an IQ of 142, he was an exceptional child.

"Your considerate little Max." She winked. "I'm not at all surprised. You must be getting excited, too."

Gen's smile answered by lighting their way to the lunch counter.

Katrina grabbed a tray. "Any other news?"

"Well, I hear Dr. Richard Jeminez is our new Dean of Teaching and Learning. He came to us from Peace College in southern Michigan. He's a psychologist by training. Do you happen to know him?"

"No, Gen. I don't know Dr. Dick."

Gen giggled, which was a bright spot. Katrina's sense of humor was alive, which meant the hurt wasn't getting the best of her.

As a safeguard against pain, Dr. Lopez didn't keep many female friends. She found women, in general, to be a self-centered breed that had difficulty keeping their mouths shut. Gossip. Untruths. Cliques. None of these were worth Katrina's emotional energy.

Gen was different from most women. Maybe it was Gen's educational background that made the difference. Or maybe it was Gen's experiences as an inconspicuous bi-racial female. Or maybe it was the fact that Gen was divorcing her husband while pregnant with their second child. Whatever it was, Gen knew the value of trust and privacy.

Gen had an inner strength that complemented Katrina's strength in just the right way. She'd proven herself worthy of Katrina's confidence by never pressing too hard or asking too much. And she never *needed*. Dr. Lopez didn't trust people who *needed*. Need required Katrina to give, and giving should never be required of a stranger, let alone a friend. Giving should be a freedom, not an expectation.

Yes, Gen was safe. A colleague-turned-girlfriend who didn't get too close. Their lunch dates and occasional texts were the extent of their relationship. It was ideal—never forcing Katrina outside her comfort zone. Never requiring anything other than support, honesty, intelligent discussion, and goofy laughter. Gen was the perfect female friend.

While Katrina was paying for her chicken salad sandwich and cranberry juice, Gen elbowed her arm. "You know, you'll have the opportunity to know a Dr. Dick intimately if you desire. Be prepared. Stevens is spying you from four o'clock."

Shit.

"Thanks." He wouldn't dare come over. Not after Saturday. Yeah, Katrina fucked up everything on Saturday.

While Gen was settling her order, Katrina put her debit card back in her purse, grabbed her items, and stepped left in hopes of avoiding Stevens only to walk into something that should not be in her way.

Stevens grabbed her arm, which sent a surge of electricity between her legs. "I'm sorry," he said. "I didn't see you there."

He was so full of shit. In order to avoid his eyes, Katrina looked at her hands, which were barely holding onto her purchases following the collision. She was as attracted to him as ever; he was so fucking hot—well, not as hot as Aaron, but she couldn't go there—and he smelled fantastic.

Working to maintain composure because a cheater wasn't good for her, she looked at his cheek. "You should watch where you're going. I almost dropped my lunch."

"Aw, come on, Dr. Lopez. Don't be mad. I'll make it up to you."

Saturday hadn't fazed him. Blood rushed through her, rousing parts that wanted a man, which was all of her body. And after lusting over Aaron for a solid twenty-six hours, she was particularly worked up. Vibrators weren't the same as hot flesh and sweat. She had to force herself to be curt. "There's no need for that. Please excuse me."

She beckoned Gen to accompany her to the patio in the courtyard off the commons. It was warm and bright outside, so the courtyard was crowded; everyone wanted some nourishing sunlight. A couple of students got up from their table, so she and Gen claimed it and took seats beneath a blooming magnolia.

Damn. Another reminder of Aaron. Why did he have to have a magnolia near his front porch? To torture her? She bit her cheek again, reminding herself to remain in the present.

She removed a tie from her purse and pulled her hair into a pony tail high on her head while scanning the space for Stevens. He hadn't followed her, but her body was reminding her that he was somewhere nearby. And she was tempted to do a thorough search.

"I've gotta say this," Gen whispered. "How in the world can you be so assertive with Stevens? He's got it so bad for you and he's so hot. If he flirted with me, I don't think I'd be able to put together a simple sentence. You amaze me."

She didn't have the energy to explain everything, so she pretended Saturday hadn't happened. "Honestly, Gen, when he touched me back there…" Her brow furrowed over what she was about to divulge. "I thought my crotch was going to explode. That man affects me exactly how he wants to affect me. He knows he's hot and he knows I think he's hot. Plus, there's our history neither of us can forget. He's not a moron."

Gen's eyes went wide, as if Katrina were missing the obvious. "Then why don't you go out with him again?"

"Genevieve," Katrina scolded and then took a bite of sandwich.

"I know. I know. I'm sorry. It's just I can't believe you can say no to him. Aren't you frustrated?"

Frustrated? Absolutely. Eleven years frustrated. She went from regular sexcapades with Connor to nothing. And then

Stevens, the only man close to the virility she'd known in Connor, turned out to be a cheat. "It's not about being frustrated or lonely. And I'm not desperate. It's about morals."

"Maybe you should report him. Then he'd *have* to leave you alone."

"I've thought about that." She took a sip of juice. "But I won't."

"Why?"

Katrina took another bite of her sandwich. There was no doubt Stevens sensed why she'd never reported him. He knew her body loved how he made her feel. He was her naughty aphrodisiac in spite of his fuck-up two years prior. And now that all her dreams of Aaron were most likely dead, literally and figuratively, Stevens was all she'd have.

"To be honest, Gen, as much as I hate to admit it, I love the thrill I feel when he flirts. Except for the fact that he's a cheat, he's my type. Intelligent, blue-eyed, and toned. Delicious."

Gen winked. "Agreed."

Katrina loved that Gen was content when company went silent. Gen didn't press or go on about anything when Katrina turned her full attention to her lunch.

Oddly, Katrina was feeling a little better than she had at the end of class. Maybe it was the good company. Or maybe...

Maybe Gen was right.

It was a stupid thought.

But...maybe Stevens deserved another chance.

AARON

"What's up, Keller?" Eric Mendez, Aaron's best friend, walked off the outdoor basketball court at the community center to greet Aaron while the other guys continue shooting hoops on Tuesday night.

Eric's red t-shirt stirred up mental images of Katrina's red panty dance—the most recent dream to make Aaron come. Hoping he'd have enough focus to concentrate on the game, he dropped his keys on the bench and took a seat to retie his shoe.

Eric sat next to him. "Stressed?"

Aaron shrugged. There was always something to stress about—like the run-around he got when placing that order of roses during his lunch break. How hard was it to understand a request for exactly thirty-five roses? Not three dozen. Just thirty-five. The fifteen minutes it took to place that order had made him late for his next patient, which pissed her off and fucked up his schedule for the rest of the day.

"How's Isaac?" Eric asked.

"Healthy."

"Glad to hear that, man."

Yeah. Isaac had just made it a full year without *any* hospital visits. No pneumonia this year. No RSV. Isaac was getting stronger.

Aaron got up to stretch. "Anything new with you?"

"Yes sir." Eric's grin was smug. "Got myself a date for Friday night. A pretty thing I met at the dog park of all places."

Aaron laughed, "Which breed is she?" After deflecting the elbow Eric attempted to ram into his pec, he said, "You opened yourself up for that one. Dock ten points from that IQ of yours."

Eric chuckled. "So you still talking to that chick you went out with last month? What was her name again?"

Aaron gave his hamstrings a good stretch. "Jenny. No."

"Yeah. Jenny. Why'd you cut it off? She ugly?"

"No. She looked alright. It was Isaac."

Eric screwed up his face. "Man, I told you to keep him out of the picture until they know you."

The familiar shock of protective anger tore through Aaron,

so he stopped stretching. Eric couldn't relate to Aaron's life. Hell, none of Aaron's buddies had any idea what it was like to be in his shoes. This was part of why Katrina mattered so much. She'd get it.

Everything was a challenge. Not in a bad way. It was just draining. For example, while making a pancake and sausage breakfast that morning, Aaron grabbed a couple of Isaac's plush toys and set them on the table so Isaac could play in his booster seat. Isaac squeezed the toys and patted them on the table for a moment before tossing them to the floor.

"You can't play with toys if you throw them down, bud." Aaron had picked them up and, again, placed them on the table. A moment later, Isaac swept his hands across the surface, sending the toys to the floor once more. But because food was more important, Aaron left them and returned to the griddles.

He'd pointed the spatula at Isaac. "She'd understand you." And that truth gave Aaron a buoyancy he hadn't felt in ages. Katrina was bound to understand that breakfast, for example, was not a simple event. No. With Isaac, it often took forty-five minutes, two thrown cups of juice, and (sometimes) a poopy diaper before they could say they were done with breakfast.

Yes, everything was a challenge. Isaac didn't talk yet, so it was hard to know what he wanted and felt. He was still in diapers with no sign of being ready to learn to use the toilet. Even though it was still pretty typical for some 3-year-old boys to be in diapers, Isaac's syndrome predicted that he may need diapers for a quite a while yet. He was likely to need special care for a very long time—maybe even his whole life.

Isaac's behavior could be confusing, unpredictable, and exhausting. He needed a lot of prompting and reminding. He made lots of messes that he couldn't help clean up. He rarely kept on his shoes and socks in public, even in the dead of winter. He was overly friendly, willing to give hugs to everyone around him even when it was inappropriate. He feared nothing, which was a safety concern. Constant vigilance—that's what was required of Isaac's caregivers. Katrina would *understand* this.

She'd be perfect.

"Sorry man." Eric's apology drew Aaron back to the present.

Knowing Eric's apology was genuine, Aaron continue explaining the Jenny situation while shooting the basketball to warm up. "When I first met her, I thought she was trying to impress me by being all Preschool Teacher to Isaac. She looked good and seemed comfortable with him, so I asked her if she wanted to meet for dinner."

Eric shrugged. "So she was trying to impress you. What's wrong with that?"

"It turned out she was Preschool Teacher all the time. Sweet and nice and way too happy."

Eric stole the ball. "Since when is there a problem with a nice woman who's sweet and happy?"

"Nothing wrong with it." Aaron shrugged. "She wasn't my type. She was nice, but no chemistry. And she wasn't bright."

"Whatcha mean?" Eric passed the ball.

"I had a little fun by asking her what she typically does after she masticates."

Eric laughed. "You didn't."

"She froze like a deer in headlights." Aaron shook his head. "I could never take her seriously."

"Poor Preschool Teacher. How many women does this make since you started trying?"

News of Katrina was too big and too new. If he told Eric now and it didn't work out...

Aaron lied, "Three since Rose."

"You know, Rose ain't ever coming back to you. And you

can't keep screening chicks through Isaac. You need to get some play before you turn into Mr. Rogers, man."

Eric didn't have kids and Aaron's other buddies had kids part-time. Smart kids. Kids who learned without trying. Aaron's buddies couldn't relate to his version of the protective-father thing because they weren't solo parents. And, beyond that, they couldn't relate to Isaac.

Eric kept it real. The world out there, in general, didn't understand a life like Aaron's, but he couldn't care about that. All that mattered was Isaac, the woman who might become his mother, and figuring out how in the hell he was going to get her to stay in his life this time around.

KATRINA

Wednesday morning was accompanied by a blessing—a weather report of sunny skies in the mid-70s—exactly what Katrina needed to rise above the funk she'd been battling. She had no school, so she'd be spending her day with the earth.

She and her intelligent comrade, Jake, went for a run after a light breakfast. Jake was the type of male she needed. Steadfast. Protective. Unwilling to take anyone's shit. And, best of all, cuddly. What woman needed a man when she had woman's best friend by her side?

As they approached home at the conclusion of their run, a floral delivery truck parked in her driveway. Such a simple event wouldn't bother most people, of course. Most people would be excited to receive whatever the floral delivery person might be bringing as a present. But Katrina's trauma brain didn't work that way. No. Instead, her nervous system decided it was time for her heart to palpitate with fear.

This was why she had Jake. Protection. Intrusions could happen anywhere, even in daylight on a quiet country road.

Thankfully, her neighbor was outside. She shouted, "Hey, Jeff! How are you today?" so the delivery person heard that she wasn't alone.

"Just fine, Katrina! And you?" Jeff replied.

"Who wouldn't be fine on such a glorious day? Enjoy!"

As desired, the deliveryman noticed her talking to Jeff, so he began to walk down her long, narrow drive, but Jake's growl stopped him.

Midway up the drive, Katrina asked, "May I help you?"

The man didn't move. "Good morning, Miss. I have a delivery for Dr. Katrina Lopez at this address. Is that you?"

"Yes."

The man set his electronic signature pad on the gravel. "If you would please sign, I'll place your flowers on the porch."

She signed the device and took it to the porch where the man placed a breathtaking bouquet of deep red roses set inside a sleek black vase.

"It's alright Jake." Jake took a seat at her feet as she handed the signature pad to the man. "If you would excuse me for a moment, I'll be right back."

She unlocked her front door, grabbed the vase and set it on the foyer table, and then locked the storm door behind her. Jake by her side, she ran to the back hall, took a five-dollar bill from her purse, and returned to the front entry. After unlocking the storm door, she handed the bill to the man. "Thank you for the flowers."

"The pleasure was all mine, Dr. Lopez. Have a nice day." He gave her a barely-there wink and returned to his truck.

She closed and locked the doors and then watched through her front window to be sure he drove away. After she unleashed Jake, she turned her attention to the bouquet.

Her palms were sweaty.

She shouldn't let her hopes rise, but it was too late. Ideas of

Aaron and roses and hugs played with her heart in the cruelest way.

But he didn't ask for her number.

He didn't know her address.

She needed to close that book.

Her shaky hand opened the card.

I'm so sorry. Please forgive me. Sincerely, Your Admirer.

Shit. "Damn, Jake, these are from Stevens. He won't give up, will he?" She counted the blooms. Thirty-five. "You should ask for your money back, prick, because they didn't deliver a full three dozen."

In spite of her disdain for cheaters, she nestled her nose against the velvet bouquet because roses were one of her favorites. Stevens knew they were.

Geez.

Roses are what heaven must smell like.

She sighed. Maybe Stevens was alright. He *had* been working to get her to try again for a long time. And he was *apologizing*. Maybe she shouldn't be so hard on him. After all, people could change for the better if they truly wanted to. Sometimes.

Or maybe these thoughts were a symptom of sexual frustration. After all, Katrina wanted it and Stevens was looking better by the minute.

She stroked her index finger up a soft petal. "He has good taste, Jake. Let's put these on the dining room table." The arrangement provided an elegant focal point on the dark walnut finish set between dark green walls.

Jake followed her upstairs where she traded running gear for warm-weather lawn-mowing attire—a cotton camisole over short cut-off blue jeans. After applying a generous layer of sunscreen to all exposed parts, she took Jake to the front yard and attached his collar to the line she'd anchored into concrete near the drive. She adjusted her ponytail so it sat toward the top of her head and put on ear protection.

Mowing the entire property took her three hours. She loved her house, a two-story built in 1900, which was set on acreage surrounded by farmland with only one close neighbor, Jeff, a fifty-something widower.

If she finished everything on the day's agenda, she would reward herself with some iced tea and maybe a book on one of her two generous covered porches where she often absorbed the quiet and let go of her ills. Her old lilacs were in full bloom, so a quiet meditation on the porch would be especially therapeutic.

She mowed around hundred-year-old oaks and maples that shaded the lawn here and there, and around the line of bountiful pear and apple trees bordering the back of her property. Yes, her home was old and comfortable and she loved it. And she'd accomplished it all without a man. Without Connor. And without Aaron Keller.

After lunch, she edged the sidewalk and garden beds, applied weed preventive and fertilizer, and pruned that which needed pruning. Her last big event for the day was a visit to the local home improvement center to buy compost for her vegetable garden.

By 7 p.m., she was pretty tired, so she used the last of her energy to fix herself breakfast for supper (homemade pancakes and fried eggs with orange juice) and headed upstairs to take a much-needed bubble bath.

Hot water penetrated her muscles. She was feeling pretty good after her day with the earth, so she allowed her mind to wander where it had gone all too often over the past week. It was a test to see if she could handle the memory without tears.

She settled in the water, bubbles pressing into her cheeks, and closed her eyes.

And she found his eyes.

And she heard his laugh.

And she felt his hand on hers.

Yes, the connection was still palpable.

Oh, Aaron. What had he done to her?

Why didn't he want her?

She breathed in the sensual scent of bubbles, thankful that he hadn't visited her dreams since their date.

Maybe it was all over and she could move past him for good.

But a solitary tear released itself, telling her she didn't want it to be over.

No.

She needed to stop the foolishness.

They were only dreams.

She dried her hands, cued the music of George Gershwin on her cell phone, and forced herself to analyze the structure of each piece, attempting to forget everything while she soaked in the hot, bubbly water.

Katrina knocked on his office door, kind of hoping he wouldn't answer and kind of hoping he would and kind of confused what led her there at all. She'd give it thirty seconds. If he didn't answer, she'd leave.

"Hi." Stevens' voice, as strong-willed as ever, was behind her.

Her heart pounded, scolding her for doing this, but her mind was made up. She turned around and looked at his feet so she didn't see the expression of triumph that was sure to be plastered on his face. "Do you want to play for me?"

"I can in ten minutes." His voice smiled at her, but she didn't look.

"Okay." Head down, she walked past him and made her way to the dance studio in the Fine Arts building next door. Thursday evenings were peaceful there. A single art class was in session down the hall, so she wouldn't have any interruptions. Or...*they* wouldn't have any.

She flipped on the lights, kicked off her street shoes, and crossed the mirrored room to the corner where she stripped to her dance camisole and leggings and tossed her clothes over the barre. He'd be there soon, and she was kind of excited he was coming.

She extended her right leg over the barre and stretched. The pull in her muscles felt fantastic, so she held the stretch nice and long before repeating on the other side.

The door clicked open. "I'm glad you invited me."

She maintained the stretch a little longer than she would have because she didn't want to look at him. Or maybe she did.

She didn't know what she wanted.

"Thank you for agreeing to come." She turned to face him. "I want to tell you I appreciate your apology and I'm sorry for having been so rude to you last Saturday. I was hoping maybe we could mend things with a little of Chopin's *Prelude in C Minor*?"

Stevens smiled, pulled out the piano bench, and played.

In the center of the floor, she stretched everything in the midst of the powerful, melancholy accompaniment, liberating her muscles from the confinement of sadness that had wrapped them so tightly over the past several days. Stevens, a gifted pianist disguised as the world's hottest professor of biology, played as well as he ever did.

He transitioned into *Valse triste* by Sibelius, like she had asked him to that one time years ago. She was warm and ready to move, so she let herself fly into the contemporary movement that was her.

He kept the music coming.

She improvised.

Winston's *Tamarack Pines*.

Brickman's *Rocket to the Moon*.

Guaraldi's *Skating*.

And Bach's *Prelude in C Major*.

Thirty minutes of movement and all of her felt glorious.

She slid to her back on the floor and closed her eyes to absorb remnants of the music. Yeah, she'd missed this. Not many dancers had a personal accompanist.

"You've still got it." He was standing over her, arm stretched out to help her rise from the floor.

She took his hand and got up. "Thank you. I never stopped coming here, you know. It was nice to have you play for me again." She went to the corner and grabbed her clothes.

"I can play any Thursday you want me to." He approached the piano and grabbed his keys.

She joined him at the piano, using her shirt as a towel to dry her forehead and neck.

He was looking at her neck, and she felt it. He always affected her body.

He almost affected her heart. Once. Maybe he would again, in time?

He was her best option.

"Would you like to..." She didn't want to say this, but she needed to move on. Dr. Lopez had protected her for so many years, but Katrina's sexual needs were...

This would help her move on. His eyes reminded her of Aaron's. Not as blue or as pretty, but pretty enough. She moved closer. "Would you like to kiss me?"

He chuckled without a smile. "You have no idea." His voice was raw, intense, and his eyes, hungry.

He was backed against the piano while she pressed into him, her most sensitive parts absorbing the masculine energy rolling off his body. He was all lust and sex—a no-strings type of guy. A live-and-ready channel for the lustful desires triggered by dreams she'd never have again. It was time for Katrina to release without involving her heart. She needed a release. She needed to move on.

He grabbed the back of her neck, weakening her limbs a little. He liked to be in charge.

But so did she.

She grabbed his hand, yanked it from her neck, and tugged his wrist so he followed her to the switch where she doused the lights in the windowless space.

He pressed into her, forcing her against the wall so she felt his cock against her ass. "Afraid someone will walk in?" His minty breath was hot on her ear.

She pushed backward to knock him off balance and yanked down her camisole, freeing her breasts. She turned, grabbed his shirt, and pulled him close. "Not one bit. Grab my ass. Hard."

His hands grabbed just right, the pain channeling arousal to her crotch as his mouth seized her neck.

Yes.

She pushed his shirt upward and clawed his chest.

"I. Knew. It." He bit the words into her shoulder. "You like it rough."

His words. His bite. For the first time ever, she wanted to be fucked and not give a shit about responsibility or trust or anything beyond the moment. She wrapped her arms over his shoulders and pulled him down, but he pinned her arms against the wooden floor, his cock pressing hard into her thigh. If she wanted it, she'd have it.

She pushed her arms into his hands and rolled on top of him, straddling his abs. His hands resumed a heavenly assault on her ass, but she stole one and placed it on her breast.

"I'm thinking you want to be fucked, Dr. Lopez." His voice was fervent, reminding her that he didn't respect women, but for some demented reason, it heightened her arousal.

And then she saw Aaron.

No.

She slid her hands under Stevens' t-shirt and kneaded his pecs while he kneaded her.

And she saw Aaron.

Fuck no!

His smiling eyes.

His wet t-shirt.

His five o'clock shadow.

She threw herself upward and shuffled to find the wall, trying to shake the visions as she pulled up her camisole.

And there was light.

Stevens was standing next to her, his hand on the light switch, but she didn't look at him. "What's up?" This was the smallest his voice had ever sounded.

She was in a tunnel, her arousal turning round and round, tumbling her in a circle of uncertainty and disbelief. *Her brief time with Aaron had fucked her up.*

"Cam, I can't do this." She forced herself to look into his eyes...and she found pain. Shit.

She walked over to the piano and picked up the clothes she'd dropped and the keys he must have dropped as well. He was standing at the door when she approached to slide into her street shoes. She offered him his keys and he replied by holding her hand a little too long.

"I promised myself if I ever got another chance, I wouldn't blow it." His voice was gentle. "How about dinner?"

Another chance. Yeah, last time around she was waiting for a more-than-mainly-lust connection to form, but he couldn't wait. She caught him fucking a married nursing instructor in his office.

Stevens was a stupid thought, but he was talented, appreciated her dancing, and was still trying to win her over after years of waiting. He was intelligent. He had a great job. She could've done much worse. But—

He squeezed her arm and her belly flipped. "Why aren't you answering?"

She stepped back to pull out of his grasp. "Dinner sounds great. How about next week Friday? After another dance-date in here on Thursday? Same time?"

He smiled. "You've made me a happy man. I promise to do better this time."

Katrina's Dreams

Last Year

WANT

LAST JUNE

Her feet nestle in sand along the great lake's edge where waves curl and flip, licking her ankles. Water begs her sweltering body to dive in, but she doesn't want to cool off. Not yet. Sunlight forces her gaze to seek shade. Given there are neither trees nor umbrellas nearby, she looks down.

Sheer red fabric clings to her sweaty breasts, which are plumper than usual. A see-through sundress over nothing. Hell, she looks hotter than she feels. And that's something.

It seems she's alone on a beach under a clear sky at noon. Free to do as she wishes, she draws up the red fabric and slips fingers between her swollen folds. Her touch is warm, welcoming, so she slides herself against it. As if it's been ages, her heart pulses faster in giddy anticipation for this unexpected opportunity. An orgasmic treat under the sky.

Her most precious part contracts against her fingers as she drops to her knees on the shore. The lake splashes her, soaking her dress so it defines her nipples, bellybutton, and hips, as she teases herself. Blood rushes through her, filling her loins as she works her way toward pleasure.

Breath coming faster, she grinds into her hand, leans back, and opens her chest to the sky. Her long hair grazes sand as excitement climbs toward the sun. Everything is white-hot. Sliding two fingers in, she rocks to a rhythm so intense it sends her blood toward the point of no return. She spreads her knees wide, falls to her back, and presses her pelvis toward the sky. Her fingertip delivers stimulation so sweet. She needs more. And more. Until...

At the mercy of convulsions, her neck arches, forcing the crown of her head into the sand.

Heat rockets across her skin.

Apparently, she's not alone.

Breath unsteady, she slides her wet fingers up her pelvis and rolls to her belly. Propping herself on her elbows, she watches Aaron Keller stare at her with a gaze fiery enough to light the moon. She's not sure why he's wearing jeans in this heat, but she doesn't care. Jeans don't matter when ripped abs and pecs are part of his attire. Barefoot and beautiful, he's lying on a beach towel not twenty feet away. A delicious circumstance.

She pushes herself to standing and prepares to brush off, but there's no need. Her glistening skin is covered only by a sparkling red bikini. She scans the beach, but there's not a sundress in sight. She bites her lip. Maybe he prefers a bikini.

He's propped on one elbow, watching her. Determined to touch this time, she strides toward him. Eagerness propels her, moving her quicker than intended. Next thing she knows, she's at his side. Thrill of proximity tempts her to straddle him, but she doesn't; instead, she plants her left foot an inch from his elbow, making it clear she welcomes his everything.

When he leans toward her left leg and looks up the length, her pussy decides she wants another turn. His eyes plead for what she wants to give him, and her heart replies with a skip of excitement. This is it.

She commands herself to kneel. To touch. But she can't, damn it.

She's frozen. *Again*.

She watches his gaze caress her legs. Her pelvis. Her face. Driving the need to fill herself with the cock hiding behind that zipper.

Yes. Aaron Keller's gaze is making her ache...for him.

RESISTANCE
LAST JUNE

Aaron has her enclosed against a car door, his body so close to hers they dance on the edge of full contact. Everything is hot and naked.

Aware she's dreaming, she commands her arms to embrace him, but they won't. She's helpless. She can neither pull herself into him nor look anywhere but at his lips; parted and wet, they implore her to taste and let him savor her. If only they could. Fate is determined to drive her wild by stirring the fire of frustration that's been growing inside her these past couple of months.

Cravings pulse, impelling her to do naughty things to this beautiful man. Oh, how she yearns to meld their carnal impulses. They're poised for a kiss but don't. Inability to move is now a sensation of resistance. A delicious restraint. An insanity that vibrates through her. Every bit of him is pulling her toward an ecstasy designed for them. An erotic burn. Slow and intoxicating. Oh yes. She'll wait like this forever and die in their exquisite flame.

Promises

"They're flowers, not fish." Marina took the hose, turned off the valve, and then dropped it on the lawn. "You need to tell me what's up, Katrina, because in the past thirty minutes, I've witnessed you overfill Jake's water dish, trip over your shovel, and drown your impatiens."

"They'll be fine." Katrina tipped the large bowl-shaped planter to drain excess water and then lugged it from her porch to the lawn where July sun would dry the soil.

"What's going on?"

Katrina straightened up and faced her mother, the most perceptive woman she knew. Sweat glistened on Marina's brow while the breeze teased her long graying pony tail. She was a picture of Katrina in thirty years.

Marina tugged off her gardening gloves, sat on the bottom porch step, and then patted the spot next to her, welcoming Katrina to sit. "You're not a klutz and you're an ace gardener. Today you're not you. Why?"

Katrina took a seat next to her mother and looked into her eyes. "Remember when you finally kicked out dad?"

"You're thinking about your father?"

Katrina shook her head. "Back when you announced your decision to get divorced, I made myself a promise. I swore I'd work hard to achieve four things." She gestured to Jake. "The easiest one sits at your feet. Own a German Shepherd to keep me safe."

As if he knew she was speaking of him, Jake turned his head to watch her, his tongue lolling in efforts to cool himself.

"Two of the achievements were more work," she continued. "I became a doctor and I own my own home. No man necessary."

Warm smile reaching her eyes, Marina said, "You're my intelligent, driven daughter. You've done well. Look at this property." She waved her hand at Katrina's acreage.

Katrina smiled at the crop of blue salvia dressing up her rock bed. Her gaze followed the rocks to the edge where red petunias lived.

Red.

Her mind flitted to the beach, the red bikini, and *him*, which sent her heart into flutters. He was her favorite distraction, just like when they were kids. Only now her fantasies were all grown up, full of muscles and heat and wanting. Given she was no longer a schoolgirl, she didn't get to see him—ever— but his continual presence in her thoughts was—

"I'm waiting for number four." Marina stroked Jake's head, which was resting on her knee.

Katrina drew a long breath and released it along with some tension. "I promised myself one more thing, but it was a little girl's dream. Silly, really, because its accomplishment relied on someone other than me."

"Oooo. Did you hear that, Jake? A little girl's silly dream."

Jake perked up and looked at them.

Marina winked. "Silly dreams tend to be the most worthwhile."

"I promised to marry a man who'd never hurt me."

"Well, I don't see anything silly about that. After everything your father did, it's the most sensible thing in the world."

"But I picked Aaron Keller."

Understanding lifted Marina's countenance. "That's a name I haven't heard in ages." Her eyes sparkled as if in celebration of renewed hope for her still-single 34-year-old daughter.

"Nothing's going on, Mom." Katrina's reached over to stroke Jake's head. "Of all my goals, that was the irrational one. A nonsense fantasy."

"No. Not nonsense. He asked you out."

Memory of that moment twisted the void left by Connor.

If she'd said yes to Aaron...

The void pulsed against her heart.

Aaron never had a chance to see how far she'd come because she'd never given him the opportunity.

Marina nudged her. "What's got you thinking about Aaron?"

Warmth flowed through her, reminding her of details best kept private. "After I found out he was married, I blocked him out of my mind. I swear I haven't thought of him in years. I've been focused on work and my property—my life—but all of a sudden, a few months ago, I started having dreams of being with him. Vivid dreams. Intimate dreams." Tears for ridiculous hopes pressed into her eyes.

"Ah." Marina chuckled. "Aaron Keller strikes again. You know what this means, don't you?"

Katrina nodded. "But I'm not ready to know. If he's divorced, there'll be baggage. If he's still married, I'll be disappointed again, which will hurt. If he's dead, I'll be devastated. I don't want baggage or hurt or devastation. I want to be happy like I am right now. I'm the happiest I've ever been."

Disappointment darkened Marina's eyes. "Katrina...you're wrong. I don't regret anything. I loved your father and he gave me you and that goofball brother of yours. And because of his way, as upsetting as it was, you became a very strong woman. But you can't keep hiding behind independence. You *are* ready to know. You *are* ready to deal with baggage and hurt and devastation because you've already done all that. And you've *prevailed*." She squeezed Katrina's hand. "Look. Him. Up."

Tears blinked out of Katrina's eyes.

Her heart *was* ready. It was crying for her to find out.

But her body...

Her mind...

She wiped away a tear.

Fear never goes away.

Belief

Autumn haze surrounds her.

Grasses blow in a breeze she cannot feel, their seed heads nodding as if in favor of her presence; tall and unruly, they tickle her hands as she walks a dirt path toward an unknown destination.

All is quiet as she ambles through open fields punctuated here and there by massive oaks. Warm and woodsy country air fills her lungs, empowering her with the strength only nature can provide.

Now Aaron's presence makes itself known. His warmth is close and her heart squeezes with longing.

He's walking next to her.

She attempts to take his hand in hers, but her arm won't obey. As usual, she cannot touch him, but she sees his strong profile as he watches the path. Their path. And she feels his energy, his gentle confidence, accompany her every step.

A strength unlike any other blossoms inside her.

In this moment, Aaron Keller is hers. Her partner. A life force meant for her.

As they walk, a powerful, heady drive consumes her. She will conquer everything: The darkest of moments. The wildest of dreams. The fiercest of passions.

Heart full and head light, she believes in the impossible. A world of wonder and hope and happiness fills her. She revels in the exquisite buoyancy of childlike belief as they walk these grassy fields.

Then their destination becomes clear.

Her heart tightens its rhythm as they approach the faded structure. Weathered wood clings to memories long forgotten, a defiance that must have prevented its collapse. When they step through the doorway, the scent of hay fills her with sadness.

Their time is ending.

Her throat constricts when his eyes meet hers. Beautiful and blue. Intimate and whole. Full of power and peace.

His gaze holds her...into their goodbye.

Part Three
Introductions
May of This Year

THREE

KATRINA

Sunlight filters through limbs of trees towering above, illuminating the dirt trail beneath her feet. The deep green wood is alive with voices of squirrels and birds and the warm breeze teasing leaves.

And she feels him. A step behind.

Belly full of anticipation and hope, she turns to face him. He takes another step to close the distance between them, his breast now brushing hers.

Long-known protective warmth envelops her. Infects her. Urges her to climb into his chest and get lost forever. She holds her breath, welcoming his energy, warm and serene, letting it flow into her darkest, emptiest places until it explodes inside her, into the painful, addictive emotion she's afraid to embrace.

She's afraid of the tear on her cheek—the one meant for him.

She doesn't want any more tears.

She doesn't want any more hurt.

She doesn't want to love him.

But she does.

Eyes full of understanding, he lifts her hand to his lips and—

Katrina's eyes opened.

She was in her room.

Alone.

She clutched her pillow, eyelids crushed in an effort to recapture the moment, but the visions faded fast. No! Nightmares echoed after she woke, but happy dreams died in an instant.

So Aaron hadn't finished visiting her dreams?

Figured.

Well, fuck it.

A fury built inside. She needed to stay strong, and if the fucking dreams were all she'd ever have, bring 'em on, damn it. She'd treat 'em like she did Stevens. As cheap titillation for the spinster she'd become because she was all messed up inside.

She couldn't care about it anymore.

She was not letting any man fuck up her life again. Fuck Aaron. Fuck Stevens. Fuck 'em all. She ripped back her curtains, veins on fire with determination. It was Saturday morning, the sun was up, and she was done. Just done.

She snapped, "Let's get breakfast, Jake," as she threw a sheer robe over her naked body and headed downstairs.

Jake joined her on a trip to the back entry where she filled his dish with kibble. She took a moment to freshen water in the vase Stevens sent her and promised herself to move on with or without him. Whatever she decided after dancing again next Thursday would be the path she'd take.

Following a breakfast of bran cereal, toast, orange, and banana, she changed into a pair of black yoga pants and a comfy red camisole. House cleaning attire. First the bathrooms, then the kitchen, and after that, the highlight of her day would be her vegetable garden. But before she could do anything, she needed music.

She put on some Queen to get on with her day. Jake stopped licking his paws to look at her, which she took as approval of her musical selection, so she cranked up the volume, let the music consume her, and threw herself into housework.

She sang every song. When she couldn't remember lyrics, she made them up, which proved effective for keeping her mind in the great escape that was music. This was exactly what she needed on the one-week anniversary of that heavenly wretched date.

While scrubbing the kitchen sink, Jake nudged her thigh with his nose.

"What's up, bud?"

He turned his head toward the foyer and whimpered.

"Is someone here?" She took off her rubber gloves and lowered the volume so she could have a conversation. In the foyer, she peered through the peephole in her front door.

Oh wow. Stevens?

She took another peek. Yeah, it was Stevens. He was facing the road, but that was the back of his head. It had been ages since he'd come to visit her. Maybe he couldn't wait to see her until next Thursday?

Wow.

She was kind of happy he'd come to visit. Maybe he did want to do better by her this time around.

She stepped away from the door and checked herself in the foyer mirror. He'd already seen her all sweaty in dance attire, which was pretty much what she was wearing, so she was presentable. She tugged her hair to tighten her ponytail and then, being careful to keep Jake back, she unlocked and opened the front door.

When her visitor turned around to face her, black spots claimed her vision. An impulse to slam the front door took over while her lungs decided it was time to hyperventilate. Damn it.

She walked through the house, in spite of the spotty vision that made it difficult to see, and went out onto the back porch even though it didn't make any sense to do so. After all, Aaron was on the front porch.

Fuck.

She trembled with confusion, so she took a seat in one of her white rockers and attempted to control her breathing.

Aaron was there. On her porch.

The other porch.

And she'd slammed the door on him.

Fuck.

What in the hell was wrong with her?

Looking at the porch floor, she forced herself to breathe properly, but before she could get herself under control, the unthinkable happened: a truck engine roared with life.

She tore out of her seat and sprinted around to the front of her house—to the driveway—in order to stop him before he drove away.

The moment she cleared the front corner, he stopped backing his truck, which was midway down her long drive, and got out.

She couldn't feel her limbs, but that didn't matter. As soon as she was close enough, she threw herself into him, wrapped her legs around his waist, and squeezed him with all her might. "I'm so glad you're here."

His strong arms held her tight. "I happened to be in the area, so I thought I'd stop by to visit an old schoolmate."

Her eyes wanted to cry and her head wanted to think, but as neither was happening for her, she continued to cling to him like a favorite dream.

"But I wonder. Do you always one-up people when they try to surprise you?"

Something inside Katrina wanted to smile at his curious comment, but she couldn't smile. Everything was numb. "What do you mean?"

The vibration of his chuckle soothed her shakiness. "I waited all week to surprise you like you surprised me and then you slammed the door in my face. Surprise number one. I figured that was my cue to leave you in peace, so I'm about to do that, and then you come running and give me the hug of my life. Surprise number two."

Even though she didn't want to, partly because of embarrassment and partly because he felt so good, she let herself slide to standing and looked into his eyes. The twinkle she found therein made it clear he wasn't upset in the least. "I appreciate you enjoyed my two surprises, but they were accidental. You could say they were wrapped in panic paper."

His belly laugh assured her she was safe from his judgment, so she smiled a small smile.

His gaze drifted down the length of her. "But I'd be lying if I didn't say that I feel cheated. A certain woman arrived on my doorstep a little over a week ago and, when I answered the door, *my* t-shirt was all wet." A to-die-for flirtatious smile swept his face. "I was hoping I'd be as lucky when you opened the door today, Dr. Lopez."

She looked at her camisole. Not a drop on it.

Reality hit her. Hard.

She didn't know how to feel. "You wanted me all this

time?"

He took her hand in his and stroked it with his thumb. "Did you get what I sent you?"

What the hell did he send her? She didn't get anyth—

"Oh, *you* sent them?"

He nodded. "All thirty-five. I have one more thing for you, too." He led her to the bed of his truck, where he grabbed a six-inch pot of stems and thorns with his free hand, and then guided her to the wooden swing on her front porch. "Sit with me."

She looked at the label on the pot: Gertrude Jekyll—Fragrant English Rose—Deep Pink. A rosebush.

"When I hugged you last week, I noticed the delicious scent of rose on you."

Her lotion. She looked into his eyes and found them glassy with emotion. Aaron Keller was a romantic?

"Each one of the thirty-five represents a year I've lived without you." He brushed her cheek. "I hope this bush will bloom for you every year to come." The wetness in his eyes shouted sincerity.

She was without words, so she did the only thing her confused, delighted, frightened body could manage. She crawled into his lap, nuzzled his neck, and wept.

His arms held her tight while she cried. Minutes passed as they sat in silence except for her sniffles and birds chirping at the feeder. Her muscles relaxed with time.

A breeze reminded her she was alive and this was real.

Of all the moments of her life, this was about the most perfect. Enveloped in strong, secure arms of a man who *felt right*.

Red nose and puffy eyes impossible to conceal, she worked up nerve to look at his face. "Aaron, you obviously affect me. Is there any chance I affect you so strongly?"

He squeezed her. "It was all I could do to keep myself from contacting you after we separated last Saturday. You've been on my mind every day since."

She slid off his lap onto the swing, entwined her fingers in his, and rested her head on his arm. In spite of the wonder of the moment, she felt small. Six days of internal hell, a week of emotional havoc, only to find all the heartbreak had been pointless. He'd wanted her the entire time.

What a fool she was.

Or was she?

The dreams.

Maybe she was wise to think they meant something after all? If it weren't for the dreams, she'd never have visited him. Because of the visit, he asked her for a date. Because of the date, he was with her now.

So why had she been telling herself it was over?

Damn her incessant fear.

Her insides had been crying all week. Maybe it was intuition screaming at her to wake up and believe in the truth—to stop listening to her damned head.

"But you didn't think of me as much as I hoped you would."

She looked up. "Why would you think that?"

Aaron raised his eyebrows. "Who did you think sent the roses?"

Oh man. She was going to have to deal with Stevens. "I thought they were from Stevens, apologizing for being a prick last Saturday."

"Oh wow." He laughed. "Today must've caught you completely off-guard."

"You have no idea." Her insides sank over her mistake. They had the same dark blonde crew cut, but the back of Aaron's head was broader than the back of Stevens' because

Aaron was bigger. Had she not been so intent on feeling rejected, she might have realized right away that it was Aaron at her door.

She looked at the pot of stems and thorns, which was an indicator that at least a small part of him cared about her. She needed to keep her head out of her way. She needed to stop thinking.

"So are you going to work on your vegetable garden today or are you open to changing your plans?"

"I'm open. What did you have in mind?"

"I'd like to take you to lunch."

Katrina stepped onto her gravel drive and walked toward his truck, looking as hot as she could manage with a fifteen-minute prep. Platform sandals, slim jeans, and a deep blue camisole underneath a silvery-blue fly-away sweater coordinated with Aaron's dark blue button up shirt and blue jeans.

He pulled her close. "You look gorgeous." His breath tickled her ear.

"So do you."

She pulled away in order to open the passenger door, but he grabbed her hand. "No, no, Dr. Lopez. You paid for dinner. I get to open the door."

Point made. She slid into her seat and enjoyed watching him walk around and settle into his.

"We're going for a long drive. How long can Jake make it before you need to let him out?"

"Around six hours. And I can always ask Jeff to let him out if need be. Jeff's my neighbor." She pointed at the house across the road.

"Convenient." He returned his gaze to her. "Music or conversation?"

"Music."

"Very well." He handed her his cell phone, which was connected to the car stereo, and backed out of the drive.

She touched the music icon to open his library. "What would you like to hear?"

He kept his eyes on the road as a smile slid across his lips. "I'd like to hear Crash."

She searched to find Crash, an album she'd never heard, which was by The Dave Matthews Band. "Do you have a favorite song on this album?"

"Yup."

She waited for him to tell her what it was, but he didn't. She looked up and found a smirk. "Do you mind telling me the name of your favorite song on this album, smart ass?"

He chuckled. "Nope."

And that was all he said. She commanded, "Tell me the name of your favorite song on this album."

"Sure. *Crash Into Me.*"

She found the track, set the phone in its cradle, and settled into her seat as trees flew by on the highway.

It was a soothing song.

Calm, inviting, and—

She took his right hand, placed it on her lap, and stroked it with her thumb while she listened.

Her belly liked getting all twisted up in the song, which made it clear that Aaron Keller wanted to do naughty things to her. She licked her lips at the thought of stroking him with her tongue...all the way there. That would be delicious indeed.

She looked over to see him spying her. Yeah, she got the message. She cleared her throat. "How long has this been your favorite song?"

His eyes penetrated her from beneath those long lashes, which felt so good she didn't mind he wasn't watching the road. "Since 5:30 last Saturday when I hugged you at the restaurant. You intoxicated me at that moment. And I'm still drunk."

Oh shit. He was good with words. She crossed her legs and pressed his palm into her thigh, and he responded by stroking the length of her muscle. Long, deep strokes. Yeah, his hand was perfect. She guessed that skill came with being a physical therapist.

"You like?" he asked.

"More than you can imagine." She was almost purring.

They drove nearly two hours without many words and she loved every minute of it because she needed the time to rearrange her emotions—the week had been quite a trial. Thankfully, Aaron didn't need to talk. He was content to just *be*. Spending time with Aaron was like spending time in her garden or soaking in a bubbly bath or rocking on her porch. Peaceful. Fulfilling. *Balanced*.

When he pulled into a parking space at The Terrace, a small eatery not far from the hotel where she had stayed last week, he ordered her to stay put, so she removed her hand from the door handle and waited while he walked around to open her door.

"You better not spoil me, Mr. Keller. I might get used to it."

He extended his elbow.

Her arm linked with his, he took her through the restaurant and out the back door onto a large patio overlooking a river where they took a seat beneath an umbrella at a table near the back rail. They had privacy and full view of the water.

She reviewed the menu, which offered a variety of specialty sandwiches, hot and chilled soups, salads, and cheesecakes—upscale offerings at a little mom-and-pop restaurant. She loved it. "Okay, I need to focus on the menu so I know what to order. Once I know what to order, I can focus on you."

He leaned forward and looked at her from beneath his eyelashes. "Your wish is my command."

Oh man. Bedroom eyes. She couldn't focus with him looking at her like that, so she put up the menu to block his face. "You're distracting me."

He placed a finger on the top edge of her menu and pulled it down. "I know."

She set down the menu and kicked him under the table, gently of course.

"Ow. Okay. Focus." He was all smiles when he picked up his menu, and, a few minutes later, their orders were placed.

"So, the note that accompanied the roses. For what were you apologizing?"

He grinned. "You'll think me vain, but during our dinner last weekend I got the feeling you were as into me as I'm into you. Before we said goodnight, I'd already decided I was somehow going to show up on your doorstep—unannounced. I needed to keep you off-guard." His eyes were dancing. "I was hoping you'd be disappointed that I didn't ask for your phone number."

Sensations of stupidity flooded her. Why hadn't she listened to her feelings. The warm ones that gave her happiness. The ones she wished to be true. The ones that were honest and real and everything she was supposed to believe.

But those were feelings of hope, and her brain was not programmed to navigate hope. Hope was an abyss—a thing unworthy of trust—because every time she rode a wave of it as a child, she'd fallen into the void. Broken promises. Broken sleep. Broken spirit. Broken bones. The only way out was by scaling her emotional walls—then building them higher for next time—until she could see clearly, without tears, again.

Again.

And again.

She'd done it so many times as a child, the walls were ridiculously easy to build. A disappointment here. A misunderstanding there. An imagined slight. Didn't matter what it was, her brain was programmed to build upon fear.

Dr. Lopez was an expert at guarding the walls; she'd kept Stevens and all the men out. But Katrina...

This week of stupidity shined a floodlight into her brain and begged Katrina to analyze what needed fixing in order to make it change course. She needed to alter something because hiding in her emotional fortress had made her a *fool*. And Katrina Lopez wasn't a fool.

"Do you forgive me?" he asked.

The pain of the past week twisted inside her. "I wasn't disappointed. I was devastated." She reached across the table and took his hand between hers. She stroked his long, strong fingers. "Please don't do something like that again." She looked into his eyes. "Forgiven."

"Thank you." His gaze caressed hers. "I wasn't surprised you slammed the door in my face, but I was devastated to think I was on par with that *Stevens*. I'm sorry."

She let his gaze hold her while that thought lingered. It was vital that he consider what he'd just said because hurting her would not be permitted.

After a long moment, she released his hand and lifted her water glass, which brought wetness to mind. "Why was your t-shirt all wet when you answered your door?"

"I was giving Isaac a bath. He was splashing water. Then both my phones and the doorbell rang—all at once, of course. I got even wetter when I lifted him out of the tub. Why? Did you like that?"

Her eyebrows replied while she cleared her throat, and then

she took a drink. "And why do I feel like you and I have known each other forever?"

He laughed at what he probably thought was obvious. "Because we've known each other forever. I have memories of you starting at age five."

"That's not what I mean. You and I never talked much. We were never what you'd call friends. We just went to school and church at the same places." But she'd always felt so close to him, from a distance.

"Yeah, but our class was small." He shrugged. "We had, what, eighteen kids in it? We spent a lot of time together and we talked some."

"I guess." But she wasn't satisfied with his answer. "So you have memories of me at the age of five. Such as?"

He grinned. "I remember chasing you around the tables in the kindergarten room. I got in trouble for that. A lot. You remember?"

The memory warmed her. "Yes, I do. You always pulled my pigtails when you caught me. It hurt."

"I'm sorry. You never told me it hurt. If I'd known, I would've stopped."

"Then I'm glad I didn't say anything because I liked that you chased me. You made me feel happy. The pain didn't matter."

Concern flashed in his eyes. "Oh no. I don't ever want you to hurt because of me. Starting today, of course." He winked. "Please always tell me how you feel. Promise?"

"Promise. I'm not the same girl I was when you knew me in school. My life is much better now." She paused while their lunches were set on the table. "But you need to promise to be honest about your feelings, too. Deal?"

"Deal."

She took a bite of her chicken salad croissant and decided

that it was the most delicious sandwich she'd ever eaten, complete with walnuts and grapes...and cherries. As a family of ducks swam by, she realized their conversations hadn't yet explored family. "Aaron, you haven't said much about Isaac. I'd like to know about him."

Aaron didn't look up from his plate. "You'll have a chance to meet him today if you wish. We can talk about him then."

"Well, yes, I'd like to meet him. I'm guessing he's quite young if you still need to give him a bath."

"Yeah. He's with my mom. He's having his lunch now. I'll text her to bring him here when they're done."

He sent a text and turned the conversation to other topics. They covered sports, Hollywood figures, current events, and politics, finding they were like-minded in everything that mattered, so, of course, she couldn't trust it.

"Are you being honest with me?" she said. "I don't want you to pretend to be someone you're not in order to impress me. You don't mind I'm not into sports?"

"Not at all as long as you don't mind me watching a game when I want to."

The waitress took their dessert orders and cleared the dishes.

"Are you a fanatic who watches sports every day all year long?" Katrina asked.

"No. Since Isaac was born, I haven't had much time to feed what used to be my sports obsession. I've gotten over it. I catch a game when I can. I'm more interested in taking care of my body these days." His eyes locked on hers as he flexed his bicep, which melted her middle. "But would you like to go to a basketball game with me sometime?"

She managed to pull her focus from his muscles, which was no easy feat. "Absolutely, as long as you don't mind I won't understand it."

He leaned forward. "Are you willing to learn?"

She leaned forward. "Absolutely. And are you willing to attend a ballet with me once in a while?"

He cocked his head. "Absolutely, as long as you don't mind I won't understand it."

"Are you willing to learn?" She winked.

But his attention was drawn somewhere else, so her gaze followed his. A woman with grey hair pulled into a tight bun was walking across the patio toward them. On her hip was a small child with a crop of light blonde hair who appeared to be around one-and-a-half years old.

Isaac.

"Hi Mom." Aaron stood to give the woman a hug.

In disbelief she was meeting his mother so soon, Katrina stood as well.

Aaron turned to Katrina. "Mom, this is Dr. Katrina Lopez."

Katrina forced her best smile for the woman, who was halfway smiling at her. "Nice to meet you, Mrs. Keller."

But the woman said nothing in reply.

Following an awkward moment of silence, Aaron said, "Feel free to call her Sarah. And this is Isaac." Aaron took Isaac from his mom and shifted him so Katrina could see his face.

As if on cue, Isaac gave her his best smile.

Oh god.

Down syndrome.

Katrina looked at the child for a long moment, hardly registering anything but the fact that he had Down syndrome.

A syndrome had never entered her mind.

But why would it?

Then again, why not?

Damn her nerves. The blasted jackhammer in her chest got

going for whatever reason, so she battled it by taking a good look at the child's smile.

This was why he didn't invite her into his house last Friday, wasn't it?

Flooding with compassion for this man and the child his wife left behind, her throat constricted, but she managed to stop the wetness in her eyes from welling. Feeling faint, she smiled at Isaac, shook his little hand, and forced herself to speak. Knowing that children with Down syndrome were often smaller than their same-age peers, she made an educated guess. "Isaac, are you three years old?"

"Yes," Aaron said. "He turned three on December 7th."

Sensing Aaron was watching her every move, she forced herself to get a grip. "May I hold him?"

"Absolutely." He passed Isaac to her.

Goodness, he was tiny.

Cuddly.

And he smelled like a baby.

"Hi, Isaac. My name is Katrina. I'm an old friend of your father's. Has he told you about me?" She sat and placed the child on her lap. He had such tiny ears and a tiny nose and adorable, stubby little fingers. His eyes were exactly the same shade as his daddy's—the color of crisp water welcoming her for a swim on a hot day. "I see you have beautiful blue eyes like your daddy, Isaac." She removed her eyeglasses so Isaac could see her eyes without obstruction. "My eyes are brown. See?"

His little fingers touched her nose, and she melted inside. The jackhammer slowed.

"Nose. That's my nose, Isaac. Where's your nose?"

Isaac touched his nose, a simple act that stole her weary heart.

"Very good, Isaac. That is your nose. And a cute little nose, it is." She tapped it with the tip of her finger, which made Isaac laugh, so she squeezed him, and he laughed some more. His was a precious little laugh—a barely-there, squeaky giggle that was so adorable, she giggled, too.

The waitress arrived.

"Oh, dessert is here." Katrina put on her eyeglasses and looked at Aaron and his mother. "Will you be joining us, Sarah?"

Sarah wasn't smiling. "No, we made a quick stop here so you could meet Isaac. We already ate lunch and now Isaac is due for his nap."

"Okay, well, thank you for coming to see me. I'm glad I was able to meet both of you today." Katrina gave Isaac another squeeze, heard him giggle once more, and handed him back to Sarah who prompted him to wave bye-bye.

Isaac just smiled instead.

Katrina waved. "Goodbye, Isaac."

While Sarah walked away, Aaron motioned for the waitress to pick up his card, and they took their seats.

Katrina stared at her dessert, processing the moment. Down syndrome and a mother who looked less than pleased to meet her. No. Not less than pleased. The woman looked like an absolute bitch.

"Is everything okay?" Aaron's voice was small, distant.

Again, she forced a smile. "Oh, yes, I'm sorry. I was thinking." But her smile faded while she searched Aaron's eyes.

"Katrina." He hesitated, so she held her breath. He looked worried. "I'm on a path that will become...painful for me if you cannot accept Isaac. Please tell me how you feel about him."

She dropped her gaze because this was too much. "You want me to do what?" She looked at her plate.

"Please tell me how you feel about Isaac."

She took a deep breath while the jackhammer got going again.

How should she respond to this?

She didn't know how she felt.

Down syndrome.

Well, she was a little freaked out.

No. A *lot* freaked out.

Isaac would be a lifelong responsibility.

There would be no moving out by age twenty.

Or, maybe there would be...but he'd need a guardian of some sort. Wouldn't he?

Oh, hell, why was she planning a future anyway?

She was nuts.

She was already in way too deep, emotionally. Now some of his *baggage* laid at her feet, and it was only their second date.

Baggage. What a cruel word. What kind of psychologist was she anyway?

A sick one.

A psychologist who was still figuring out her own fears.

Down syndrome.

Down syndrome came with *needs*.

Needs came with *expectations*.

Expectations restricted freedom.

She'd been free.

She'd been safe.

She'd been...*alone*.

Frustrated by her inability to identify an answer that wouldn't embarrass herself, she sputtered something. "I don't—I don't know. I don't know how I feel. I just met him."

The waitress dropped off the receipt for Aaron to sign, but he ignored it. He was searching Katrina's face while she stared back, the hammer pounding her ribs the entire time.

Why was he putting pressure on her?

What did he want her to say?

Maybe he was imbalanced.

He was too good to be true. That was it, wasn't it? She never trusted things that felt too good to be true.

She looked at her dessert and focused on breathing.

He put his credit card away, signed the receipt, and set it aside. After what seemed an eternity, he spoke. "You gave me the answer I should've expected. You aren't fake."

"Have I ever given you reason to believe I'm fake?" Her voice was tinier than it should have been. She took a small bite of her strawberry cheesecake, but didn't taste it.

Aaron leaned forward and lifted her chin so her eyes met his. "You've never given me reason to believe you're fake, but lots of women are. I've learned that over time, especially since I lost Rose." He took a bite of sherbet. "Anyway, you'll find Isaac is one of the most easy-going, happy kids you'll ever meet."

Of course. That was the stereotype. People with Down syndrome love to love.

Kind of the opposite of her, really.

She was afraid to love.

Love hurt.

How messed up it was. She'd held Isaac's little body for not even five minutes, and, in that short time, he'd loved her without fear, without condition. He'd given her a moment of something sunshiny—giggles and smiles.

And her brain called him baggage?

No.

She was all tangles and heartbreak, but little Isaac was...liberation.

They ate silently until most of the dessert was gone, her mind racing over one of Aaron's comments while she wallowed in shame. "Aaron, will you tell me what you meant when you said you're going down a path that'll be painful for you if I can't accept Isaac?"

Aaron's gaze burned into hers. "You know the answer to that question."

Her insides quivered, reminding her she was a desired woman—not a heartless monster. He could be assertive, and she liked it. She wanted more because it felt better than shame, so she asserted back. "Maybe I do, but I want you to tell me anyway."

"I thought my roses said enough." His over-enunciation of those words excited her.

"Don't. Be. Coy."

"Simple." His eyes were intense, his tone was serious, and his voice was firm. "I'm yours. I've always been yours, but only if you can love Isaac, too. If you can't, I'll need to say goodbye. Isaac is my top priority."

She shook her head because this was fucking crazy. Her defenses sharpened her tongue. "What do you mean you've always been mine? Where did that come from? And I could never respect you if Isaac weren't your top priority. What's this all about?"

He stood and took her hand. "Let's get out of here."

He wasn't answering her questions. He'd always been hers? Since when? He hadn't seen her in fifteen years. Bullshit. He was handing her a line. No lines. No lies. No hurting!

Next thing she knew, she was holding his hand next to the passenger door of his truck.

"I want to be alone with you." His voice and his eyes were sincere. "Would you mind a walk in the woods?"

She looked at her feet. "I love to walk in the woods, but I'm not wearing the shoes for it right now." Damn it, her voice was shaking.

"I know. We won't walk far. I can carry you if you wish. I want to show you something."

"No need to carry me." Unless all her blood drained from her head by the time they got to their destination, of course.

Katrina sorted through her mess of feelings while Aaron drove them wherever they were going.

Down syndrome. Bitch mother. And he'd always been hers?

It was a line. No man talked about devotion on a second date.

But...

His wife was dead. She'd left behind a child with special needs, and Aaron was raising that little boy *all by himself*. The thought tugged her heart. Isaac's smile flashed in her mind, spurring something like happiness.

But being happy didn't fit.

Did Aaron want something from her? Maybe. Would that something be bad for her? Unlikely. Was he telling falsehoods in order to win her over? Maybe, but only if he was a jerk, and she didn't think he was a jerk.

Was she ready for a relationship?

She didn't know.

He pulled into a lonely parking space next to the woods, a nature reserve open to the public for walks along various trails. After he opened her door, she allowed him to take her hand.

Platform sandals and a walk in the woods; the perfect pairing for a twisted ankle. She watched her feet, taking care to avoid stones and twigs as they ventured down a dirt trail. The contrast of shadows and sunlight made it difficult to see everything on the path, but she didn't want him to carry her.

The warm breeze teased her hair, causing strands to dance about her shoulders. Squirrels chirped somewhere as the call of a red-winged blackbird floated by.

She stopped.

She *remembered* this.

Aaron turned to her, and she felt his energy.

She felt...love.

Then her eyes...cried.

He wiped her cheek. "What's making you cry?" he asked, his voice as gentle as the moment should have felt.

But it didn't feel gentle.

It felt frighteningly surreal.

"Nothing," she said.

"You aren't a good liar."

"I..." She'd dreamt this. This morning. Aaron was with her. In this place. *Just like this.*

He lifted her hand to his lips and kissed it.

Whoa. Black spots. She threw her hands out for support, but couldn't get a firm grip. Whatever she was grabbing was too large for her hands. His biceps maybe? "Aaron, I'm dizzy." She felt his hands holding her up.

"What's wrong?"

Blood rushed past her ears. "I need to sit down."

A panic attack.

Fuck.

Her cells buzzed as she breathed too fast. This was bad energy, and her body was sure to collapse at any moment. She needed to sit. Damn the blood rushing past her ears. Slow down. Please.

"Here." He led her to a bench several steps away. The bench faced away from the trail, toward a small river running through the woods. She closed her eyes and focused on slowing her breath. Her blood needed to slow down.

He sat next to her. "Are you okay?"

She looked out at the river while her nerves continued their riot. "I'm feeling a bit light-headed right now. Maybe I'm dehydrated." How many lies would she tell him to cover up her defenses?

She closed her eyes. It must have been precognition. That dream was so clear and so real. She couldn't hold back her tears. She was so in love with the idea of him. A year of dreams had made every fiber of her being connect with him and he didn't have a clue.

She was in too deep.

Her nose was running. Damn it. "I need a tissue. I don't have one."

"I don't have one either."

"I need a moment to gather myself and I need a tissue." She looked at him, her eyes wide with desperation. "Now. All of this is too much for me."

He unbuttoned the rest of his shirt.

"What are you doing?"

He took off his button up, removed his undershirt, and handed it to her. "Here's a tissue."

Oh, damn her tears. She couldn't see his body through the film!

He pulled on his shirt and walked away.

She wiped her eyes and nose, closed her eyes, and worked on centering herself.

She was going to be fine.

She *had* to be fine.

Over the course of several embarrassing minutes, her body settled and relaxed.

She sat still, looking at the water through tear-spattered eyeglasses. Aaron's undershirt was settled in her hands on her lap, so she used it to clean her lenses.

He cared for her.

He must, right?

When she felt strong enough to stand, she found him standing several feet behind the bench.

"Are you okay?" he asked, concern in his voice and eyes.

"I will be. I was overwhelmed by my feelings for all of this." She looked at the undershirt in her hands. "I'm overwhelmed by my feelings for you." She looked at the trees. "It's so beautiful here and you're with me and I love it." She bit her lip and looked into his eyes.

He walked over and tucked a stray piece of her hair behind her ear. "Something's bothering you. What is it? You promised to tell me what you feel."

Her body was spent so, what the hell, she'd just say it. "I love the idea of you. Already. Too soon. And I'm scared to death. This just can't be real."

Right. It couldn't be real, so she let it fly. "And you're feeding me a line. You've always been mine? Who do you think you're kidding?" She stepped away and turned her back on him. "You're scaring me."

"That's what this is about?" He touched her hand. "I don't know what's going on, either, but after thirty years, I don't think this is too soon. It is what it is. I don't want it to stop."

She turned and buried her face in his chest. "I don't want it to stop either."

He wrapped his arms around her. "Then no worries. Okay?"

His arms made her feel safe, which reminded her that she promised herself to stop thinking. She peeked at him. "Okay. No worries."

"Katrina." His face was serious. "You were in my heart first. Before Rose. Before Isaac. If you hadn't turned me down fifteen years ago, who knows what would've happened between us. But I think it all would've headed in the same direction."

She closed her eyes. "Yes."

Entwining her fingers with his, she lifted her chin. This was it. After eleven years, her fire would be fed. His lips grazed her neck, sending thrills down her arms and into her belly. It was a thousand times more erotic than in the dreams.

"Your lips are heaven." She released his fingers, slid her hands around his waist, and pulled him into her. He was solid —all man—and she wanted to be inside him. "There's no turning back. Promise you're mine?"

He took her head between his hands, breathed his promise, and crushed his lips to hers.

Oh god.

His tongue made long strokes against hers, making it clear he was as starved as she. Hot. Needful. Tasting a delicacy after a lifetime of wanting.

Making her burn.

Everything was lips and tongues and the scent of him. Yes. One hand firm on his back, she slid the other to his pec and fondled it. He proved his strength by kneading deep into her ass, pulling her into his erection. Yes. Her moan encouraged him, so he intensified everything. Big, beautiful Aaron. He was so irresistible, her arousal would cripple her. She broke from his lips. "I want to rip you open and crawl inside your chest."

He groaned and took her mouth again, turning sensations into impulses. Determined to press her naked body to his, she untucked his shirt. He exhaled into her mouth when her fingers traced the warm, smooth skin along his waistline.

"I'll catch you first!"

She froze. It was a child's voice. A family was coming down the trail.

"Fuck." Her words were muffled in his mouth. He wasn't releasing her, so she pushed against his chest to break the dance. "Aaron, we have to go."

Expression full of reverence, he tucked his shirt while she straightened herself.

"Fuck, huh?" When finished tucking, he scooped her into his arms. "You've got a dirty mouth. I like it."

AARON

Katrina said *fuck*.

Rose *never* said fuck.

Rose never cursed.

Rose was the proper, polished, and only child of Riley and Juliana Williamson, two of the kindest, most generous, people on earth. If any home was what you'd call "healthy" or "well-adjusted", it was the Williamson's. They'd raised Rose to be a lady. Their family didn't swear. Their family didn't get drunk. Their home was peaceful. Welcoming. Full of love.

Rose was the type of woman Aaron's mother had wanted him to marry. Rose was a whiz in the kitchen—like his mother. She was a phenomenal hostess—like his mother wished to be. She doted on Aaron—like his mother. And she was as stylish as a Vogue magazine—like his mother wished to be. But Aaron hadn't married Rose for any of those reasons. He'd married her because she was pretty, loving, faithful, and *there*.

Rose was the perfect woman.

But she wasn't.

Not really.

Not for *him*. He realized this now.

Yes, she was the perfect wife. Yes, she would have been the perfect mother. Yes, she was the perfect hostess. The perfect friend. The perfect beauty. But now that Aaron had a taste of Katrina...

Rose's friends were Rose's friends. Not Aaron's.

Rose's interests were Rose's interests. Not Aaron's.

The only interest Aaron shared with Rose was art. She'd

loved interior design and fashion, so she adored that he could draw. He was damn good at drawing, too.

Well...he used to be, anyway.

She loved romantic comedies and dramas. He loved action flicks, but he never watched them.

She loved organized (tame) cocktail parties. He loved hanging out around a campfire with a cooler of (cheap) beer, but he never did.

And Aaron's friends—the ones he hadn't made time for until after Rose died—they made mistakes. They were divorced. They were raunchy. Raw. *Real*.

Like Katrina.

The man he had been with Rose wasn't a truthful version of himself. And that was okay. Then. He'd been young and happy. Then. He'd been well-cared for. Then. Life was easy. Then. But now...with Katrina...

Katrina had a fire inside her. Brutal honesty. Sexuality hiding behind those indecisive eyes. She had *imperfections*, and those imperfections were a heady draw. Her fire burned so hot, he felt it inside himself—a sensation he'd never felt with any other woman. He wanted more of it. He wanted to burn with the passions she was stirring in his darkest places.

But before he could lose himself in her flames, he needed assurance Isaac would be safe. Katrina had proven herself at lunch, but there was another big risk that Aaron needed to investigate. After all, if Katrina's beloved Jake were inclined to maul Isaac, they were going to have a problem.

After their hot kiss in the woods, they picked up Isaac and then drove to Katrina's home where she packed up Jake for a trip to the desired locale for the all-important introduction. The dog park was neutral territory.

And the introduction was a success.

"I can't believe this," Aaron said as Isaac grabbed a fistful of Jake's coat without repercussion.

Katrina beamed. "He's never been around a child before now." She shrugged. "I guess he likes little ones. Or at least he likes Isaac. I'm not surprised. He's a loving dog."

Jake continued to hold still while Isaac worked his fingers through his fur.

Katrina offered Aaron a ball. "Would you like to play with Jake so I can have some time with Isaac?"

Aaron scooped Isaac from the ground, handed him to her, and then slid the ball out of her fingers.

It was surreal. He'd never felt comfortable handing Isaac to a woman before. In fact, the only people who ever provided personal care to Isaac were the grandparents, preschool staff, and himself. Yet here Aaron was, playing fetch with a dog while his son was in the arms of the most special lady. *And Aaron wasn't worried about it.*

Yeah, Aaron knew he had her on a mile-high pedestal. Maybe it was because she felt so *right*. He'd always gone with his gut. Rose was the right choice—absolutely—for that time in his life. Starting up his own PT clinic—and then expanding the business—was another right choice made by following his gut. And asking Katrina out for a date—twice—was the right choice, too. His gut was telling him she was all kinds of right, which fed his confidence that he was on his way to something amazing.

As he played with Jake, he noticed Katrina doing something odd with Isaac's hands. Isaac was sitting on her lap—facing her—and watching her hands go up and down in patterns. It looked like...

Aaron, with Jake trotting beside him, approached her park bench.

"Are you using sign language?"

Her body jolted as if she'd been caught doing something naughty. She looked up. "Yes. Is that okay?"

He shrugged. "I guess it's okay. But why use it?"

She sat there for a long moment, eyes averted, and then held Isaac up for Aaron to take. "What do you want me to say? Do you want me to give you my educated response or my don't-make-parent-feel-stupid response?"

Her words bit him, giving him a better understanding why the asshole at Greene's interrupted their date. Her sharp tongue was one hell of a turn-on. "Educate me."

She stood. "Is he in Early Childhood Special Education?"

"Yes."

"Has the teacher or speech therapist discussed how valuable sign language can be in language development?"

He thought about the millions of handouts that came home in Isaac's backpack each month and recalled something about it. "They told me they use sign language in school. They gave me some sheets with signs on it, but I didn't think much about it."

"Have you been practicing any signs at home?"

"No," he replied, feeling uncertain about his parenting skills.

"Well that's too bad, but it isn't too late. We can start today. Isaac will need a lot of repetition to learn basic skills. Lots of repetition. Every day. We were practicing the sign for *more* and he already learned it. Do you know it?"

She modeled the sign and Aaron copied while blood rushed from his head over what she just said. "What do you mean, 'He already learned it?' He doesn't talk—at all."

She smirked while she took Isaac from Aaron and settled him on her lap. "Watch."

Katrina resumed the hand movements Aaron had seen from across the park, which was sign language for *The Itsy Bitsy*

Spider. When she finished the song, Isaac bumped his little fists together, which meant he wanted more.

Isaac signed a request for something.

Aaron's heart thrummed against his ribs while he stared at her for a long moment, trying like hell to tame the erection that wanted to bust out of his pants. Her intelligence—her skills—what she'd just taught his son—damn, he wanted to fuck her—yes, fuck her—for being *exactly* his type of perfect.

KATRINA

"What is a trisomy? And don't look in your books or notes." Katrina was beginning week two in the classroom with a more positive attitude than she had begun week one, but her energy was lacking. Her emotional roller coaster ride had worn her out.

How fitting it was that she was teaching Child Development and this particular lesson at this particular time. If someone were reading a book about this chapter of her life, they'd roll their eyes at how ridiculously obvious it all was. Obvious. Predictable. *Unbelievable.* But, it *was* really happening like this.

Since Saturday, Down syndrome had become her world, and it prompted her mind to question things. Was Aaron being his genuine self? Or was he pretending to be someone she could love in order to win her love *for Isaac*? Did Aaron truly have feelings for her? Or was he settling for her because her educational background was a good fit *for Isaac*? If Isaac did not have Down syndrome, would Aaron still want her in his life? After all, Aaron had already said things like *I'm yours but only if you can love Isaac, too. If you can't, I'll need to say good-bye.* She knew this statement indicated that he loved his son and would never allow a disagreeable woman into their lives, but her irrational mind questioned nonetheless.

These thoughts were ridiculous, of course, because what she could do for Isaac was a part of herself that she treasured. Her education and knowledge were a vital part of *self*, but the other parts of self—the dancer, the gardener, the lonely girl inside—needed to know that they were appreciated, too. She could never be happy knowing that he only wanted her *for Isaac*.

This mental chaos was exhausting, and she'd had enough. It was time to develop a new cognitive skill—the practice of "no worries" and ignoring the naysayer in her head—which meant this lesson was perfectly timed. It would serve as a session for dismantling her scaffolding for fear and reworking it into a framework for trust.

Elijah raised his hand, but she didn't call on him. He'd been confident since he spoke up during the first class. He was intelligent and possibly bored at the moment, but she couldn't let the other students rely on him to be their spokesperson, which was becoming the pattern.

Given nobody else raised a hand, she took the pressure off. "Everyone take out a sheet of paper, write down what you think the answer is, and fold your paper in half. Go."

She passed through the aisles, collected all thirty sheets, and separated them into two piles on her table. It turned out that twenty-six students were correct.

"Let's get something straight. This class is going to be a lot more interesting if you tell me what you know and engage in conversation. Twenty-six of you have the correct answer. A trisomy is when a human cell has an extra chromosome. One too many."

She led them in a discussion of trisomies of the sex chromosomes, which they'd need to know for the exam, and then she turned to the topic of her new world.

"Do any of you know someone who has Down syndrome?"

Two hands went up, and she was relieved to see they'd hear new voices. "Jane, may I ask who you know?"

Jane presented herself with professionalism. "My grandma had a little brother with Down syndrome. I never met him, but I've heard about him."

"Would you mind sharing a bit?"

Jane sat up a little more and crossed her legs. "I don't know much, but I know he was sent to an institution as a baby and lived in a group home as an adult. My grandma once said the doctors felt it was better for the family to put babies like that in an institution, so she grew up without him. He died when he was around thirty or something. She says it was sad that he died without ever having lived with his family."

Jane's disclosure shifted the energy in the room. Interest piqued.

Katrina turned her attention to the other student who'd raised a hand. "Do you mind sharing about the person you know, Manuel?"

Manuel didn't stop doodling on his notebook when he said, "My wife's sister had it."

Manuel's voice was as rough as his exterior, delivering a warning that further discussion was unwelcome. But Katrina waited a few beats to be sure.

When he didn't look up or say anything more, she continued the lesson. "Down syndrome is when the twenty-first chromosome has a third copy. And did you know there are three different types of Down syndrome?

Manuel's gaze snapped to hers, his face hard.

Now *her* curiosity piqued.

She continued. "For those of you who pay attention to and remember what I'm about to teach, you may find a reward in the form of extra credit points on the exam because there will be an essay question related to this.

"The most common type of Down syndrome is Trisomy 21 in which every cell in the human body contains a nucleus with a full third copy of chromosome twenty-one. This is the result of faulty cell division in either the egg or sperm cell prior to or at conception.

"A small percentage of people with Down syndrome have something called translocation Down syndrome in which an extra twenty-first chromosome is attached to a different chromosome.

"And an even smaller percentage of people with Down syndrome have mosaic Down syndrome in which the person has some typical cells with the proper number of twenty-first chromosomes and also some atypical cells that carry the extra chromosome.

"So what might be the difference in presentation between someone with mosaicism and someone with full Trisomy 21?"

Elijah and Jane raised their hands at the same time, so she called on Jane, who replied, "The mosaic form would be less involved maybe? The person would not have as many symptoms? Or maybe the symptoms would be less severe?"

"Exactly," Katrina replied, "and I expect everyone to know the common and uncommon symptoms of Down syndrome for the exam. Not as extra credit. But here's the big bonus item for today, and if anyone can tell me the answer right now without looking it up on the internet, the entire class gets five extra credit points. Can Down syndrome be inherited and, if so, how?" This question always stumped students, but she wasn't surprised Elijah's hand went up. She called on him.

"If Down syndrome results from abnormal cell division,

you can't say it's inherited. It's just an aberration. Also, people with Down syndrome are sterile, so they can't pass their genes on to the next generation. So, I'd say it can't be inherited."

"Be careful." Katrina's gaze roamed the room. "Some men and women with Down syndrome are fertile, although the thought that males with Down syndrome are sterile has been around for a long time. Class, what do you think? Does everyone agree with Elijah that Down syndrome cannot be inherited?"

To her surprise, Manuel raised his hand but didn't wait for her to call on him. "Elijah's wrong." The assuredness in his tone sparked smiles among his classmates, and some students turned to get a better look. But Manuel just kept doodling while addressing nobody in particular. "One type can be inherited." The rancor in his voice was unexpected, unsettling her a little.

"Translocation," he continued. "A person can carry it, you know? But not be affected as long as its *balanced*, whatever that means. There's no saying the baby will have Down syndrome, but that's why my wife doesn't wanna get pregnant. She carries it."

His disclosure had them frozen in their seats. Quiet, rough-edged Manuel Martinez, who was still doodling, had weight pressing on the room. He wanted a baby.

Fear of Down syndrome was real, and Katrina wasn't the only one in this room facing a decision. She, too, wanted a child of her own. She always had. Someday. But given her age, *someday* was running out of time. Every day that passed increased her chances of having a child with Down syndrome all her own. Youth was slipping away. She was still alone. And now she'd fallen for a guy who had a child with…

Her throat tightened as emotion churned inside. She'd cry if she weren't careful—because this reality was very new and very real—so she cleared her throat in an effort to ensure her voice was strong.

"Manuel is right." She waited a few moments while the attention of the room returned to her. "And for being the first student ever to answer correctly without use of the internet, I'll give everyone present today not five but eight extra credit points. Heck, I'll dismiss you early in just a moment. But before you go, I have one thing to add. Some food for thought.

"When someone learns their baby will be born with a condition that causes lifelong disability, as does Down syndrome, it's common for that person to grieve. The person grieves the death of the perfect child they'd been planning for."

She paused a moment to let her words sink in. And they did. She thought she heard a pin drop.

"Upon first hearing a diagnosis such as Down syndrome," she continued, "many parents feel stunned. They may go into denial or fail to comprehend what the doctor has said, so repetition of the information may be necessary until the news sinks in.

"But once tears are shed and grieving is done, and the mind is educated about what to expect and which supportive resources are available, the baby is welcomed and loved. By most parents who choose to keep their baby, at least.

"Sadly, Down syndrome is feared by the masses, and fetuses with Down syndrome are aborted often. But once parents open their hearts, they find their perfect child still exists. Just with one extra chromosome that makes him or her much more special. It's not easy. But it's life."

Damn. Her voice quavered on the last sentence. She needed to keep her emotions in check, so she added a quick, "Class dismissed," and stacked papers at her desk to avoid eye contact while students filed out of the room.

They were quieter than usual as they departed, and she was thankful for it because she was spent.

This shouldn't be hard. There was not much to decide, really. Isaac was part of Aaron, and, with her education, she had nothing to fear. She could handle it. In fact, her situation was fortunate in a morbid sort of way. Rose had passed, so the path was clear for her to become a mother figure. Not that Isaac needed one. Aaron was an amazing dad and Isaac had two loving grandmas. Well, at least one loving grandma, she was sure. The jury was out on Sarah Keller at the moment. But...

If Katrina and Aaron worked out long-term, Isaac might be better off with her in his life.

Maybe.

She needed to find strength in that possibility and believe that Aaron wanted her for more than what she could do *for Isaac.*

"So," Gen pointed her lettuce-laden fork at Katrina during Monday lunch, "you're in love with a widowed man who lives almost two hours away and has a kid with a disability. Are you prepared to survive another long-distance relationship?"

Distance was a test, and Katrina was okay with that. When it came to relationships, distance made truth salient. After all, it was distance that taught her she wasn't a priority in Connor's life.

Aaron had a child—priority one. He had a flourishing business—priority two. The distance between them would prove what their relationship could be. If their bond strengthened in spite of the distance, it would be proof they could last. Her own responsibilities—Jake, her house, her career—were a security blanket that gave her confidence she could handle being priority three.

While their trek between the homes last Saturday had been fun, it wasn't an easy distance for any sort of long-term intimate relationship, especially during a Michigan winter where ice and snow turned the morning commute into a session of prayer for more than a few months. She wasn't naïve. But at the moment, her priority was sorting through her feelings about the whole thing. Distance wasn't a top concern.

"Two hours isn't really long distance. He's not in another state like Connor was."

Gen shook her head. "It's far enough away that you can't be with him all the time. How do you know he's not a player? He sounds too perfect."

"First-of-all, it's not healthy to be with your partner all the time. Clingy relationships don't work out. And second-of-all... he's not a player."

"And how do you know this?"

"One, he's already introduced me to his mother and son. Two, he let me handle his phone to select music while he was driving. Three, he never had a reputation as a player when we were younger. I knew who his girlfriends were and he seemed to treat them well." Damn. She sounded like a middle schooler.

Gen focused on her soup, so Katrina turned attention to her own salad. One of the reasons she enjoyed Gen's company was because of how alike they were. Independent. And—

"Katrina, I'm happy for you, but I wouldn't be a friend if I didn't say I'm little worried. Within the space of a week, you've fallen head-over-heels in love with a man who has some baggage and lives in another part of the state. How do you know he won't break that heart you've been protecting all these years?"

—she told it like she saw it.

"Gen, you don't need to worry about me. I'm still the same

strong woman I was two weeks ago. It's like a car accident that amputates a person's leg." Katrina grinned, thankful her humor was getting stronger by the day in spite of the internal reconstruction that was underway around the clock.

Gen set down her soup spoon and folded her arms on the table. "What in the hell does that mean?"

Katrina pointed her lettuce-laden fork at her friend. "The accident happens unexpectedly and changes life forever. There's no going back."

"You're comparing your relationship to a tragic car accident? Oh, Katrina." Gen shook her head but smiled nonetheless.

"No. I'm saying that sometimes unexpected and significant life changes happen in an instant." She took a bite of salad, determined to stand by her declaration. It did sound odd, but it was her truth.

Her life had changed.

There was no going back.

Yet she had no idea where she was headed.

"Do you have a picture of this superman?"

Katrina pulled out her cell phone and showed Gen the wallpaper, an image of Katrina with Aaron, Isaac, and Jake at the dog park.

Her eyes went wide. "Hell, he's hotter than Stevens. No wonder you're hooked."

Katrina considered the image. Yeah, Aaron *was* smoking hot, but that wasn't the whole of it. "Trust me, his beauty runs deep."

Gen's expression was playful skepticism.

"It does." Katrina laughed. "But I have to admit he's the most attractive man I've ever known." She turned off her phone. "He's so beautiful I find it hard to believe he's mine."

"Girl, turn that thing back on." After Katrina did as told,

Gen took the phone and held it out for Katrina to analyze. "Look at that photo. You and hottie are a fantastic match, physically, but what about the boy? How does he fit into your life plans?"

Katrina took the phone and put it away. Isaac had run through her mind so often over the past couple of days, he'd worn a path. A path that led in a single direction. A path that was dim, but not dark. A path that led somewhere foreign, but not frightening. And Manuel's disclosure during her morning lesson provided the lantern she needed to navigate her steps. Isaac and Manuel were *signs*.

"It's simple." Kind of. Not really. But one thing was clear. She'd never be able to live with the decision to cut Aaron out of her life because of Down syndrome. That decision would create regret. Only a fool would choose regret, and only a monster would exclude such a special child from her life. Katrina was neither fool nor monster. "Isaac is part of me now. He, Aaron, and I seem to be three puzzle pieces that make the whole. I know Isaac's disability will be a challenge, but I'm up for it."

She *had* to be.

***

Katrina had been busy all week. Between long phone conversations with Aaron, working outside, and exercising with Jake, she'd completed all of next week's class preparation. She was looking forward to her first overnight with Aaron—which would happen tomorrow—and the only thing that had her feelings all twisted was this moment.

It was Thursday.

She'd give Stevens the option. He could play for her if he wanted to, but that would be it. Friends only.

She finished stretching and moved onto practicing pirouettes—doubles and triples—thankful the movement was spending some of the nervous energy built up in expectation of letting Stevens down when he arrived.

Then Joplin's *Maple Leaf Rag* joined her, giving the pirouettes a cartoonish feel. She spun and spun as best as she could, but it was no use. Her giggles emerged in spite of her nerves, making it too hard to carry on, just like every time before.

"Is this your way of telling me my turns suck?"

Stevens stopped playing. "What was that?" His smile was as childlike as she felt. Probably because he remembered all the times before, too. She could never keep spinning when he made her laugh.

She approached the piano. "Is this your way of telling me my turns suck?"

"Not at all. Your turns are amazing. I was just having some fun." He winked at her.

Her heart sank, taking her smile with it.

She had to ruin the fun.

She ran her fingers along the sleek edge of the black piano top. "Cam, I can't do this. I'm not interested in a relationship. I won't go out with you tomorrow night and because of that I don't think it's fair to have you play for me tonight. This isn't going to work."

His smile faded. "Why?"

Oh, she didn't like hurting him. Yes, he was a cheat, but... "I've changed my mind. Like I said, I'm not interested in a relationship. It's better everything stops now so nobody gets hurt."

He turned to the keys, silent.

She felt wretched but resisted the impulse to touch his shoulder. She shouldn't feel bad. He hurt her long ago.

But she didn't like hurting him back.

Then he played something she'd never heard before. Something haunting. And for the first time ever, she watched him get lost in music.

His hands were sure, long and strong masters of the instrument. His arms, muscled and tanned, flexed and flowed while his hands danced on the keys.

His profile was fierce, ablaze with the emotion he was channeling into the piano, making her feel disconnected. Melancholy and fluid, the melody washed over her, tugging her toward movement. She stepped back and let her body turn into the floor.

His music swelled, became wilder, and carried her to another realm. She closed her eyes and felt. All she needed to do was feel and the movement happened.

Ultimate peace.

Ultimate power.

Ultimate freedom.

She was in an ethereal dimension, a place where nothing could touch her.

She was all emotion and movement and connectivity.

She wasn't sure how many minutes passed before fatigue pulled her into the floor to rest.

His music slowed with her.

She closed her eyes when a pang of guilt stole her peace.

She'd robbed him of something. He'd given her his precious music, but she hadn't given him the truth. He didn't know she was in love with someone else. She didn't know why, but she couldn't bring herself to say the words.

She rose to face him.

He was standing next to the instrument, his back to her, watching her in the mirror. His eyes were still fierce. "That music is yours. You're a beautiful dancer and I want to play for you. Whenever you wish it."

Part of her felt sad. Part of her felt elated. Part of her felt unworthy.

"Are you sure?"

He snatched his keys from atop the piano and turned toward the door. "Like I said, whenever you wish it."

"Have you decided where you're going to plant that rose bush Aaron gave you?" Marina's question had Katrina scanning her property as she rocked in a chair on her back porch at sunset on Thursday evening.

"You know what? I can't decide where to put it. For some reason, all the places I think of don't seem right. I'll figure it out at some point."

"Why not put it in your perennial garden?"

"It won't work in there. I'll figure it out. It has to be the right spot." Holding her wine glass steady in one hand, Katrina clutched the phone with her shoulder and used her other hand to pull a blanket over her legs because the sun had dipped beneath the horizon.

"I know you'll find the perfect spot when the time is right. I'm glad to hear you're so happy. And little Isaac sounds sweet. You sure you're okay with everything?"

"Yes. I am. No regrets. Going to see Aaron was the best thing I've ever done."

"Good. Aaron is a good man."

Those were predictable words, which reduced their value. Part of the reason Marina stayed with Katrina's father for so long was because she always looked for the good no matter the cost. Her positivity was a blessing, but it also was once her curse. Some people were not good. Marina still had trouble seeing that, though she'd gotten much better over the years.

"How do you know he's a good man?" Katrina said. "You don't know him."

"He's a gentleman, sweetie. He called me the morning after your first date to ask permission to court you before he sent the roses. And he actually used the word *court*. He needed your address, so I gave it to him."

What? Her mother had known all this time? Even that morning after their first date? Then why—

"Also, Sarah, his mother, contacted me this past Sunday. She gave me some insight into his situation. Do you know how his wife died?"

Sarah talked to her mom? Katrina was feeling a little disembodied. A little violated. Like her boyfriend's scary mom was looking down her nose. Again.

"No, I haven't asked yet because it's a sensitive topic. More importantly, why in the world did his mother contact you?"

"Well, remember Sarah and I were acquaintances through the church choir before she and Robert moved away to live near Aaron and his wife. Sarah wanted to talk about the two of you because she's worried. She mentioned Aaron's wife died of brain cancer shortly after Isaac was born. Aaron was devastated. Sarah said he hasn't been himself since. That is, until two weeks ago. You show up on his doorstep and he's become the happiest man in the world."

These words should've made her happy, but they didn't. It was too good to be true, so she couldn't trust it. "You're just saying that because you're my mom."

"No." Marina's tone was serious. "Sarah told me this is the happiest she's ever seen Aaron in her life. He's so happy, it scares her. It's like he's a different person. She's worried about him. Those dreams must have come from somewhere. You were right to follow them. And if you don't mind me being bold, I think he might be as fragile as you. Take care."

Katrina really made him *that* happy? The power of that thought was humbling. She needed to respect it. "Mom, will you promise me something?"

Marina chuckled. "Depends on what you want me to promise."

"Promise you'll be there when all of this rips me to pieces. I'm being strong, but..."

"Stop. You don't need to worry about this. Think of it this way. You've never been impulsive or thoughtless in your actions. And look what you've accomplished. Expect wonderful things, sweetie. Enjoy it."

PART FOUR
TRANSITIONS
MAY

Four

KATRINA

"I hope your drive was pleasant."

Katrina's belly full of butterflies attempted to carry her away as she took her first step into Aaron's home. Once inside, she wrapped her arms around him and squeezed to keep herself grounded. "My drive was beyond pleasant, thank you."

"I'm very happy you're here." Aaron kissed the top of her head, making the butterflies cartwheel. His arms felt like home and, to be honest, if hugging were the only thing they'd do all weekend, she'd be okay with it.

"Let me show you the guest suite." He stepped back and took her hand. "Did you bring Jake?"

"Yeah, he's waiting in the SUV. I've got his dog crate, too." She followed Aaron through the two-story foyer into a hallway that ran through the middle of the house.

Hung in the hall was a set of three large black-ink drawings on white background. They were beautifully detailed pieces, matted in olive green, and set inside sleek black frames, a wonderful accent for the appealing neutral palate of the home's transitional décor. One drawing, the face of a sleeping baby, hung between two drawings of a breathtaking woman whose stunning full-lipped smile (complete with dimples) was so warm and welcoming Katrina could feel it.

She tugged Aaron's hand to stop him. "Aaron, she's beautiful. Who is she?"

His eyes appraised Katrina before he nodded toward the wall. "That's Rosalie. How I remember her."

Katrina's lungs pulled a quick breath. "*You* drew these?"

He nodded.

His drawings were exquisite. Art without question. And his subject...

"You never told me you're an artist. And Rosalie is...stunning."

He turned his eyes to the drawing closest to her. "Yes, she was."

She squeezed his hand. "No. She *is*." She looked into his eyes, which were regarding her with something that made her insides all warm. "Do you draw often?"

He rolled his lips inward and shook his head. "Not anymore."

His countenance teetered on the edge of emotion, so she squeezed his hand again and whispered, "You were going to show me the guest suite."

He whispered back, "I was, wasn't I?" and then led her to the end of the hall where he gestured for her to open a door.

She stepped forward and opened it.

It was absolutely cliché. Unnecessary. And totally over the top. But the way her heart was pattering over his efforts—the planning and thoughtfulness—it was five hundred percent perfect for her.

It was the grandest gesture any man had ever given her—Connor never did anything grand because she'd never asked him to—and she'd take it a million times over because Aaron Keller was making one thing clear: for whatever reason, she mattered to him.

Six massive bouquets of roses, each a different color, were placed here and there around the space. She walked to the table in front of the large bay window and took in the full, sweet scent of the room.

"I hope you like them."

"You didn't need to do this, Aaron." She breathed in a little bit of heaven. "But I love them."

He embraced her from behind. "I'm used to treating a woman like a lady. It feels good. But there's more to this than you think." He gave her a squeeze. "The pink are for happiness...peach are for appreciation...yellow are for friendship...red are for romance...orange are for the fire you feed."

He stopped talking, so she looked up and found that his eyes were glistening just like hers.

"And what about the white?" She stepped out of his embrace and turned toward the flowers on the table in front of the window.

He sniffed once and cleared his throat. "The white represent our beginning as little kids."

Shit. To say he was romantic wasn't quite right. The man was *sentimental*. He *felt*. And only he knew how deeply. Apparently, her mom's advice was on the right track. He must be fragile in some way, but how?

She wrapped her arms around him. "I love it all, you beautiful, beautiful man."

He lifted and landed her on the bed, his lips pressing into hers long enough to send her blood south. But then he pulled away. "I can't wait to take you out tonight. My mom is coming over to pick up Isaac at 5:30. You've got forty minutes to get ready. Does that work?"

She beamed. "Yes. Where'll we be going? I need to dress properly."

"I won't tell you where. But we'll have some fine dining in an upper-end casual place and then go for drinks and music. I'll help you get Jake settled, but be ready by 5:40." He winked and left the room.

Yeah, she needed to keep her head out of her way because it was telling her he was too perfect. Don't get too comfortable. Something was sure to go wrong. Do. Not. Trust. But...

Maybe dreams do come true?

She walked over to the bouquet of white roses and ran her hands over the soft blooms. Such a beautiful thing...Aaron Keller treated her like a *priority*.

Katrina found out he was an artist and now this? She smacked Aaron's rear as punishment for keeping secrets from her. "You never told me you have a customized Road Runner."

Her excitement for tonight surged as she approached the classic muscle car in the garage. The exterior was crisp black with a set of subtle black metal-flake racing stripes. The chrome rims were bright, either well-cared for, rarely driven, or both.

He opened the passenger door for her, revealing a sight more unexpected than a roomful of roses. The interior of this gorgeous beast was deep red crushed...

"Velvet?"

Aaron, who was standing next to the open door waiting for her to get in, winked.

She settled into the seat (because sliding in was impossible) and took a moment to assess the situation. Former high school basketball star, Aaron Keller, was an artist with a naughtily-upholstered classic car. She hadn't seen that coming.

She'd always loved running her fingers over velvet, so she gave it a go. With the grain. Against the grain. Drawing patterns. Hell, to be honest, the seat was enough to make her wet just playing with the sexy, blood-red upholstery.

"A car like this needs to drive a beautiful woman." He settled into the driver's seat. "And here you are, beautiful. Buckle up."

She was loving the sensations this night had gifted her so far. His roses. His lips. His...upholstery. And the best was about to come because his hand was on the key. Her body prepared by settling deep into the seat.

When the engine roared with life, rumbly vibrations penetrated her. Raw power. She. Loved. It.

He backed out and they were on their way.

"Yet again, I find myself impressed by your knowledge, Dr. Lopez. This is a Road Runner. A '68 to be exact. Do you know much about cars?"

"Some but not much. My father was a mechanic. He had some favorite classic cars and I learned a bit about them when I was little. We went to lots of car shows together and I always liked the Road Runners. He'd always wanted to customize a car, but it never happened."

"Why not?"

"Guess the opportunity never presented itself. We didn't have money for that sort of thing. And then he died young."

"I'm sorry to hear that." He stroked the back of her left hand with his thumb.

One of a handful of good memories of her father popped into her head, so she asked, "Will we be taking the freeway?"

"Yes, we're heading to Saginaw."

A cool thing about having a mechanic as a father was the opportunity to ride in muscle cars after he fixed them. He always offered to take her for a too-fast drive on the highway after he finished a job. He called it his little reward for working hard. Those joy rides were pretty much the only thing that made him happy. He enjoyed sharing those rides with her, so she joined him every time he offered.

Aaron would be pulling on in about a mile, so she secured the orange rose she'd brought with her under her clutch on the floor, cranked the handle to roll down her window, and settled back into the seat, eyes closed. Aaron took the cue and rolled down his window as well.

It had been ages. Her last ride like this was when she was... ten. Yeah, on a summer night when Dad had finished rebuilding the engine on a GTO for that asshole friend who never paid him. His drunken rage following that fallout was the one that landed Mom in the hospital for a couple of days. The hospital stay that opened Mom's eyes to—

The Road Runner was turning...

Her hair took flight as the car tore onto the freeway. The seat sucked her close, so she ground her body into its naughty red fabric. "I love this!"

She opened her eyes to look at Aaron, who was gripping the wheel with his left hand, powerful and sure of himself. Damn, he was hot.

They flew for twenty exhilarating miles before exiting.

When the ride slowed, she worked on untangling her hair. "Did you customize this yourself?"

"No. No time. I bought it five years ago for a good price. Figured it would be a good project for me but didn't do anything with it for the first couple years. Then Isaac came and Rose died. My dad took the car at that point. He wanted me to be happy, so he worked on it. He'd run ideas by me. I paid. And here it is."

"And here it is." She squeezed his hand. "Has your dad customized many cars?"

"Two, not including this one. He got the idea for the velvet from a lowrider he saw at a car show in Texas. I was nervous about the idea at first. It's..." He gave her a sideways glance. "...different."

His gaze returned to the road. "But my dad had just recovered from a heart attack and with my life being all...chaotic, he thought we should go for it. Add some whimsy to our lives, as he put it. Hope you like it."

She rubbed her hand over the seat. "I love it. It's hot." She leaned forward to pick up the rose.

"I see you decided to bring a rose. Why orange?"

All smiles because he noticed the color, her reply was flirty. "Because tonight my favorite color is orange."

"Is that so? And do your color preferences change by time of day?"

"Nope. Until tonight, my long-standing favorite color had been purple, but there's something about this orange I like very much."

He raised an eyebrow. "Fire?"

She winked. "Fire. So do you take this sexy beast out often?"

Aaron cut the engine in an angled spot in front of a set of windows on a downtown street lined with bars, restaurants, and some specialty shops, including a tattoo parlor. The car was getting stares.

"Very rarely. I'm protective of it. But I think I'll be taking her out more often in the future. Hungry?" He opened his door, walked around the vehicle, and helped her out.

Hand-in-hand, they walked through the front door of a

place called Vintage. Arranged on the old brick interior walls were oil paintings under spotlights. The space was dim, themed in black and red, with tall black booths lining the back wall. Tables finished the perimeter and the bar sat in the center. It was a sophisticated, adult environment without a child in sight.

"Table, booth, or bar?"

"Booth."

Aaron talked to the hostess, who led them away from foot traffic to the back corner of the room. After taking their seats, Aaron craned his neck in what appeared to be an effort to look out the front windows. Then the waiter came and took their drink orders. Aaron requested an Old Fashioned and, Katrina, a bottle of Pinot Noir.

Katrina reviewed her menu. "Is a crowd forming?"

"I can't see. Just feeling protective. This is my first time leaving her alone in public. I usually just take her for a cruise."

"Don't worry. She's a big girl. Relax." Katrina looked up from her menu. "Do you know what you want to order?" She nodded toward his untouched menu.

He picked it up, a movement that caused his biceps to flex just right. Black shirt sleeves tugged against muscles and the fabric hugged his pecs. The hollow of his neck, which peeked out from behind the unbuttoned collar, looked as delicious as it had tasted last week Saturday when she had forced herself to say goodbye. She pressed herself into her seat as his long-lashed eyes reviewed the menu. Damn. Who knew watching him read a menu could be so arousing? A smile swept her face.

Aaron set down the menu and looked up. "What?"

She rubbed her glossy lips together. "I'm curious about something and I'm wondering if you're prepared to discuss it."

The waiter delivered their drinks and took their orders. Both selected filet mignon.

"We can discuss anything. Shoot."

She cocked her head. "When is the last time you were with a woman?"

He took a drink—a long one considering his drink was pretty much 100% alcohol—and then looked into her eyes. "The last woman I had sex with was my wife."

Heat rocketed through her and settled into her pelvis. Something about being the *next* woman made her heavier with want. "How did you manage to go three years without sex? I'm sure you've had to beat women off with a stick. And you don't seem the violent type."

He took a deep breath. "The first, rather large, portion of those three years was spent in mourning for my wife while I was a first-time dad raising a baby with special needs."

When he put it that way, her question felt childish. But feeling stupid at the moment didn't stop her from wanting to know more. "Continue."

"You really want to hear this?"

She nodded.

"After a long while—rather recently actually—I tried dating a few women, but none of them compared to Rose. And I don't have meaningless sex."

Not having meaningless sex was a plus, but he compared the women to his deceased wife? That stunning, full-lipped beauty he'd lovingly drawn up and hung in the art gallery he called a hallway outside his guest suite? Hurt tugged her face and she kind of spat the words, "I'm not Rose, either."

He looked away without a word.

He'd better not expect her to be like Rosalie.

"No, you're not Rose."

She held her breath while he drained his glass.

"Don't you realize?" His brow knitted. "Those other women couldn't compare to Rose, but..."

Her breath held while he decided how to finish his

sentence. His eyes were searching her, but she couldn't tell if they saw Katrina or some sickening illusion of his dead wife.

He tilted his head forward, brow raised, and said, "But Rose couldn't compare to you. I've always loved you."

No way.

She couldn't believe him.

No man talked about love this soon.

Heat of a different kind rocketed past her heart and settled in her head, fueling her mouth. "You've always *loved* me? You're lying. Don't you *ever* lie to me."

"Katrina—" He ran a hand through his hair. "Katrina, I—"

"Don't. Lie. To. Me." Her voice was bile. If he couldn't be trusted, she didn't know what she'd do.

No. Not true.

She would run. She could always run. But to run away from Aaron?

No.

Her messed up brain was trying to take charge. Telling her to protect herself. To be afraid.

No.

No worries.

No worries.

No worries.

She needed to hear him out.

"You look totally pissed, but you're going to hear this anyway." He offered a little smile. "It's hard to explain. When we were little, I loved your hair. I remember daydreaming about it during school. I always wanted to run my fingers through it."

She thought back to one of her dearest memories—a time when he stroked her hair while they listened to the teacher read a story during carpet time—and then the heat settled back down into her belly.

She'd been so young, yet so aware of how he made her feel. Even back in second grade, he was gentle. He made her feel protected, which was something she'd imagined to be love.

He wasn't lying.

"I loved seeing you smile," he said, "and I always wondered why you didn't. I felt the need to watch out for you. I guess I felt protective. Remember when we used to pick teams in elementary school, like at recess?"

She gave a little smile. "Yes."

"And do you remember how rotten you were at sports?"

She rolled her eyes. "Yes."

"Did you ever notice you weren't the last one picked?"

The stupid, innocent, childlike truth in his words dismantled her defenses. "Oh, I just thought you didn't like Brandon. He and I were always the last available and he was less athletic than I. At least *I* was coordinated.

"During elementary school, my home life was shit. My dad was abusive. I was always afraid of the next attack. I avoided others and protected myself, usually by snapping at people who I thought were being mean.

"As I got older, I realized the world wasn't nearly as cruel as I had thought it was. But because I'd been so quiet and defensive all those years, I didn't have friends. And it didn't help my self-esteem that I was skinny. Girls made fun of me. A lot. My mom always told me they were jealous, but I didn't believe it. Boys didn't pay me any attention like they did the other girls and—"

"I paid attention." He held out his hand, so she gave him hers. He squeezed. "I remember one time when I heard the girls teasing you because you had strings hanging from your skirt. You looked down to find the strings, but there weren't any. They burst out laughing and said they were mistaken. They were looking at your legs."

She laughed. "Oh, I remember that day. We were playing tag and they stopped the game to tease me. You know, the teasing hurt. I didn't fit in. Mom didn't dress me well enough to fit in. And I couldn't read fast enough. And I sucked at math. I felt stupid and ugly. I was so insecure. And I felt that way until high school."

"You felt that way all those years? We didn't think of you like that."

"Who are *we*?"

"The boys. And the girls. We couldn't understand why you didn't talk. And when you did, you attacked people. I guess that's what you meant by being defensive? I didn't talk to you much, but I listened as much as I could. I didn't always know why you were hurting, but it hurt me to see it. I did what I could to make you feel better, like picking you for my team. When I got a chance to sit next to you, I took it.

"And there was one time when we were a bit older, in middle school, some girls grilled me about who I wanted for a girlfriend and without even thinking about what I was saying, I said you. My answer surprised me. Maybe I was yet again trying to raise you up. When they laughed, I told them I thought you were nice. I found out later they were nasty to you about what I said."

The pain of that moment flashed through her. "Gosh, that was ages ago. Those girls were evil and you knew your words hurt me?"

He gave her a barely-there nod. "I've had some regret all these years because I was too much of a coward to talk to you about what happened that day. Back then, I was too worried about being cool."

"Gee. Thanks." She pulled her hand from his, grabbed her glass of wine, and took a sip. "Did you have more to say?"

He pressed his lips together, stifling a smile. "I kept an eye on you through high school. I saw you were coming out of your shell. Slowly. I saw you were on honor roll. I saw you smiling more."

"Yeah, I was gaining confidence. My parents divorced when I was ten, following my mom's hospital stay that opened her eyes to the dangers of raising children amidst violence. The divorce helped the home life and my dad died when I was fifteen.

"This sounds sick but, to be honest, his death liberated me. I was finally able to venture forth without being held down by emotional manipulation and pain. I was able to work myself out of the defensiveness for the most part. I was happier."

Aaron smiled. "You were. I saw it. And during senior year, from a distance, I was realizing what you meant to me. I had a crush."

"Then why didn't you do anything about it? Why didn't you tell me?"

"Come on now. Think Dr. Lopez."

"I don't want to think. Tell me."

"Because. I'm a guy."

"You're still a guy. Why didn't you tell me?"

He cocked his head. "You're a psychologist and you can't figure that out?"

Damn, he was cute. Nervous energy and wine had her all... she didn't know. She wanted to be inside him. That's all she wanted.

"Fine," he said, "because I was an insecure boy back then. The person talking to you now is a grown man who's buried a wife and is raising a child by himself." He shrugged. "I had to grow up."

"You were insecure, too? I never would've guessed."

"Yeah," he said as if she'd missed the obvious. "Why do you think I never said much? I was too afraid of what other people would think. Even worse, I was afraid you'd attack me, Miss Defensive. I was too insecure to be your friend."

She exhaled and then said to herself more than him, "And the whole time I was crushing on you, I thought you didn't know I existed."

Aaron did a double-blink. "Wait. You were crushing on me? When?"

"Oh, like from kindergarten all the way through high school graduation." A tiny smile played on Katrina's lips. "My heart melted a little every time you sat by me and picked me for your team. My heart broke when those girls made that joke about you wanting me to be your girlfriend. That hurt more than anything. You never talked to me unless you had to and you were so distant. I never thought I had a chance, but I adored you anyway."

Aaron shook his head. "You did a great job covering your feelings. I never would've guessed you liked me at all. Guys need encouragement."

"I know. I learned that soon after we graduated. I met Connor in biology class that fall. He did everything he could to get me to notice him without talking to me. He made me laugh and so I started talking to him. He was putty in my hands after that. For a while anyway."

"Katrina, when I saw you that one day after two years apart..." He shook his head. "I finally found the courage to ask you out, and then you rejected me in an instant. You were sweet about it, too. I knew I never had a chance."

"I was committed to Connor at that time. I wasn't available. It was as simple as that. But I did lay awake that night, after I turned you down. I realized I could have made a different choice. I, myself, was in disbelief I'd turned you down so easily. But I loved Connor and you'd been locked in the back of my mind because I knew I never had a chance with you. Guess we were both way wrong, huh?"

He nodded.

"I'm wondering something more, but I'm kind of afraid to ask." Her voice was small, but his eyes encouraged her. "Before I arrived at your house the other day, had you ever thought about me since Rose died? If you *loved* me so much, wouldn't you have looked me up?"

He took a long drink of water, emptying his glass, and then examined the ice for a moment. "To tell the truth, I think I've been thinking about you for over a year now, but I didn't realize it was you until after you came to visit me."

His eyes held apprehension. "I never considered you as an option after you turned me down, so, no, I never consciously thought of you after Rose died. It turns out I was thinking of you during my sleep. I've been dreaming about you, but I didn't know it until after you came to see me."

She waited, heart pounding.

"Don't think me weird, okay? But I'd been dreaming of someone for over a year. Her face was always a blur. We never talked. We never touched but came close. Almost always innocent, as if I was protecting her.

"Last week, I saw her face clearly for the first time. It was you. Maybe I wanted it to be you, but I believe it had been you all along. I'd been seeing her more frequently before your visit. I've only had one more dream since that night you showed up."

Her chest was thumping. She cleared her throat. "Tell me what happened in the last dream."

"Think of last week when I took you for a walk in the woods."

She nodded.

"In the dream, I was following you down that trail. It was sunny, like the day we went. You turned toward me and—"

"I know. You saw me crying."

Aaron's eyes went wide.

Her voice strained through the tension in her throat. "Your eyes told me how much you loved me. You lifted my hand and kissed it."

"You had the same dream." He'd whispered more to himself than to her.

She nodded. "That's why I got so emotional and needed to sit down during our walk. I thought I was experiencing precognition. I had that dream the night before you took me to the woods."

He nodded.

"I was so affected by the power of that dream, and being with you, I had a mild panic attack. I so wanted that dream to be real." She wiped a tear from her cheek. "Aaron..." She looked at the table.

"Yes."

The table was marred on the corner. "Did you ever dream of her—me—being at your parents' house?" She ran her finger over the damage.

"Yes, you were there to meet my family, but for some reason you spent all your time—"

She interrupted again. "In the guest bedroom, waiting for you."

"Yes."

Heart still racing, she looked at him. "Did you ever dream of being with her—me—on the beach on a sunny day?"

"Yes." He cleared his throat. "I recall enjoying my view of your legs."

Yeah, she enjoyed that, too. "And the next night we were in a parking lot near that same beach. We were so close to each other, I could feel your breath on my lips."

"But resisting the kiss." He gave her a sexy smile. "That dream made me come."

His words sent a jolt of passion through her. "Yes, it did."

"You too?"

She nodded. "And I almost came again a couple of weeks ago, the morning after my surprise visit. I dreamed of dancing for you."

"Yes," he replied. "That one was a...doozy."

"And yet my favorite dream was when we were walking, side-by-side, through that grassy field in the country."

He nodded. "I wanted to walk with you forever that night, and I wished our walk didn't end when we—"

"—got to the barn." Their voices, together, had finished the sentence.

"I felt absolutely complete during that walk. Like nothing could stop us." She tried to smile, but her lip quivered. While reason screamed impossibility, her soul was crying truth, and the conflict of assuredness and disbelief was making her head swim.

Now she could tell him.

"The dreams are the reason I came to see you. They always felt so real. They were so wonderful and so powerful. But unlike your dreams, your face was never blurry in mine. I always knew it was you. I couldn't understand why I kept dreaming of you. And the dreams were becoming so frequent, they began to bother me—in a good way.

"I felt a strong drive to visit you. I needed to see you in person. I knew if I mentioned the dreams, you'd think I was crazy and so I didn't say a word about them. And here we are."

The waiter arrived at a silent table and placed their dishes. "Is everything alright?" His voice was full of concern.

The tension was tangible, so Katrina gave the waiter a

gentle smile. "Everything is perfect. He's just made me a very happy woman."

The waiter gave a slight nod before leaving.

She laid a napkin on her lap and cut her filet without looking at Aaron. They'd shared dreams. *That* wasn't in any credible textbook. Enter the realm of psychics, Katrina. How in the hell did this happen?

"So it's only fair you tell me the last time you were with a man."

She stopped cutting and looked up.

"That's how the conversation got started, isn't it? You asked me to tell the last time I was with a woman." His eyes challenged her, a playful turn on the corner of his mouth.

Surprised and pleased with the avenue he'd chosen for continued conversation, she put it all on the table. "I'm a good girl. I've been with only one man—a man I thought I was going to marry—and I told you how that ended. It's been eleven years since Connor. Yes, I've been pursued. Yes, I've dated other guys. But I never let it get that far because none of them measured up."

He laughed. "You've only been with *one* guy? You must have beaten them off with a stick. And you *do* seem the violent type."

"I'm not easy, Aaron." She finished cutting and put down her knife. "So now I'm wondering how many women you've been with."

He pretended to count beyond ten fingers. "Several."

"You bad boy. You don't have anything catchy, do you?"

His eyes flared. "No."

"How can I be sure, you slut?"

"It was a long time ago. I was young. All of them happened to be virgins and I used condoms. They all were girlfriends. No one-nighters. I'm a good guy."

"Oh yes, good guys regularly go around deflowering women they aren't married to."

"I smell hypocrisy. Did you not have sex out of wedlock?"

"I fully intended to marry him."

"But you didn't. And I wonder how many women he deflowered before he stole you from me. Did you grill him with all these questions before your first time?"

"Absolutely. He was a young college freshman, only seventeen when we met in the fall. He was a virgin, too. A late bloomer like me." She bit her cheek to repress the smile that was trying to bust out. "He was a gentleman. We dated a year before we had sex because I needed to know he was committed to me first. And a year was enough time to prove that."

Aaron looked at his plate.

Gotcha.

They ate their meals in silence while occasional flirty glances and more alcohol provided entertainment.

After the longest lull in conversation to date, she took a final swallow of wine and walked around to Aaron's side of the table. She leaned down so she could whisper in his ear. "No worries, Aaron. I'm wet for you. You need to decide what you're going to do about that and when."

Then she dropped the orange rose on his lap.

"Open your eyes."

Curiosity piqued following that mysterious after-dinner car ride, Katrina opened her eyes and found herself standing in the middle of an upscale jewelry store where two salespeople were poised behind the counter. Their smiling eyes gazed at them, the only two customers in the store.

"We have one hour."

"One hour for what, Aaron?"

"To select your engagement ring."

Nervous laughter tore out of her. He was out of his mind. "You can't be serious."

He pulled her close. "I'm one hundred percent serious."

"Aaron," her whisper was harsh, "you can't be serious." She was feeling pretty dizzy at the moment, partly due to the wine and partly due to the fact that this night had to be a joke. Unbelievable. It was either a joke or she was losing her sanity.

"You're intelligent, successful, independent, confident, and beautiful. You're perfect for me and my son. I want you forever. Please be my wife."

Shit. "I need to sit. Take me out of here." She didn't register anything she saw, but she felt his hands guide her to a seat somewhere outside the jewelry store. She sat, leaned forward, and took five slow breaths. When her heart rate slowed, she sat up and found herself on a park bench on the sidewalk facing the jewelry store window.

This kind of thing just didn't happen. Well, it did, but not to rational, educated, responsible people like her. She had simply wanted to know if the dreams meant anything.

No. Maybe someone put something in one of her drinks.

No. She wasn't drugged.

She wasn't even that drunk.

The man of her dreams—literally of her dreams—just asked her to marry him.

There he was, pacing the sidewalk in front of her, quite possibly more nervous than she was at the moment.

What did Mom say?

He was fragile?

Here they were, not even three full weeks in, and they'd discussed more about feelings than some married couples do in a lifetime.

Not many women could add a proposal to a night of surprise roses and surprise dreams. And surprise upholstery.

She watched him pace, but he wasn't looking at her.

Marriage?

She just wanted to see where this would go. But...time.

She needed time.

Engagement wasn't marriage.

Engagement was no big deal.

At her age, engagement would be kind of...cool.

Nothing official needed to be rushed.

She took a deep breath. "Aaron, please sit by me."

He did.

Given she couldn't bring herself to look at him, she stared at their reflection in the store window.

He was a beautiful single father who had lost a wife already.

He wanted to marry her.

But she wasn't looking for marriage.

She didn't know what she was looking for.

She only knew she was looking for *him*. The dreams made her look for *him*.

But marriage?

The reflection told her he was staring at her profile. What was he feeling? Fear? Hope? Insanity?

Insanity. That must be it.

Because she was about to say the unthinkable. "A million times..."

His head turned and his eyes found hers in the reflection.

She couldn't let him down.

Engagement wasn't marriage.

Engagement could last *years*.

"A million times..."

She turned to him but couldn't smile because none of it felt real.

He waited.

Her heart drummed the answer she feared. The answer he wanted to hear. The answer that would make her certifiable.

She forced out the word. "Yes."

"Hell yeah!" He jumped, punched the air, and then swept her into his arms.

God, he was strong. She felt like a rag doll. "Put me down before we fall."

He did as she wished and slid his hands to her hips. "I was sure you'd turn me down again."

"Well you nearly shocked me to death. Who proposes after two weeks?"

He kissed her forehead. "I'm proposing after thirty years. We don't have to select the ring tonight if you don't want to."

His voice was so buoyant, she thought he might float. She couldn't disappoint him no matter how frightened she was. "I want you to go into the store, select the ring you want me to have, buy it, and present it to me sometime tonight. I'll love whatever you pick."

AARON

Aaron hadn't *planned* to propose so soon, but the dreams and whiskey had their way—thankfully, without destroying his fledgling relationship.

"We're all set." Aaron approached Katrina, who was still seated on the bench outside the jewelry store.

She looked at the white bag in his hand and shook her head. "You got me an engagement ring." Disbelief colored her words.

"Yes." He took a seat next to her, feeling smaller than he had a moment ago.

She took his hand and squeezed it hard. "We're moving extremely fast. Does that scare you at all?"

The only thing that scared him was the thought of losing her, and the fear in her eyes wasn't helping him feel confident. He pulled a long breath. "Not one bit."

She searched his eyes. "But we haven't even had sex yet. How do you know we're compatible enough to last in marriage? We're being impulsive."

He stroked the back of her hand with his thumb, wishing he could erase her fear. "I have no doubts that I want you with me for the rest of my life. I don't care that we haven't had sex. I was married to Rose for eight years before she died. Trust me. Sex doesn't hold a marriage together."

"Then what held it together? Friendship?"

Her question forced him to face the truth he'd recently realized. Rose was his sweet, kind-hearted beauty. Anyone would love her. Everyone did. But friendship?

No. Rose was a partner. Someone to make a family with. Someone good and loving. Someone to call his. But friendship?

No. She had her friends and he had his. Nice people, all of them, but not the type to travel in the same circle. Her friends were proper, sometimes too nice—not the type to hang out with earthy people like his buddy, Eric...or the man Aaron spent years pretending *not* to be. And here was Katrina, clueless about what she'd unlocked in him, so he shook his head in reply to her question.

"Well," she continued, "if friendship didn't hold your marriage together, what did?"

Her eyes begged for truth, so he gave it to her in a shrug. "Commitment."

"You weren't *friends*?"

Admitting this truth felt good. Life was giving him a new beginning in the form of this amazing woman, so he told it like it was. "Not friends like we should've been. We were a great partnership more than great friends."

She blinked as if this news was distasteful...alien. "Then who's your best friend?"

He sniffed and cleared his throat, preparing to tell the truth. "My best friend was Eric."

"Was? Who's your best friend now?"

Warmth flowed through him at the thought of having found her. She was the only woman who'd ever shown enough strength for Aaron to be himself. A woman who didn't *need* him to take care of her even though he wanted to. A woman who loved steak and action flicks. Who was comfortable in her own skin. Who swore without blushing. Who was so like the person he'd pretended not to be. He put his arm around her shoulders and squeezed. "I just asked her to marry me."

She returned her gaze to the window. "How do you know all these feelings aren't just the sexual tension you and I feel when we're together? Maybe it's all an illusion."

He sat back and looked at the window. She was doubtful. She said she didn't trust as a kid. Maybe she still didn't trust? He couldn't blame her. He *was* rushing things, but he didn't care. He'd lost everything once already, and he couldn't lose her, too. She was perfect for Isaac, and they were short on time.

"I think our dreams say it all. I want you to be my wife. I want you to be Isaac's mother. Those are the most important things to me. Great sex would be a bonus but not a requirement. If you're willing to have sex with me at all, I'll be happy. Hell, just looking at you nearly makes me come."

"You actually said that." A tiny smile was on her lips when she turned to face him. "You know, you're a mature man. As I can't imagine you'd go to these lengths with the sole goal of getting into my pants, I'd say I'm the luckiest woman on the planet. I feel a little better now. This is just the biggest impulsive thing I've ever done. It'll take a while for me to adjust to the idea of being engaged. Heck, a couple of weeks ago, I didn't even have a boyfriend." She looked at the bag holding her engagement ring. "I'm going to be Aaron Keller's wife."

Thank god. He pulled her close and kissed her head.

"So are you taking me out for drinks now?" she asked.

"You want more drinks?"

"I just got engaged to my childhood crush. Yeah, I'd like a drink or three."

Katrina was blowing his mind. After-proposal drinks had become a session of foreplay right in front of the crowded tables surrounding them. The woman had no fear. She had a way with her fingers and words. He'd simply asked the color of her panties, and she showed them to him. Right there. While a bunch of twenty-somethings watched.

He'd never been with anyone like her. He burned for her fire. He wanted to lick it. Taste it. Savor it.

The pressure was on. If he wanted to keep her, he needed to *blow her mind*. The problem was, he was so fucking horny, simply touching her was likely to make him come.

After returning home, Katrina went out back with Jake. Aaron used that moment to steal three vases of roses—pink, red, and orange—from the guest suite and rushed them up to the master bedroom. He placed red roses on one bedside table, pink on the other, and orange on the dresser along the wall. After stripping the king-sized four-poster down to the fitted white sheet and pillows, he discarded the coverings in the walk-in closet off the master bath.

"I'm bringing Jake in!" Her voice carried up the stairs. "I'll need about ten minutes to freshen up!"

"I'll meet you in the kitchen in ten!" After pulling tight the sheets and straightening the pillows, he removed blooms from six orange roses, tore petals from each one, and sprinkled them over the surface of the bed.

Given he'd thrown out all of Rose's candles after she died in order to stop himself from breathing memories, he'd purchased a new set this morning—all lilac, one of Katrina's favorite scents. He placed three purple pillars on each bedside table and six on the dresser.

After lighting each wick, he doused the overhead light. Mahogany furniture stood strong against goldenrod walls now glowing in candlelight. He removed his shirt and flexed his upper body—all of it—for the mirror. Yes. The illumination was enough to highlight his muscles and her curves. The stage was set.

In the bathroom, he freshened up and pulled on his favorite pair of old button-fly jeans, which were soft and worn. Wearing nothing else, he headed to the kitchen.

When he reached his destination, she was already there, on a barstool in front of the kitchen island. Her crossed legs were dressed in thigh-high black stockings and black heels, which matched her black lace bra and panties. Her hair was pulled into a thick pony tail high on her head. She looked at him from beneath long black eyelashes. "You have no idea how much I want you."

When he drew close, he bent just enough to grab her ass. "Hold on." Her legs wrapped around his waist as he lifted her from the barstool. Then, he pinned her against the wall. "I guarantee I want you more."

She was soft and warm against his abs and the palms of his hands. And she smelled like roses. Fucking heavenly. He brushed his lips against hers, and then he hovered. Just like in their dreams.

"You're a tease, Mr. Keller." She grabbed his head and crushed her lips to his, stroking her minty tongue with sweet determination, nice and deep. "You ready? Because I'm ready."

His erection escaped his fly as if her words were giving it directives. "But the condom is upstairs. And the bed."

"You mean you don't want to fuck me against the wall?" Her grin was wicked. Her breath, impatient.

His heart drummed hard because she wasn't joking. Against the wall? No. It didn't matter that his dick was dying to get inside. It didn't matter that she was a hot little fire-cracker. It didn't matter that she wanted to be *fucked*. This first time would not be against his kitchen wall. This first time, he would treat her like a lady. "How about we take a little break?"

Her head vacillated between a nod and a shake, making him smile.

"Hold still." He carried her to the barstool and bent his knees to set her on it. "If I'm not careful, I'm going to hook you." He flared his eyes as he rose, giving her a moment to see what was busting out of his pants before adjusting himself to hide the goods again.

"No need to be modest, Mr. Keller." She traced her fingers along the v-line above his waistband. "I'm dying to see all of it."

"Patience, Dr. Lopez." He took her hand. "Come." He led her up the stairs to his bedroom door. "You go in. In sixty seconds, I'll join."

She closed the door behind her, leaving him in the hall.

He'd never been this wound up. And after more than three years without sex. Fuck. His heart was pumping hot, heady lust through his veins.

Breathe, man, breathe.

But attempts to calm himself were in vain. His body was

on the brink, so he pleaded for his soldiers to hold off on firing the artillery until *after* she exploded. Their future—his and Isaac's—depended on Aaron's triumph in the bedroom. Tonight. He couldn't disappoint her. Not now. Not *ever*.

When he opened the door, she looked at him and dropped the petals. "Orange. I love it." She approached. In command. In heels. "Do you like what you see?" She turned and bent over to showcase her ass and legs, her supple dancer's body holding the position without wavering. Even after all that wine.

His head was light. Long, lean legs. And panties that hugged just right, wrapping above her toned cheeks, calling him to bury his face in them.

She looked at him, upside down, between her legs. "I'm waiting."

Too intoxicated to smile, he managed a whisper. "Love it."

"I can see that."

His erection had busted open the buttons again.

She stood and circled him, trailing her fingers just above his waistline as she went. "I want to see everything, Aaron." All confidence, she knelt in front of him, unfastened the last buttons of his fly, and then pulled the jeans down, freeing his cock. She smiled that wicked smile. "Fuck. Your dick…"

His erection jumped at her words. Hell, it would do cartwheels, backflips, and fucking skydive if she so commanded it to.

And then she did the unthinkable.

Impulses forced his hand to grip that sexy ponytail while her tongue, warm and wet, slid up his shaft.

"Shit." His pounding heart felt as good as his cock.

Green-brown devil eyes looked up from their position next to his package. "You're gonna have to pull my hair harder than *that* if you want more of *this*." Her tongue stroked him again, and then her lips wrapped around the head.

Breath escaped him as he tugged her head away. Not because he wanted to, but because he needed to. "It's too much right now."

She smiled. "Let's see all of you then." She worked his jeans to the floor. "Step out."

Unsure how he was managing to stay upright, he did as she commanded. After throwing his jeans to the side, she locked her eyes on his and slid feather-light fingertips up the inner side of each leg, stopping short of the boys. His erection jumped again.

She rose, sliding her fingertips over his hips...his abs...his sides...his back, and then she pulled him into an embrace, pressing her pelvis hard into his cock. "Am I driving you wild?"

"Absolut— " His throat swallowed impulsively. "Absolutely."

She flashed a grin. "Now it's your turn." She took two steps back and placed her hands on her hips.

"Not sure I want to take much off you. You're extraordinary just as you are."

She licked the corner of her mouth. "The choice is yours."

"Lean over the bed and show me your ass again."

"Your wish." She turned to face the foot of the bed, placed her feet just beyond shoulder-width, and bent forward.

Unsteady, he knelt and kneaded her ass with his thumbs, resisting the urge to slide the crotch of her panties to the side so that he could bury his tongue in the folds hidden there.

"Go ahead and have a taste."

His heart pounded. She *wanted* him to lick her pussy? Unsure whether his dick could handle much more, he ventured a taste.

Oh hell, she tasted as good as she smelled.

"Mm, your tongue is divine, but I must agree. It's too much right now."

He slid her panties down. After she stepped out, he stood to undo her bra and let it fall to the floor.

She turned to face him wearing nothing but those seductive stockings and heels in the soft candlelight dancing on her feminine curves. His gaze trailed from the curve of her collar bone...to the swell of her breast...to the dip in her navel...to the sultry little patch, waxed and trimmed, that was calling his name.

"Like what you see?"

He cleared his throat to find a voice. "A piece of heaven."

"Thank you Mr. Keller, but I'm no angel." She stepped forward and slipped her fingers into his. "I wish we could extend this erotica forever, but I'm near my limit. How about you?"

He nodded, thankful that his soldiers hadn't fired anything yet. He led her to the dresser where he grabbed the engagement ring and condom. "Do you still want to be my wife?"

Her breath caught. "Yes."

"Then you must wear this." He placed the ring on her finger.

She held up her left hand, examining the ring for the first time. "I can't see it well in this light. And it's loose."

"No worries. Just hold it in place for now. Put your hands on your hips so I can admire you with that ring on your finger."

She did as she was told, and he stepped back, taking another moment to savor the spectacular view. This woman was by far one of the wonders of the world.

"Aaron, you can look at me later." Her breath was coming hard. She crawled onto the mattress.

He followed. "How do you want it?"

She held firm on hands and knees and pressed her ass into his cock. "This is how I want it, baby."

His stomach flipped. "In the ass?"

She laughed. "I didn't know you were into that sort of thing. Maybe another time."

He'd never been in an ass before.

Surprised his head was able to think with such little blood flow, he forced himself to focus on what she must've meant. Doggy. On his knees between her legs, he stroked his cock against her clit. "You're so wet."

"Yes. And I'm on the brink. Just fuck me."

The bite in her words warned him to obey so he tore open the foil wrapper.

She turned her head, which caused her hair to tumble off her neck. "What are you doing?"

His gut turned at the sight of the pitted scar staring at him from the base of her neck. He'd never been in a position to notice it before. Damn it. *Someone hurt her.*

She pressed up into a full kneel, her hair tumbling over the scar, and reached back and around to squeeze his ass. "Please tell me you haven't changed your mind."

While his left hand enjoyed her left breast, his right held the little package in front of her eyes. "The condom."

She pushed his hands away, slid to her belly, rolled over, and spread her legs. "I'll be your wife. I want your skin to fuck me."

Those words and the view were almost his undoing. He tossed the condom aside, settled his body over hers, and slid into her tight walls, burying himself deep.

"Fuck. You fit me just right." Her fingernails seared the length of his back. "Oh, Aaron, I want to watch you come undone." Her breath came faster, her eyes as intense as her voice. "Pound the hell out of me."

Her pussy massaged his cock. Damn, she was strong and so

hot his arms were trembling under his weight. He couldn't blow this.

"You aren't pounding me yet. I told you to pound me." Her nails made another searing trek across his back, ordering him to get going.

He thrust into her so hard he couldn't believe she hadn't cried in pain.

"Fuck yes." Her devil eyes were watching his. "Keep going and tell me when you're about to come."

Damn, she was...he didn't even know. Her eyes commanded him to watch her watch him fuck her.

She had no fear.

She was all intensity.

She was all about them.

So he pounded the hell out of her.

And she took it. Again and again.

His cock swelled.

And rushed.

"Now!" he shouted.

"Oh Aaron!"

He pounded through his convulsions as her sweet voice cried his name.

He pounded until she cried no more.

He pounded until her sweaty body was limp.

He pounded until he couldn't anymore.

Then he pressed into her, his bare chest sticking to hers, and breathed. Heavy breaths. Exhausted.

But he didn't pull out. No. He was home.

She rested beneath him, watching his eyes, her brow tranquil. Intimate.

Still trembling, he placed a gentle kiss on her forehead.

Everything rested on this moment.

If he'd made her happy enough, maybe she'd truly be his.

Only his.

Forever.

Morning light shone through Aaron's eyelids, waking him. Anticipation slid his hand across the bed to find her and pull her close, but he found nothing.

Shit.

He bolted to sitting, blood thick with fear, in hopes of finding evidence that he was mistaken.

But she wasn't there.

Shit.

His body spiked with sensations he'd forced away a couple years ago—sensations that could *never* come back—he scrambled out of bed.

Where the hell was she?

Heart pounding, he scanned the room. Her stuff was still on the floor, so she couldn't have taken off.

Relief hit him, but he didn't trust it.

He tried to laugh at his insecurity but failed.

He needed to see her.

He headed into the master bathroom, but she wasn't there either.

Forcing himself to behave sensibly, he took a moment to pull on some boxer briefs and brush his teeth. It was irrational to think she was gone, so he needed to calm down.

After making his way downstairs, he checked the guest suite. Jake's crate was still there, which was a good sign, but there was no Jake. On edge, he headed to the kitchen.

On the kitchen island, he found a note.

Took Jake for a run.

See you soon.

Love, Katrina

He placed his palms on the counter, welcoming the relief that flowed through him. She hadn't left.

Of course, she hadn't left.

But his emotional reaction—his worry—wasn't a good sign. It had been irrational. Just like his darkness was irrational.

Still rattled, he gathered the makings for breakfast. He tied his apron and cued Harry Connick, Jr., on the sound system.

He scrambled eggs with salt and pepper and set some coffee to brew. Then he turned his attention to toast, placing yogurt in serving dishes, and setting two places at the island.

A knock jolted him.

Katrina, in running shorts and a cropped top, was standing on the patio step outside his door, a sight that should have calmed his nerves.

She slid the door open. "Do you mind if I let Jake run loose in your backyard? He won't get into anything."

Aaron smiled in spite of himself. "Go ahead."

"I need a dish of water."

He grabbed a large dish, filled it, and handed it to her.

"Go explore."

While she watched Jake begin investigation of the yard, Aaron grabbed her hand and pulled her close. He needed to feel her. He needed her in his arms. "You're covered in sweat. Let me taste." He sucked her collarbone.

"I'm wondering, Mr. Keller." Her hands explored his back. "Do you always wear an apron over a bare chest when you work in the kitchen?"

He slid his mouth to the other side of her neck and enjoyed more of her. Tasting her. Holding her. Loving her. It was all he wanted.

She moved her hands south. "Oh. And boxer briefs, too. Boxer briefs are my favorite." She ran her fingers around his waistband to the front, under his apron, and tucked them inside, teasing the hair next to his erection. "Your mouth is turning me on, Aaron."

"Your hands are turning me on, Katrina." He moved his lips to hers, lifted her onto the counter, and placed himself between her legs. His tongue went deep while his thumb found her sweet spot.

She rocked her hips in time with the rhythm his thumb was circling against her running shorts. "Mm." She pulled his lower lip into her mouth for a delicious moment. When she released it, she breathed into his ear, "Keep this up and I'm going to come."

"Oh yeah?" Anything to please this woman.

She continued rocking with the rhythm while he sucked her neck. "Oh Aaron." Her pussy pressed into his hand, so he kept it going. And a moment later, she fell apart on the counter. But as her body released, her eyes flew open and she ducked for cover. Her face was white as a sheet.

His laugh released his tension. "What was that?"

She chuckled. "Well, your thumb was an ace, but my orgasm was foiled by fear of knocking my head on a cupboard."

"Oh." He opened his arms to showcase his kitchen, which had no upper cabinetry. "Cabinets rank number one in reasons why women don't enjoy orgasm."

She surveyed the room. "Where the hell do you keep all your stuff?"

He stroked her thighs. "Where do you think?"

She surveyed the room again, likely taking note of the excessive number of base drawers he had trouble filling. "Your kitchen is huge. And beautiful."

Yes, Rose designed an amazing kitchen. White granite countertops with a hint of grey veining, white tile backsplash, and white walls. An airy space anchored by ebony base cabinets and tied down by ebony ceiling beams.

She tugged his hands away from her hips. "I'm hungry. What's for breakfast?"

"Me." His hopes were high.

She sucked the skin below his ear, causing it to stand at attention. "Sounds fantastic. I'm quite hungry." Her eyes teased him from beneath those eyelashes.

He managed to keep his head together. "I was about to make a spinach and mushroom scramble. Sound good?"

She replied by pushing him away and sliding off the counter, so he headed over to the stove.

"You know, you're total eye candy. I love, love, love your bod in boxer briefs and an apron." She walked past, slapped his rear, and proceeded to a stool at the island. "A spinach and mushroom scramble sounds great."

He tended the skillet.

"You enjoy cooking?"

"It's alright. I enjoy it most when I have a lady to cook for." He gave her a wink.

"Thank you. And I enjoy watching my fiancée cook for me in his skivvies."

"Your pleasure is my desire." He suspected she was admiring his domestic masculinity, so he took care to make sure the eggs were tender.

"Love your choice of music. Harry, yes?"

"Right again, Doc." He set the hot skillet on the island and offered toast and yogurt. "I've asked you to marry me, but I don't know what you like to drink for breakfast. What would you like?"

"Orange juice is my favorite followed by tea. I rarely drink coffee and never for breakfast. And do you like your coffee regular or decaf? Black or with cream?"

He poured her a big glass of orange juice. "I'm supposed to drink decaf and I drink it black."

"Oh. This scramble is perfect. Thank you. Why is your coffee supposed to be decaf?"

He'd asked her to marry him, so he better tell her. He needed to tell her.

So...he'd tell her just enough.

"After Rose died, I developed high blood pressure and a bit of a problem with anxiety. The caffeine isn't good for my system. Messes with me. But I do drink some regular on occasion. I also enjoy an occasional cola." He grabbed his coffee, filled his plate, and took a seat next to her.

"Aaron, do you mind if I ask some questions?"

He shrugged. "You can ask me anything."

"Well, now I know you have high blood pressure and an anxiety problem. What sort of problem with anxiety?"

His fork teased the egg on his plate so he didn't have to look at her. "Oh...I was having panic attacks during the year following Rose's death, but those have been under control for a couple years. I got over them after seeing a therapist for a while."

Disgusted by the memory of what he once was, he continued teasing the egg on his plate. Why did it ever have to happen? If it never happened, he wouldn't need to hide it from her at this moment. Hoping his partially-true disclosure hadn't frightened her, he looked up.

Her eyes were big. "I have problems with anxiety, too. My anxiety developed when I was little, living with an unpredictable, abusive father. As a result, my body is too emotionally reactive, often perceiving non-threatening things as threatening. Primarily when I'm feeling lack of control over a situation. Deep breathing and self-talk help me through the majority of the time.

"When my father died, I went into a severe stress reaction. I had some horrific dreams during that phase of my life. And got sick, too. Scary stuff, stress reactions. I got a diagnosis of post-traumatic stress disorder."

He understood a little better now. She was pretty emotional. More than Rose ever was. "I noticed the scar on your neck last night." Memory of that vicious mark turned his stomach. "What happened?"

And now *she* was the one teasing egg with a fork.

After a moment of quiet, she said, "I was carrying his glass across the cement slab out back to where he was sitting in a lawn chair. The glass was full of the whiskey and water he'd just ordered me to pour for him. Three-quarters full with whiskey and topped off with water. Like always. And he told me never to spill.

"Then a bee buzzed in my ear, so close I felt its vibrations. I panicked and dropped the glass at his feet. When I threw myself to the ground to pick up the pieces, he drove his cigarette into my neck as punishment. It hurt like hell. Seemed to go on forever. I didn't scream. I knew better than to scream. If I screamed, Mom would've come running and he'd have beaten her for standing up to him.

"A few hours later, the burn was oozing so badly I had to show her. She feared taking me to the hospital because he'd threatened her life more than once. She was too afraid, so I didn't get proper treatment. That scar is a remnant of those dark years."

Hatred for a man he never met rocketed through Aaron. "How old were you when this happened?"

"Five." She looked at him as if this bit of information was as ordinary as a weather report. "Thankfully, Mom eventually wised up and booted his ass for good when I was ten. Her epiphany came after he threw her down the stairs, which broke her collar bone and could've killed her. The hospital stay gave her the strength she needed to push her husband out of her home."

No wonder Aaron wanted to protect her when they were little. No wonder she rarely smiled. And the worst of his childhood was breaking an arm when he flew off a trampoline. "I'm so sorry. I had no idea you lived with that."

She shrugged and gave half a smile. "It made me stronger in lots of ways. Don't be sorry."

Yeah. She was strong. That was clear. Aaron needed to force himself to take a few more bites because his appetite was gone. "Do you have any other health conditions?"

But she didn't answer. She appeared to be lost in thought.

It was a bit of a mind-fuck to realize he was sensing the truth way back when he was five. Damn. He'd always wanted to give her that hug. Of course, he did. Some part of him knew she was hurting. But he didn't do the one thing that could've taken away some of her pain. A simple hug.

Her gaze was still directed out the window, so he gave a gentle nudge. "Hey, you still with me? I was wondering if you had any other health conditions."

She pulled her gaze back to the moment and looked at him. "Nope, I'm healthy. I get too many cavities for someone who takes excellent care of her teeth, but other than that, I'm in great shape. The only other thing is my eyes, of course. I'm legally blind without corrective lenses, so I have the unfortunate situation of not being able to see you clearly if I fuck you without contacts or eyeglasses."

She commanded the word *fuck* in a way that channeled directly to his... "You being blind is a good thing for me when I get old and ugly. I'll make sure you don't wear lenses when I let you have me."

"When you *let* me have you?" She laughed. "Let's just

promise we'll always work to stay healthy no matter how old we are. Deal?"

"Deal."

"And what about you?" She took the last bite of her breakfast. "Any other health conditions?"

He couldn't tell her.

Not yet.

Maybe not ever.

There was no point in mentioning it if symptoms were absent. Plus, she'd been through enough as it was. "Nope. I work out a lot. I'm healthy." He took another bite.

"It helps to know what you're doing, Mr. Physical Therapist. I bet you give terrific massages, yes?"

The thought of giving her the massage of her life made him smile. "How about you be the judge later?"

She flared her eyes and took her dishes to the dishwasher. He finished the rest of his meal while she wiped the counters.

"I love your kitchen and your yard. Who was your designer?"

"Rose."

She stopped working. "*She* designed the kitchen and the yard?"

"Yes." He got up to put things away.

"Wow." She ran her hand over the countertop. "They're gorgeous."

"Designing, cooking, and entertaining were her hobbies. She would search through magazines and books and run ideas by me. I would tell her what I liked and she would run with it. Like my dad did with the Road Runner."

"Rose was talented. I love what I've seen here and I'm looking forward to a full tour sometime soon."

"Want a tour now?"

She shook her head. "I need to feed Jake and refill his water dish. Then I'd like to take a shower." Her wink told him she had other things on her mind, too.

She watched him untie his apron, so he flexed his upper body as he lifted it over his head. "Alright Doc, after you feed Jake, meet me in my bathroom."

<hr>

Katrina was trembling, so she must have enjoyed it. Again. Three orgasms in the space of an hour. Not bad.

She sank into his naked chest. "I love having you inside me."

Aaron's fingers traced the line of her shoulder blades. "I'd set up residence inside you if I could. You know, I never would have guessed you'd be so..." He wasn't sure the word to use. The fact she'd sucked him off like that... "...diverse."

"Diverse?" She chuckled. "That's an interesting choice of words. I'm not into nipple clamps or things in my ass, though. Does that disappoint you?"

Deep down, an unsettled part of him knew, but he asked anyway. "Have you tried those things?"

"Yeah."

Damn it.

She rolled to her side, propped her head on her hand, and traced his pec. "If you want to fuck my ass, I'll let you, but I don't like things in my ass. And I don't want to hear any bullshit that I haven't done it right. It's not for everyone. I know what I like."

Damn Connor. He stole her, her virginity, and her—

"And my nipples..."

There was *more*?

"...you can do whatever you want with them, but nipple play doesn't arouse me. Light touch on all parts of my breasts turns me on. Except the nipple. But my most favorite body parts are my legs."

He couldn't argue with that. Her legs were his favorite body part, too. She brought her knee to his abdomen, so he stroked her thigh.

"I love it when you play with the back of my calves. Knees. Thighs. Ass. I love being spanked and bitten. And I love when my neck is suckled. Hard. Especially with fingers in my pussy, but I ask you to hold back on the sucking unless its winter and I can wear a turtleneck. And avoid my carotid artery so I don't have a stroke. Okay?"

What? He'd need to look that up.

"And sometime soon I'll pull out one of my vibrators. You like fucking with a vibrator?"

Damn. What was she? An instruction book? *How to Please Katrina for Idiots?*

"Have you ever fucked with a vibrator?"

He shook his head.

"Oh, I'm sorry." She propped herself on her elbow and looked into his eyes. "Am I saying too much? Am I freaking you out?"

Yup. He swallowed his disappointment. "Not at all."

"Well…" Her eyes were cute. Sheepish. "…I guess you could say I enjoy some kink. Last night, I really wanted you to fuck me against the wall. And today, I would've loved to fuck in the back yard. It's so sunny out. Just perfect."

In the back yard? What the hell did Connor do to her?

"Is something bothering you?"

He shook his head. "But what about the neighbors?"

Her brow furrowed. "You aren't into kinky stuff?"

Shit. He was disappointing her. He couldn't disappoint her. Not ever.

Kinky stuff? He didn't know.

Was he?

He and Rose just had sex. They made love. Rose was a good girl. And he was happy with that.

Katrina sat up and covered her lap with the bedsheet, her fingers running themselves along the seam. "Well…" Her voice was small. "…to answer your question, I scoped out your back yard this morning. Before my run. I saw the privacy fence and the trees and the shrubbery. Nobody can see in. And your neighbors are, what, like a hundred feet away in each direction, right?" She looked into his eyes. "I thought it would be fun out in the open, you know? And I saw your gazebo. A hot tub. Nice."

Oh man.

Rose never sucked him off. Not once. And licking her was out of the question no matter how much he wanted to. Katrina was raw. Free. Demanding.

He loved it.

But out in the back yard?

He needed to reassure her, so he forced a smile. "I don't want the neighbors to hear. What we do isn't their business."

Her wicked smile returned. "I can keep quiet."

Oh man. That smile was his new addiction. It killed him to think she gave it to Connor or to anyone. "I'm kind of wondering how you got so diverse when you've only been with one guy and haven't been with a man in a decade. What aren't you telling me?"

She twisted the bedsheet in her hands. "You want to know?"

No. But…"Yes."

"Simple. Connor and I were virgins."

Virgins? That didn't explain anything. And no way was Connor was a virgin if he did all this with her. "Go on."

"You really want to hear this?"

"Yes," he lied again, his heart heavy.

"Well...we learned together. It was easy for us to let go and explore because we weren't being compared to previous partners. We had lots of interest in exploring and, as a result, had a great sex life."

"Oh." She explored. Lots. With *Connor*.

"What's wrong?" she asked.

A pang of jealousy claimed his gut. "I missed out I guess."

"Explain."

"Connor was lucky. That's all."

"You're hiding something. I can tell."

Dark sensations were creeping back. They couldn't come back. Ever. His nerves couldn't get the best of him. Maybe asking would keep them at bay. "What do you think of our sex life so far?"

"See? It sucks being compared to someone who came before you, literally."

Not funny. He tried to keep hurt out of his voice. "I just think I missed out. It could've been me. We could've explored together."

"Oh no, don't you do this. You're wishing for an alternative story for us and, trust me, it would have been a disappointment."

"Gee. *Thanks*."

She sat astride him. "Aaron, you and I never would have been so good together back then."

Fuck. She was disappointed. "*That* makes me feel better."

"No. You don't get it." She grabbed his head and attempted to look into his eyes, but he looked over her shoulder instead. At the spider on the ceiling.

"As you said last night, you'd been with several girls. I'm sure you had some experience by senior year. And, if we'd gone out, I'm sure you would've had difficulty waiting a year for sex."

She was right, but he gave her his best poker face and continued looking at the spider.

"Who do you think you're fooling?" Her tongue was sharp. Strong and perfect. "Of course, you wouldn't have waited. And if you stuck with me long enough to get sex, I would've been so nervous. So worried about measuring up to those girls you deflowered before me." She twisted his nipple.

And his tension released.

Beautiful green-brown eyes smiled down on him.

"It took me a long time to get comfortable with the idea of some of the stuff Connor and I tried. Oral sex. Anal…"

"Alright that's enough." He didn't want to know any more about her and Connor and anything anal.

"Aaron, think. We've both matured into confident, responsible adults. I think we're incredible together because our past is our past. Don't ruin this."

Okay. She said *incredible*. So she liked it.

"You know, I could have asked how I measure up to all those girls who came before me, but that question isn't fair to either of us. Please don't think about the past. It's not healthy."

He pulled her to his chest and hugged her tight. He would never get enough, so he was glad to have forever. "I told you I have trouble with anxiety at times. And for the record, you're the best I've ever had. I guess I need to thank Connor."

Damn.

"Isaac still takes an afternoon nap." Aaron tossed his keys onto the kitchen counter after returning from errands (dropping off the ring for sizing and picking up Isaac from Grandma and

Grandpa Keller's house). Isaac on his arm, he led Katrina upstairs. "Do you want to help me put him down?"

"Actually," she replied, "I'd like to put him down myself so we get to know each other better. Would that be okay?"

"Sure." He led Katrina to the changing table. "Here are wipes and diapers." He pointed to the dresser. "And you'll find comfies in there. Some fleece pants and a long-sleeved t-shirt will work. He still sleeps without a blanket or pillow. Any questions?"

"Nope."

"Okay. I'll be in my—our bedroom." He swung Isaac into the air. "You have a good nap, bud." After blowing a raspberry on Isaac's cheek, Aaron handed him to her.

Isaac gave her a big smile as she kissed him on the head.

"See you soon." He went to the master bedroom, appreciating that she was there.

If all went well, Isaac would have little brothers or sisters someday. Isaac wouldn't have to grow up alone. A vision of Katrina's belly swollen with a sibling settled Aaron's nerves a little more.

Then, he heard it.

Her voice was carrying an unfamiliar lullaby. Soft and sweet. Beautiful. Like her.

He sneaked to Isaac's door and turned the handle with his well-practiced hand. Without a sound, it opened so Aaron could see.

She was leaning over the crib, stroking Isaac's back.

Three full versus. Every word, every note, tranquility.

Throat clenched, he closed the door and rushed to the master bath.

KATRINA

"There you are." Aaron was standing at the bathroom window, looking out over the backyard, so Katrina wrapped her arms around his waist and nuzzled his back. "Isaac was starting to nod off while I changed his clothes, so we didn't even try a book. He must've had a wild night with grandma and grandpa."

Aaron's chuckle gave her a grin.

"You still think we're moving too fast?" he asked.

"Of course, we're moving too fast. Don't you think?" The breeze coming in through the window chilled her arms, so she nuzzled her hunk a little harder. It was pretty peaceful at his house. Not as quiet as her home in the country, but quiet enough. And a breeze that carried in voices of birds like this was welcome any time. Maybe someday she'd feel as at home here as she did in her old farmhouse.

"I don't think we're moving fast enough."

She stepped back and tugged his shirt to make him turn away from the window.

He looked into her eyes, all serious.

His eyes didn't waver while she searched them for evidence of humor. For evidence of the joke he must be playing on her. For some shred of evidence that he didn't mean what he was saying.

But, fuck no. He was serious.

He took her hand and squeezed it. "I want us to get married next month."

Her heart took off. "What?" Taking a step back, she pulled her hand out of his.

Three weeks ago, they weren't even talking.

She couldn't wrap her head around the engagement.

She lived two hours away.

What about her house?

Her job?

What if they found out they don't get along after a couple of months?

Divorce?

What would their families think?

No. What would *Bitch Mom* think?

Her heart was thumping so hard, she felt it in her throat.

Fuck. She was losing it.

She walked over to the vanity and held on. "Aaron. We're engaged after two weeks. That's crazy enough. The ring doesn't even fit me yet. Why in the hell are you in such a rush?"

He didn't respond but turned back to the window and leaned into his hands against the frame.

Oh, she needed sanity. All rational thought screamed for them to slow down.

She tried deep breathing, but her heart wouldn't listen. Fear writhed under her skin. Her grip on the vanity tightened. "Aaron." Her voice was shaking. "Please answer me."

He faced her, his eyes gentle. "It's clear as day. You're Isaac's mother—I—"

Anger blistered inside. "No. I'm not."

"Yes, you are. I—"

What the fuck? He was disrespecting his dead wife? What was *wrong* with him? "Isaac already has a mother. Didn't you love her?"

Aaron's eyes flickered. "Yes, but that doesn't have anything to do with—"

"Doesn't have anything to do with it? What the hell?" Her face felt as hard as her heart was pounding. "Isaac's mother was named Rose or has my *pussy* caused you to forget that?"

Black spots.

Oh no.

She didn't.

She looked at her feet as horror flooded her.

Yes, she did.

She did.

She'd said the words *aloud*.

Her head floated above her body...

"That. Was. Low." His voice was black.

She couldn't see through the spots in her eyes, but she heard the door close too hard as she crumpled to the ground, head spinning, in a torrent of tears.

How did this happen?

Damn her.

She'd destroyed the best thing that had ever come into her life.

Damn her tongue.

Damn her heart.

Damn her *head*.

Floating in a nightmare of panic after a morning of bliss?

She was fucked up.

She pressed her cheek into the floor. The cold tile felt good, so she let the tears puddle there.

How mad was he?

Would he forgive her?

Or would he write her off as a bitch?

Maybe they hadn't started sizing the ring yet and he could get a refund. Her throat clenched. He'd wanted *marriage*.

And there she was, on the floor, crying.

Hadn't he explained, not twenty-four hours ago, that he'd always felt protective of her? That he'd always loved her?

He'd forgive her.

Right?

She let tears puddle for she didn't know how long.

When her emotions exhausted themselves, she used her t-shirt to wipe the floor. Given no black spots visited her when she sat, she took a firm grasp on the vanity and pulled herself to standing in front of the mirror. Her eyes were bloodshot and she looked like hell.

But it didn't matter.

She needed to apologize...and pray for him to know she wasn't a monster.

***

"I'm sorry. Can we please talk?"

Aaron was sitting on a bench in the basement, lifting weights. He didn't look at her. "I was trying to talk, but you kept interrupting."

The distance in his voice thickened the lump in her throat.

"Aaron, I'm so sorry. I'm afraid you'll hate me for the vile thing I said. The thing is..." Standing in the doorway of his workout room, feeling childish and exposed, she continued explaining to a man who wouldn't look at her. "I'm not ready for marriage. I'm scared to death. And I panicked. And when I panic, I get defensive. And when I get defensive, I say stupid things to keep people out. Remember? I told you I was always defensive as a kid."

His face was blank, but he nodded.

"Well...that defensiveness will always live in me. I've tamed it, but it's a neurological thing that will never go away. It hasn't come out in a long time because I avoid known triggers—the biggest of which is the unexpected. I promise it's been years since it last happened. And I was handling the situation well enough until you disrespected Rose."

"What?" His gaze snapped to her face, and his voice cut. "Damn it, Katrina. You're highly educated, not psychic. You need to let people finish their sentences before you tear into them for disrespecting their dead loved ones."

The pain in his face was killing her. Her body shuddered under more tears. "I-I know. I'm sorry. I-I wasn't thinking clearly. I wasn't listening. I was panicking."

He got up, went into an adjacent room, and closed the door.

She waited.

And waited.

Several minutes passed.

And it became clear.

She'd fucked it up.

Just like her father had always said. She was a bitch. An unappreciative little bitch and nobody could ever love her.

She needed to hide.

"Aaron, I'll leave if you want me to. I'm sorry."

This wasn't right. They were supposed to be *together*. But he remained silent behind the closed door.

She was sorry. Sorry for showing him that person. That wretched person she used to be.

That person she still was. The girl who didn't let people get close for fear of being hurt. But who was the fool? She was. She was hurting them *both*.

Through the haze, she found her way upstairs and put Jake in the backyard. On the guest room floor, she worked on dismantling his crate because it was time to leave.

Fuck, it was hard to see the metal parts through the tears.

Pain surged up her arm when her pinky finger got caught between a side wall and the ceiling piece. "Damn it."

"What are you doing?"

His voice was behind her, but she didn't look. She yanked back her hands and the structure collapsed. "I'm giving you space." At least her finger wasn't bleeding. Too bad her nose was so runny. She wiped it on her shoulder.

"I never said I wanted space."

Tears were still streaming when she, all crouched and small on the floor, turned to look at him. "I know. But I apologized and you walked away. I figured I better leave."

He ran his hand through his hair. "You know what? For a psychologist, you can be thick." He walked over and pulled her up, his hands gripping her arms so she couldn't avoid his gaze like she wanted to. "Forgiveness is more than words. You pissed me off. I needed to deal with my feelings before I could say I forgive you. And here you are, ready to run. What's up with that?"

She shrugged. "You know..." Her voice was queer, feeble. "If you never stopped me, I would know it's over."

His arms enveloped her nice and tight.

Her body shuddered, but he didn't let go. And after a while, her tears subsided. Hope set down frail roots to try again.

He kissed her on the head. "You do have some baggage, don't you?"

Yeah. Baggage. Baggage that taught her to always protect herself. To always be her own strength.

But she shouldn't be the only one protecting her, should she? Here she was, crying, emotionally naked, in Aaron's arms. *Protected*.

The sensation was foreign.

This man wasn't pushing her away.

This man wasn't laughing at her tears.

This man was supporting her. The emotional wreck that was her at this moment.

Peace was claiming her prickly edginess. "Why do you

think I studied psychology? Believe it or not, I'm much better these days. Will you forgive me?"

"I'll forgive you on one condition."

She peeked at him. "Okay. What is it?"

"Let me finish my sentence."

She nodded into his chest.

"My sentence was going to be this: You're Isaac's mother—I know it in my soul."

Shame burned every cell.

"And this has nothing to do with Rose," he said. "You put that spin on it yourself."

She pulled out of his embrace to look in his eyes. "But don't you see how that's disrespectful of her? I've only known Isaac for a week. She gave birth to him."

"And that's all she could do for him. This isn't about her—"

"But she was his mom."

"Sit down."

She sat on the loveseat.

"I loved Rose. She was a wonderful woman and, if she hadn't died, I'd still be happily married. But she's dead. Isaac has no mother. Pretend he's an orphan. Are you following?"

She nodded to acknowledge she was following and, more privately to herself, to acknowledge she was an idiot.

"I heard you singing the lullaby and I peeked in. Right then, I knew." He knelt in front of her and took her hands into his. His eyes tried to convince her. "You are the one who is supposed to be his mother. Not Rose. You. If it were supposed to be Rose, she'd be here. You're the one. The only one. And I want to get married."

She bit her lip. "But Aaron, we don't have to rush into marriage. Why the rush?"

He looked into her eyes for a long moment and then

released her hands. Relief and fear fought for territory inside her while she awaited his reply.

He walked to the window and looked out. "Rose and I were only children. Isaac has no uncles or aunts. No close cousins. My closest friends are single with occasional kids. He's going to be *alone*. And that thought haunts me every day. It was Rose's wish, and mine, that I find a good woman who'd love him and give him a brother or sister so he won't be alone."

He looked at her, his face stoic. "Rose lost three babies over the course of four years. Sometimes it's tough to get pregnant. Sometimes it's tough to stay pregnant."

He turned back to the window. "You and I are thirty-five. Risks increase each year. I already have one with Down syndrome. It could take us years to get pregnant and there are no guarantees. I want a family. That's the rush. And if you think this is crazy, I need to ask you to leave."

Without a glance, he left the room.

She locked the door and ran to the bed, her head pounding with wretchedness. He was the prince in shining armor little girls dream about and she was scared to death to ride into the sunset.

What was *wrong* with her?

She climbed under the covers and clutched the pillow to her chest, her mind a flurry of anxieties and possibilities and hopes.

The chime jolted her.

Katrina crawled out of bed to get her cell phone, which was lying on the table across the room, and found a text from Aaron asking if she was okay.

Shit. She'd slept for two hours.

She went to the bathroom and enlisted her hairbrush, mouthwash, and makeup to help fix the train wreck in the mirror.

Marriage.

What about her job?

Would they live apart during the week?

She could commute for a while, but she'd eventually need to find a new position.

She'd chosen a career with options. So...

She'd find another job when she needed to.

Or maybe the commute wouldn't be so bad.

She pulled her hair into a pony tail.

It wouldn't be too difficult to sell her house.

The thought stuck in her throat. She *loved* her house. She didn't want to leave it.

Oh no.

Jake!

She rushed to the bedroom window that overlooked the backyard and found him running with a ball in his mouth.

And there was Aaron, with Isaac, getting ready to throw the ball again.

Everyone was smiling. Even Jake.

She was tangled inside, her wants and fears twisted and taught among threads of dreams. She knew she was a mess. Aaron knew she was a mess. *But he wanted to marry her in spite of it.*

Something righted itself deep inside. Ringing Aaron's doorbell on that Friday night was the beginning of this unfamiliar life. She knew it was a risk, yet she'd been brave that night.

Only a fool wouldn't be brave now.

While she watched her family—yes, her family—play outside, her future became clear. The fear would never go away, but she wouldn't let it control her. Scared as she was, she wouldn't let fear hurt Aaron again.

The achievement-driven resolve of Dr. Lopez mixed with Katrina's bravery to spark a plan. She *would* do this. For Aaron. But more importantly—for herself.

First, Aaron needed a response, so she texted: *I'm okay. I fell asleep.* She pressed send and watched through the window.

A second later, he pulled his phone from his pocket and turned toward the house.

She headed into the other room, unlocked the door, and waited.

After several minutes, the door flew open. "I'm sorry." He rushed over and pulled her into a hug. "We'll wait as long as you want to wait. I shouldn't have been in such a rush. I feel like an ass for pressuring you. A family can't be forced. Will you forgive me?"

His hug felt so good. "Aaron, you have nothing to apologize for. I always had the option to say no. You weren't pressuring me." A familiar tune caught her ear. It was coming from the hall. "Where's Isaac?"

Aaron released her. "You should see this."

He led her by the hand to the living room where Isaac was sitting on the floor, Jake by his side. Both were watching an educational program designed to teach children American Sign Language. She always showed a clip of this program in her Child Development class.

"If you decide not to marry me sometime soon, I think Jake might want to have some sleepovers here. He and Isaac are best buds. They watched two episodes during your nap. I purchased the program after you told me about sign language last week. Isaac already knows the signs for *milk* and *go*." Aaron demonstrated.

Katrina's resolve took over. "How about the fourth of July?"

Aaron was watching the program. "For what?"

"It's the nation's birthday, and mine. That would be a cool day for an anniversary. What do you think?" She waited for it to register.

He turned to her, his eyes huge. "What did you say?"

Her smile felt good. "My birthday is on the Fourth of July and I thought that would be a cool day for an anniversary. What do you think?"

"Hell yeah!" He spun her around, making her laugh in spite of herself. "Are you sure you're ready for this? Your freak-out had me thinking we'd need to wait a couple years." He lowered her to the ground.

"Yeah, well I've had a talk with myself about letting my fear get the better of me. I'm sorry for—" But his kiss cut her off.

Part Five
Resolutions
May through July

FIVE

KATRINA

Scoring exams was hard because Katrina kept imagining what that platinum band was going to look like on her finger. A trio of brilliant cut diamonds. A family of three. The perfect ring for her. For them.

It was the end of week three and one last student was finishing her exam. Life changed fast during those first three weeks of class, hadn't it? A month ago, she was Dr. Katrina Lopez, associate professor of psychology and owner of a wonderful home and dedicated dog. But today...

It was hard to admit after so many prideful years being single, but she didn't like being away from him. She wanted to be close. Physically.

Stifling her smile, she focused on the task in front of her.

She was proud that many students were earning extra credit for remembering the three types of Down syndrome. Maybe it was because the topic meant a whole lot more to her than it had before, or maybe it was because Manuel's disclosure about his wife stuck in their heads; either way, she was proud.

"I'm all set." Jaz grabbed her things and handed in her exam.

"How do you feel about it?" Katrina asked, confident Jaz had done well.

"Pretty good. Thanks." Jaz smiled. "Have a good weekend."

"You too." After Jaz left, Katrina gathered her things, placed them in her bag, and left the building to go to her office. It was only ninety minutes before she could leave—office hours, during which she'd finish scoring and post grades.

The sun was welcoming, so she opened the glass door to cut through the courtyard. A line of red tulips stood tall along the well-worn pebble path that separated the gardens. As she neared the steps, she—

Stevens was coming down. And fuck it all. It was Thursday.

She stepped to the side to make room for him on the path. "Hi." She sounded as curt as ever.

He stopped next to her at the bottom of the steps, a little too close, but she didn't want to step on the tulips so she was stuck.

"How are you today?" he asked. His smiling eyes forced her to look down to avoid his gaze.

"Okay." Which wasn't true. Her body hadn't forgotten that his tight muscles were beneath his red polo shirt.

He put a hand in his pocket and pulled out some keys while they stood there saying nothing. Maybe he was waiting for her to ask about dancing tonight, but that wouldn't happen.

That couldn't happen.

"Have a good one." She headed up the steps without

waiting for a response. At least he hadn't touched her. He used to touch her arm any chance he got.

She went inside and down the hall to her office where she found Manuel Martinez waiting. "Hi Manuel." She unlocked the door and welcomed him inside.

"Hi Dr. Lopez." He took a seat in front of her desk.

"How can I help you today?" She set down her things and sat across from him.

"Well." He leaned forward, placed his elbows on his knees, and folded his hands. "I just wanna say thanks." By the look in his eyes, you'd think she'd saved his life. "I think you're a great teacher. You make it real, you know?"

He stood as if about to leave, but didn't. "Just wanna say my wife is willing to try for a baby now. We both want one, but she's scared. I talked to her about what you said about the whole perfect-baby-dying-and-grieving thing and we realize we've already been doing that. You know, because we weren't trying for the baby we want. We both lived through hell and wanted to start over once we left the bad elements behind, you know? She finished school last year and here I am now. She's a dental assistant." The corner of his mouth turned up at those words.

He was proud of her.

"We want a family. And now we gonna try because of what you said. Because of you."

Warmth spread through Katrina like cider on an autumn day. "You're going to be great, Manuel." She gave him the smile she felt everywhere. "Good luck and, if you don't mind, keep me posted. Okay?"

"Sure thing, Dr. Lopez." He grabbed the doorknob and gave her his casual salute. "See you Monday."

After he closed the door, she fired up her laptop and pulled exams out of her bag. Curious, she finished Manuel's exam first.

He earned every essay point, including the extra credit, and only made a few mistakes on multiple-choice. Overall score was ninety-five percent. Well done, friend.

She glanced at her laptop and saw the list of unread emails from students, the social science department, and...Cam Stevens.

Shit. He hadn't emailed her since their undoing.

She clicked on his name.

```
From: Camden Stevens
To: Katrina Lopez
Date: Thursday, May 24 at 10:57 AM
Subject: sorry
--
Look, I'm sorry for messing everything
up like I did. Can we please be
friends?
--
Camden Stevens, Ph.D.
Professor of Biology
Great Lakes Community College
```

Oh no. She needed to stay away from him. Far away. But she didn't want to hurt him. She didn't *want* to hurt anyone. So she told him the blunt truth.

```
From: Katrina Lopez
To: Camden Stevens
Date: Thursday, May 24 at 11:11 AM
Subject: sorry
--
```

```
Apology accepted. And be friends? I'm
not sure you can be just friends
with me.
Be clear on this- I'm not interested
in a relationship.
And I'm not dancing tonight.
--
Katrina Lopez, Ph.D., Associate
Professor of Psychology, Assessment
Committee Chairperson, GLCC
```

"I've only got a couple minutes. I'm between patients. What's up?"

Katrina smiled into her phone and continued rocking in a chair on her back porch. "How's your day going?"

Aaron's voice smiled back. "Okay, I guess. Miss you."

"Miss you, too. Any more thoughts about my request?" She wanted the prenuptial agreement for one simple reason: she couldn't risk her future.

"I don't think we need to go that far. No worries, please."

"But I would feel better about it." She rubbed her lips together. "You know, if things don't work."

"A ray of sunshine, aren't you? What about 'til death do us part?'"

"I thought you understood why I wanted this."

"I do. It's because you think too much."

Yeah, yeah. She didn't respond.

"I checked with my lawyer on Monday. Papers can be drawn up within the week."

Relief lifted her. "Why didn't you tell me? Tell him to get on it."

"I was hoping you'd change your mind. *She's* already on it. But you owe me."

She smiled. "What do I owe you?"

"A private dance. Soon."

"Create some floor space and it's a deal. Thank you."

"Your wish, my command. Gotta go. Love you."

"Love you."

Her head kept screaming at her. Don't get married without protection. She'd worked so hard for security. She couldn't risk her pension, her savings, her independence. She needed to hold onto it. All of it.

And how the hell were they going to break the news to their families anyway? Aaron seemed so confident. Not worried in the least, but seriously, what would they think? Especially Bitch Mom. How does a couple break the news they're getting married after dating for three weeks?

She texted him.

> We could get married without telling anyone.

> Hm. Let's think for a sec. Unless you don't plan to live with me after we're married, they'll all just think we're living together. What would they think of that? :-o

> Living together before marriage makes perfect sense. It would be a good trial period to be sure we work.

> Sounds like you want to wait before starting a family.

> I don't want to wait.

LMAO You're scared to death to tell people we're getting married, but you don't care if they think we're having a baby out of wedlock. Or do you plan to stage a shotgun wedding at that point?

Jerk. ;)

You're the one with the issues, not me.

:(

For someone who says the past is the past, you worry a lot about the future. Live in the moment. We'll tell them together, in person. It'll be fine.

Okay, but will you do the talking? I don't want to panic.

Oh brother. Please don't panic. LOL Yes, I'll talk.

When?

Sometime after you have the ring. Gotta get back to my patient. Love you.

Love you.

She put down her phone. Jake was taking a nap in the shade of her favorite oak tree.

She was going to miss that tree.

And her gardens. And her house and her road.

But she would be brave and let them go.

She stepped onto the cool grass and lay down next to Jake.

Sunlight flickered on her skin, blanketing her as she snuggled Jake's soft coat. For the hundred-millionth time, she closed her eyes to envision her future with Aaron, Isaac, and Jake. And for the hundred-millionth time, peace consumed her.

She had to stop letting her head get in the way.

The evidence was clear: Worry turned her stomach and upset her heart. But letting go felt healthy and peaceful.

What was that song? Don't worry. Be happy.

And it all falls into place.

That was her guide. Her hope. A new way to approach life —her new life.

Plus, the dreams.

She smiled.

It was official.

The worry was done.

It was Friday date night, and Katrina was wearing the black dress and heels she'd hastily thrown on after receiving Aaron's last-minute call to dress up before she left her house for his.

Aaron, looking fantastic in dark grey slacks with matching vest and tie over a form-fitting light grey shirt, pulled the Road Runner into a parking spot outside a restaurant she'd never heard of before, Bel Fiore.

Delicious aromas floated about the sophisticated interior of the restaurant. It was a world of soft light, greenery, and garlicky yumminess. But when Aaron whispered something to the host, the man led them down a long hallway, away from the wonderful world, and through a door.

They stepped onto a large patio covered by a massive pergola adorned with decorative string lights and flowering vines. The space held many tables, all of which were occupied.

The host led them to a large table under the center of the pergola where the gazes of all eight people seated there shifted to Katrina.

Uh oh.

She needed to start practicing her rational thinking.

There was no need for a racing heart, but if it raced...no big deal, right?

Positive thoughts. This was just another date with her man. *And a boatload of other people.*

She scanned the faces sitting around the table.

What was her brother doing there? And her sister-in-law? Mom? And Isaac and Bitch—Sarah?

She didn't recognize the other faces.

Yeah, her heart was pattering inside her frozen chest.

She guessed the man next to Sarah was Aaron's father, but she had no idea who the other two were.

The host led her to the end of the table where Isaac was sitting next to an unfamiliar woman, a pretty lady with long grey hair swept into an elegant French twist. Everyone stood, except Isaac, who was seated in a high chair wearing a little grey suit and tie like his daddy's. If her face weren't frozen, she'd be smiling. Maybe.

Aaron took his place behind the head seat.

What the hell was he up to?

She forced a weak smile because it was all she had at the moment. And eye contact. She needed to make eye contact. She made herself look into each set of eyes looking at her.

"Hi everyone," Aaron said.

Thank goodness he was taking the attention from her. She looked at his necktie and found his clean-shaven neck below that five o'clock shadow. The perfect distraction.

"Thank you for coming on such short notice. Just so you know, Katrina has no idea what's going on right now and she's probably having a mild panic attack." His eyes grinned at her. "I'm hoping she won't faint."

Oh, shit, he was right. Edginess was cutting through her, so she reminded herself not to lock her knees with the goal of remaining upright.

He gestured to the beautiful woman standing next to Isaac and the gentleman next to her. It was clear this couple had money, but their warm smiles were welcoming. "Katrina, this is Juliana and Riley Williamson, Isaac's maternal grandparents."

Oh man. Rose's parents. Her head was feeling too light for her shoulders, so she gripped the back of her chair.

"And next to Riley is my dad, Robert." Mr. Keller, who had the same blue eyes as his son, smiled and bowed his head.

Aaron gestured to his mother, who was seated on the end, opposite Aaron, and looked like a prune compared to everyone else. "You know my mom and the rest."

Marina was sitting next to Sarah, opposite Mr. Keller, and, between Marina and Katrina's little brother, Kevin, was sister-in-law Jenny.

"Hi everyone," Katrina said with more confidence than she felt.

Aaron continued, "I wanted all of us to have some time to get to know each other, so relax and enjoy. Order anything you wish." He took his seat, as did everyone else.

Still trying to process all this, Katrina was the last one standing. In an unusual moment of clumsiness, she knocked her kneecap on the leg of the table as she took her seat. Pain wrenched through her leg to her stomach, but she pretended nothing happened.

Damn, it hurt.

While she massaged her knee, she looked at her brother and whispered. "Do you have any idea what this is about?"

Kevin whispered back. "Hell, I didn't know you were even dating anyone. Then Mom calls me Wednesday night telling me your boyfriend asked her to bring all of us up here for dinner tonight. His treat. Jen and I didn't have plans, so here we are." He elbowed Katrina. "This is a nice place. He must have some bucks."

She didn't have a response.

She looked to her left.

Aaron was seated next to her, reviewing the menu with Isaac. Everyone else had resumed conversation.

She picked up her menu.

Yeah, it was going to be expensive.

He was up to something big.

But what?

It was difficult to focus on the menu, so she picked the first entrée on the list— angel hair, feta, and sundried tomatoes. And she ordered a bottle of Chardonnay.

"Holding up?" Aaron winked at her.

She forced a smile and turned to Mr. and Mrs. Williamson. "It's nice to meet you. You have a beautiful grandson." In her peripheral vision, Aaron played peek-a-boo behind a napkin with Isaac.

The Williamsons beamed.

Juliana said, "Thank you, Katrina. And it is nice to meet you. We've heard a lot about you since last week. It sounds like you and Aaron have been friends for a long time."

They already knew a lot about her and they were smiling? She fought the cloudiness in her head. "Yes, we've known each other practically forever."

"Oh yeah," Kevin piped up in an off-putting little brother voice. "They've known each other forever alright. Aaron was her biggest crush through school. He's all I ever heard about." He turned to Katrina. "So when did you two start dating anyway? You didn't mention anything about having a boyfriend when we talked last month."

Why the hell did Kevin have a pain-in-the-ass troublemaker grin on his face?

"I guess it slipped my mind." The tension in Katrina's jaw gave her voice its edge.

"I'm sure you wouldn't have forgotten a detail like that. Anyhoo, Mom said you two have only been together like three weeks, huh?"

She stared at him as he took a long drink of his beer. Her heart was beyond pounding. It was crying. Why was he doing this?

He didn't *look* drunk.

Or high.

The table was silent, except for the rhythm in her ears. All eyes were on her.

Kevin set down his beer and continued. "Next thing I know, you're going to tell us you're getting engaged." His eyes popped with enlightenment and he leaned forward to look at Aaron. "Oh my gosh." He smiled. "That's what this is all about isn't it?" He looked back at her and laughed in her face. "Are you two getting engaged?"

Jenny leaned forward maybe to get a better look at the impending disaster that was Katrina. Her chest was a frozen jackhammer.

Veins livid, she glared at her brother through the wet film on her eyes.

How could he? In front of Rose's parents?

Half of her wanted to beat him to a pulp and half of her wanted to bolt. She looked down the table to find Marina's eyes, but it was too hard to see through the blur of tears that wanted to bust free, so she blinked and let them fall.

Mom was...smiling? Marina's eyes encouraged her while she nodded toward Aaron, so Katrina turned to look at him.

He was on the floor with Isaac, who was holding a small box, perched on his knee.

She fought the lightheadedness and tears because she needed to hear.

He set Isaac in her lap and took the box. Isaac's warm frame helped. He was something solid—something to hold onto while she floated in this surreal cloud, so she held him tight.

Still on one knee, Aaron opened the box, removed the ring, and looked into her eyes. She'd never seen a man's gaze hold so much adoration.

"Isaac and I are hoping you'll be in our family. I want you to be my wife. And he wants you to be his mommy. He told me it would make him happy." Aaron looked at Isaac. "That would make you happy, right Isaac?" Aaron signed the word *happy* on his chest.

Without missing a beat, Isaac smiled, copied his daddy, and shouted, "Peee!"

His first spoken word.

For her.

Aaron's smile was larger than life as a tear trickled down his cheek. "See? He's talking because of you. You're supposed to be his mommy. Will you please marry me?"

She shifted Isaac to her right and felt Kevin take him. Her body was jelly, but it was moving for her, so she slid onto Aaron's knee and held out her left hand.

The ring fit.

They all knew this was going to happen tonight. Of course, they knew.

He said he'd take care of it.

And he did.

She looked into those eyes.

Yes, he loved her. With all his heart.

She wrapped her arms around him and squeezed. "Yes, I will marry you."

AARON

Dinner went better than planned. Juliana and Riley adored Katrina, as Aaron knew they would. His dad was in love, too. And Kevin? Enlisting his future brother-in-law to throw Katrina off-balance so Aaron could save the day was a wise move. Kevin had style. Eric was gonna love him.

"I'm not sure this is a good idea. I've had a lot of wine."

So maybe the necktie blindfold was overkill. Katrina's grip on Aaron's hand tightened as he led her down the basement steps. They went through the media room to what used to be his weight room, which was now a vacant space, twenty by twenty-five feet. In the center of the room, he removed her blindfold.

Eyes wide, she asked, "Where did you put all your equipment?"

"I split it between the spare bedroom and the workshop down here."

She took a turn and jumped into his chest. "I love it."

He wrapped his arms around her, squeezed, and then lowered her to the floor. "It's a floating subfloor, laminate over plywood, so you won't be dancing on concrete. Don't want to have to replace your knees anytime soon. So when do I get my first show?"

She walked to the center of the space like she owned it—an artist claiming her canvas. "Well, Mr. Keller, a performance can be arranged tonight as long as I have time to warm up. You've earned it with the big surprise dinner and engagement and all. Do you have a chair?"

He went into the workshop and brought back the old teacher's chair, painted black, that Rose had wanted to strip and repaint bright green as an accent for the guest bedroom.

"That'll work." She took the chair from him. "We'll go our separate ways now. I'm going to change in the guest suite. Then I'll come down and warm up. I'll text you when I want you to come down. Deal?"

"Deal."

"And the only thing I want you to wear is a towel." She winked and bounced out of the room.

When her footsteps disappeared into the guest suite, he rushed upstairs. On his way, an image formulated. Her gorgeous legs spread eagle on the hood of his car. Hell yes. Someday. He'd fuck her there. Hard. Against the shining black finish. Because she'd love it.

When he reached his bathroom, he undressed and hopped in the shower for a quick clean-up. White towel around his waist, he headed to the kitchen to grab his cell phone and check for her text.

Nothing.

Damn.

Well it had only been what, ten minutes?

Excitement necessitating distraction, he went out the patio door to the gazebo where his hot tub was enclosed by four cedar walls under a lattice ceiling open to the sky. He set his phone and towel on the bench next to the tub and climbed in to sit on the rim.

There was something in the bromine-scented humidity that he craved, so he drew in a lungful.

Rose.

She was the last woman in the tub.

His excitement took a tumble.

He'd begged her to join him for a soak that night. Her birthday.

She'd been careful for so many years. Always worried she might be pregnant. Always wanting to protect the baby she'd hoped was in her belly. The heat would hurt the baby, so no hot tub. And no drinks.

Her favorite bottles of red wine still rested in the racks beneath the wet bar in the basement. He'd forgotten about those.

No. Not forgotten. Just not thought about in a while. He hadn't been using the bar.

But he'd never been an entertainer. That was Rose's thing. One of the big differences between them, actually.

Rose. She was alive that night. She'd agreed to ten minutes in the tub. Only ten. And during those ten minutes, Aaron gave her the massage of her life. For her birthday because she deserved it.

At least she let go that once. She needed to. Always putting the maybe-baby first. Always being careful for the last four years of her life. It was half their marriage. And was it—

The chime jolted him, so he climbed out and grabbed his phone.

She was ready.

But his hand was trembling.

He wrapped the towel around his waist, closed the gazebo, and went into the house. But before heading down to his fiancée, he stopped at the mirror in the half-bath off the kitchen.

He needed to get his head back on Katrina. They had a wonderful family dinner. Everyone was happy he proposed. Everyone except Mom, of course, but Katrina was ecstatic he took care of everything.

And she was downstairs, waiting for him.

He looked himself hard in the eyes.

Katrina wanted a man who took chances with sex. She wanted someone strong and spontaneous. He needed to stop being sensitive. He needed to stop thinking about Rose. He needed to find his inner cock and go fuck his fiancée.

He drew a long breath, gave his body a good shake to loosen up, and went downstairs.

Katrina's skin, luscious warm cream, glowed in the dimmed light of her new dance studio. She was straddling the chair set a few feet in front of the center of the back wall, beckoning him to come closer.

When she stood, he gripped the towel because his erection was loosening it.

Her nipples stood beneath the cropped white t-shirt that hugged her shining skin. And the pony tail he loved sat high on her head. But the most delicious sight of all was the blush on those long legs.

She gestured for him to sit, so he obeyed, anticipation clawing at his insides. It was all he could do to stop himself from ramming her on his cock.

Then she bent over. All the way.

He clutched the towel to keep his hands occupied. Her backside was covered in sheer red fabric with a seam down the center, between her cheeks, tugging red-sequin stripes horizontally across her flesh. His head was light as her sparkling ass and blushing legs skipped to the far wall to cue music on the sound system.

The music was soft piano. Melancholy. Like a music box.

Then her movement began as if he weren't there.

This was not a sexual prelude.

Her movement was not cheap.

Her movement was...longing...pain...loneliness...lust.

And he was a voyeur. A silent, appreciative watcher of this private, forbidden thing. This raw display of strength and independence that was her.

Her extensions. Her articulations. Her breath. They filled him.

This movement was priceless. Powerful. Elegant. Real. So beyond what he imagined.

And now the second verse.

The movement changed. A stolen glance punctuated each phrase, her eyes making it clear her body wanted him. And his body responded in kind, flushing in the presence of this heady artwork created just for him.

She moved closer without touching him, creating electricity that heightened his craving.

Next verse.

She was closer. He felt her heat. Still not touching but making her need clear. And he burned. He needed to put his hands on her. But he remained still. He wouldn't move for fear of disrespecting this moment.

Then she wrapped her arms around herself and pulled off her top. Choreographed to the music, it was.

Just. For. Him.

Her lips were close. And her legs grazed him, expressing more power and need with the crescendo in the music.

She slid to the floor and tugged his towel, freeing his cock as the third verse ended. He swam in the cool rush while she removed her panties, her hair sweeping over his erection. Oh, her hair. He wanted to fuck it. Just grab a handful and—

A crescendo intensified the music.

She sat astride him, her eyes burning through his, so he slid his hands around her hips and kneaded her ass in time with the music. The perfect handful. But not as perfect as her—

Oh, hell yes. She was rubbing her pussy against his cock. Wetting it.

Yeah, baby. She could rub all she wanted.

The perfect massage.

Then she slid him inside, welcoming him to pulsing heaven.

He sucked the salty sweetness of her neck as the music, loud and strong, pushed him upward. Up. In long strides. Higher and higher. He rocked with her rhythm, watching her eyes as she used him to get off.

He wanted to hear those sweet, sweet words.

"Fuck. Aaron. You ready?"

"Yeah, baby." But he was determined to hold back. "Go for it." He held still and enjoyed her warm, wet ride.

"Oh, Aaron!" He grabbed her to prevent a fall while she tremored.

When her body let go, he seized his moment by taking her to the floor and pushing himself deep inside. "Damn, Katrina you feel so good."

He drove in and pressed. Harder. And harder.

"Yes! Fuck me Aaron."

Convulsions seized him.

Everything was his orgasm.

And he floated, continuing the perfect dance to the echo of the final chords replaying in his brain.

Echoing.

Until he could move no more.

"Did I hurt you?" Katrina reclined against Aaron's chest in the hot tub where he had her wrapped in his arms.

"Huh? Hurt me?"

"When I took you to the floor a few minutes ago. I didn't think about what I was doing. I'm worried I hurt you."

She laughed. "Seriously? Um. No. Dancers are used to floor work." She pulled his arms tight and squeezed.

She was amazing. Talented beyond anything he imagined. And wonderful with Isaac.

Damn that Connor.

"Penny for your thoughts?" she asked.

Pushing his jealousy down, he lied, "Was thinking about how I don't ever want to let you go."

She broke free from his arms and rolled into his chest, her smile illuminated by the wavering light from the tub. "But if you never let me go, we would never know the joy of reuniting." She gave him a soft kiss.

"Very true." He pulled her hips into a straddle on his abs and she took another kiss, so he let his tongue go deep. "Penny for your thoughts?"

She grabbed his wrists and placed his hands on her breasts, so he massaged them. "I was wondering what ran through your head when you found me at your front door that first night. I thought for sure you were pissed at me and I couldn't get out of there fast enough. And now, just a few weeks later, we've told our families we're getting married. It's unbelievable how fast everything is happening. But I wonder. Why did you look so pissed that day?"

Oh man, he loved how she was rubbing her palms into his pecs.

She could keep rubbing all night if she wanted.

"Hey." She twisted his nipple. "I asked you a question."

The pain made him laugh. "I need a break from the heat." He slid her back so he could get out of the water and sit on the rim of the tub. "To be honest, I was awestruck when I realized it was you standing on my porch. I panicked. I didn't want you coming inside and seeing Isaac."

She took a seat next to him and stroked his thigh. Her head found a spot on his shoulder and settled in. "I guess I can understand why you'd be afraid for a new woman to see Isaac right away."

"I really don't care what women think. But in that moment, what you would think mattered. Lots. I wanted to impress you, but I was all wet and in shock. I did the best I could."

"I'm really glad you asked me out."

"Me too." He rubbed her thigh. "Do you ever wonder what might've happened if I'd asked you out in high school?"

"Yeah. I don't think it matters, though. We've got each other now. It's all good. It was worth the wait."

A breeze came in through the gazebo windows, reminding him of her hair brushing his cock. "Where did you learn to dance like that? I can't get it out of my brain."

"Do you want to get it out of your brain?"

"No, but I need to work on Monday. I'll need my focus."

She laughed. "I guarantee the memories will be less vivid by Monday."

"I'm sorry to hear that." And he was.

"You liked the dance?"

"More than you can imagine." Jealousy pushed itself upward. "I'm wondering if Connor ever had a dance like that."

Her head snapped up. "Why are you bringing up Connor?"

He shrugged. "You wondered what I was thinking and that popped into my head." Unhappy with his weakness, Aaron lowered himself into the water.

She straddled him again, but he couldn't look at her. He

didn't like that Connor was there first. And he didn't like the idea she gave him *that* sort of dance.

She grabbed his face and made him look. "What's wrong?"

What *was* wrong with him? He should've been enjoying this.

But an image of a faceless man receiving a red-panty dance was causing anxiety to worm its way into his head. "You're just so... Damn. It kills me to think he was there first."

She rolled her lips. "You know we're quite a pair, aren't we?" Her finger stroked his brow, easing his tension a little. "I have to fight against worrying about the future and you, obviously, have to fight against worrying about the past. Well, my past anyway."

She was right. He was being an idiot. "I'm sorry."

A small smile on her lips, she tucked her head into the crook of his neck and snuggled him. "What do you mean, I'm so... I'm so what?"

He wasn't sure.

She was so much more than he ever wished for.

He stroked her back as her body relaxed into him.

She was so... "You're so perfect for me."

He felt her smile. "And you're perfect for me."

"Isaac. No! Don't stick your hand down your pants." Aaron abandoned dishes in the kitchen sink and ran to the living room where Isaac was rubbing his hands together.

Shit. Aaron filled his lungs to douse the flare of his temper. "Alright, I guess it's bath time." He scooped Isaac from the floor and pinned his wrists together so he wouldn't get poop on anything else. "You can't stick your hand down your pants, buddy. It's disgusting."

Isaac looked at Aaron and smiled.

That smile got him every time, so Aaron had to look away so Isaac wouldn't see him chuckle.

Aaron rushed upstairs to the baby wipes, an item he'd never live without. They remove everything, even sap from hands that grab pinecones. After wiping Isaac as clean as possible, Aaron took him to the bathroom.

As he was putting Isaac into the tub, his cell phone went off downstairs. Mom's ringtone. But she'd have to wait.

As usual, Isaac held still while Aaron washed him, which was a good thing because Aaron wanted to get back to the dishes so he had time to work out before hitting the sack. It would be nice when Katrina moved in. All the responsibilities wouldn't be piled on Aaron anymore. Not that he was looking to push things off on her. No way. That's not what marriage was about. Parenting was just...tiring.

The landline rang just as he was lifting Isaac out of the tub, so Aaron clutched him to his chest and listened for the answering machine in the master bedroom.

It was Mom again, but he couldn't understand her, so he grabbed a towel and carried Isaac to the phone. "Hi. Isaac's all wet from a bath, so I've got my hands full. I'm guessing you called my cell a few minutes ago, too. Is Dad okay?"

"Yes, your father is fine." Then she went silent.

Aaron carried the receiver on his shoulder as he went to Isaac's room for diapering. She remained silent, so Aaron prompted her. "Then what is it? I can talk."

"You know what I'm going to say."

Not. Again. He'd been dealing with this all week. She wouldn't quit. "Mom, I'm marrying her."

"I know you think you're in love, but this is too much too fast, Aaron. Please listen to reason. You don't know enough about her. You don't know she's right for you. Please give it more time."

He knew she was saying these things out of love, but he didn't want to hear it. He wasn't waiting any longer. "She's perfect for us, Mom. I'm not waiting." He set a diapered Isaac on the floor.

"But what does *perfect* mean?" Her voice was constricted.

"We've been through this. I'm done talking about it."

"I still think you're moving too fast. This isn't normal." And now she was crying. Again. "I just don't want anyone to hurt you, honey. You've been through so much. And you finally got past your problem. I don't want it haunting you ever again."

Her words were sickening because they dredged up memories of the man he feared. Katrina was a psychologist, so she'd understand his OCD to an extent. The problem was the nature of it. His OCD was all sorts of fucked up. It was violent. And Katrina...she'd grown up with physical and mental abuse. She had PTSD. He could *never* tell her that he'd once had thoughts...visions of killing Isaac.

He wasn't a monster, but his brain had made him *feel* like one.

He didn't want to talk about it anymore. "If it helps you feel better, Katrina wants a prenup. So please stop now. For me."

His mother went silent.

His decision was made.

He was moving forward no matter what.

KATRINA

"It was intense. Fantastic, but intense. Manuel is a treasure." Katrina settled into her bubbly tub, candlelight flickering in the darkened room where she had Aaron on speakerphone.

It was Thursday night—a week and four days since she and Aaron had been together—and she wasn't necessarily liking her decision to remain apart until they were married. But she wasn't disliking it either. She still loved her single life and wanted to savor her remaining days.

Besides, she had a lot to do before the big day, like preparing her house for sale and finishing Child Development. Today's class marked the end of week five, and it was one of her most memorable classes yet.

The class had divided themselves into teams—Team Nature and Team Nurture. She'd asked her students to provide arguments for their team related to how nature (or nurture) affects intellectual development. Both teams had provided strong arguments. And Manuel, who was among the few students who elected to support Team Nurture, was feeling it.

Agitated by one of Team Nature's arguments, which suggested that intelligence always *found* a way to develop in spite of a child's environment, he'd blurted, "My grandpa was a musical genius."

Katrina's eyes caught some students on Team Nature shift in their seats. Manuel had made some friends in class, but the majority of the students still seemed uncomfortable around him. He was a little older, more worn, wiser, but could come off as unintelligent due to the simple direct nature of his interactions. The middle-class late-teen and early-twenty-somethings couldn't relate. Katrina smiled to encourage him to continue.

"He was a migrant worker," Manuel said. "His family didn't have anything except a one-bedroom house and a love of music. Yeah, they were born with it, the music. I got it, too, you know. As a kid, abuelo taught himself to play guitar. Wasn't a nice guitar. The family got a used one cheap and everyone shared it. All fifteen of them in that house.

"He always struggled in school, you know. Couldn't do math. Struggled to read. Was in detention all the time for goofing off. And then one day the high school band teacher heard him drumming on his desk in the detention room. Abuelo was drumming the rhythm he'd heard the marching band playing the day before. Perfectly. The band teacher invited him to join the marching band that day.

"For the first time ever, someone that mattered—a educated white teacher—invited abuelo to be part of something good, you know? Invited him to be part of music in school. A great opportunity for someone like him, you know?"

The students remained still while Manuel's glassy gaze held Katrina's.

"He lasted two days. Abuelo could play anything. He was a genius. But you know what? In order to join the band, he had to read music. He promised the teacher he could play percussion as long as he heard the music once, just once. But no. He couldn't read music, so he was kicked out of band. He dropped out of high school that year.

"Maybe he wasn't smart with reading and math. Maybe he didn't write too well. Maybe he wasn't college material. But abuelo was smart in his special way. Music. Maybe if education thought about that a little bit, they'd teach kids different, you know? Prepare them for life instead of college. Maybe then there'd be less kids dropping out of high school."

Manuel had resumed doodling on his notebook and then drove home his point. "So, maybe Team Nature is right. Maybe it is born in you, but if the environment beats you down and doesn't let you shine and doesn't nurture your special skills, that intelligence only goes so far."

Katrina shifted her legs under the bubbly water as she finished explaining to Aaron over the phone. "His disclosure had been so honest. So powerful. His story was the perfect lead-in for today's lesson and it reminded me that we must give Isaac all the opportunities we can. His brain may have a knack for music or art or even reading or math. We must expose him early and often. Yes, it's likely to take him longer to develop most skills, but he's bound to have special talents beyond his ability to love. We need to find out what they are." A breeze flitted in through the open window, teasing her ponytail.

Aaron laughed. "Do you have any idea how much I love you for saying that?"

"Maybe." She removed her hair tie, tossed it to the floor, and clutched the roots of her hair, pulling in sections to release tension.

"Any other news?"

"No. I've just been super busy cleaning the house. I've cleaned all walls, trim, and doors."

"I told you I'd hire someone to do that for you."

"I know, but I've told you a million times I can do it myself. I like working with my hands." Under the water, she slid her fingertips up her inner thighs.

"I know, but if you weren't working so hard, you'd have time to visit me."

She smiled.

"I miss you."

"I miss you, too." Her fingertips found their way across her pelvis and down her inner thighs. "But I'm giving up a lot, you know. I love this house and I want my time with it before I have to say goodbye." She also wanted more of her fingertips on her inner thighs, so she kept stroking while crickets sang in the distance.

Up and down.

"I prefer to think you're gaining a lot, not giving up a lot." Disappointment bled into his voice. "You know, you don't have to sell it if you don't want to."

She stopped stroking.

"You could stay there when the roads are bad. I worry about you driving so far in the winter."

She sat up, energized, splashing a little in the process. "You mean it?"

"Of course, I do. It's not my decision whether or not you keep your house, is it? Aren't you Miss Independent?"

She sank into the water.

He was right. She'd assumed she needed to sell. But why?

She had her own income. The prenup was keeping everything separate. She could afford it, so why in the world did she need to sell?

She didn't.

She didn't need to do anything she didn't want to do.

She scanned her bathroom. Ten-foot ceiling. Spacious. Clean white and worn with large windows framing the clawfoot tub she was reclining in. Aaron's master bath had nothing on this beautiful old room.

"I love the idea of keeping my house."

"Then keep it as long as you want. And now that you won't be selling, you'll have time to visit me. Like now."

But she wouldn't be visiting him. Not before the wedding. And it didn't matter how much he pleaded. She needed time alone while she worked on organizing the mess inside herself. She'd boxed fears on her left and hopes on her right, and this new Katrina forced herself to remain objective—rational— when the fears (or hopes) attempted to sneak out of storage and wreak internal havoc. After all, unfulfilled hopes were just as painful as realized fears.

Her biggest hope had been to keep the house, but she'd kept a level head. She'd been brave. She was going to let it go in spite of her fear of doing so. She didn't obsess on her sadness. She didn't let herself worry. Instead, she thought about a happy future. And now...

Her biggest hope—fulfilled.

Another week passed into a Thursday afternoon. And Katrina, again, found herself on her knees in her perennial garden out back, pulling weeds. Avoiding campus. Avoiding *him*.

Stevens.

He'd given her space. No emails. No accidental run-ins anywhere, not even in the commons during Monday lunches with Gen. This was good. Maybe he'd decided to move on like she had.

The one thing she needed to avoid more than anything was the campus dance studio. She couldn't dance for Stevens ever again. Not after Aaron got weird over the thought of her dancing for Connor.

Stevens wasn't safe. He was a liar. A cheater. He—

A rumble in Jake's chest made Katrina turn around and look toward the house.

What was *she* doing here?

"It's alright Jake." She tossed a handful of bull thistle into her wheelbarrow and got up off her knees.

Jake took a seat at her feet and, like Katrina, watched Sarah approach. She stopped next to Katrina's crop of blue salvia looking as if she'd been forced to come. Not a trace of a smile.

Katrina dropped her gloves into the wheelbarrow and approached her soon-to-be mother-in-law for a hug, which was accepted with rigidity.

"Why, this is a pleasant surprise." Katrina smiled at the woman.

"Is it?" Sarah asked, not smiling back.

Awkward. It sounded like the woman was calling Katrina a liar. On her property.

Katrina's smile died. "Yes, that's what I said. Shouldn't it be?"

Sarah stood there, like ice.

Unable to run from the ill-will she sensed in this unexpected visitor, Katrina forced herself to rise above and do the talking. "Would you like a tour?"

The creases around Sarah's eyes deepened because the clouds just drifted past the sun or maybe because she didn't trust Katrina or maybe because she was just a crotchety woman. Katrina wasn't sure. Sarah had been reserved each time Katrina had seen her since that first meeting with Isaac at The Terrace.

"Is everything okay?" Katrina asked.

"I'm not sure." Sarah's eyes softened a little. "That's why I'm here."

Alright. The woman wasn't *attacking* Katrina, which was a positive. "How about some lemonade?"

"Okay." Sarah followed to the covered porch off the back of the house where Katrina offered her a seat in one of the rockers.

Katrina gave the woman a little smile as she opened the screen door to let herself in. She filled a couple of glasses with muddled mint, ice cubes, sliced lemon, and her own special lemonade. She took a sip to be sure it was perfect. "Please have this go well," she said to the glasses as she carried them outside.

Katrina handed the woman a glass and then took a seat. "What's on your mind?"

Sarah cupped the drink between her hands in her lap, examining it, not tasting it. "Please don't hurt my son."

A lump in Katrina's throat killed her desire to take a drink, so she set her glass on the side table between the rockers. "Why would you think I'd hurt Aaron?"

Sarah set her glass on the table and looked at Katrina. Tears flooded Sarah's eyes. "He's been through so much. Losing Rosie hurt him very deeply. More deeply than you can imagine. I can't bear to think of him in that state again."

The woman's words should've filled Katrina with compassion, but they didn't.

"You two hardly know each other." Sarah wiped her eyes with a tissue. "I wish you'd take more time."

"Well, I'm with you there." Katrina gave a tiny smile. "Aaron knows I wanted more time."

Sarah's eyes widened. "You do?"

"I *did*." She chuckled. "Your son convinced me that waiting was pointless. And to be honest, I'm glad he did. I'm looking forward to becoming part of your family."

Sarah picked up her glass and took a sip. After a long moment of silence, she said, "This is delicious."

Her words didn't really sound like a compliment, but whatever. "Thank you." Katrina picked up her glass and enjoyed another taste.

"Aaron told me you asked for a prenuptial agreement." Sarah waved at the yard. "I can see why."

Katrina smiled. "Do you like it?"

"Yes. You've clearly done well for yourself. This is a beautiful property. Are you sure you want to sell it?"

"Oh, I'm not selling it."

"Not selling?"

"No."

"But you're getting married."

"Yes, but that doesn't mean I need to sell my property." Katrina's heart pounded a reminder not to trust this woman.

"You're going to keep living down here?"

"No. I'll live with Aaron, but I'm not ready to let go of this property. I'll keep it until I'm ready. Like you said, we're moving ahead really fast. I need some time to let go. I love my property. Plus, I can stay here when the roads are bad in the winter. Aaron wants me to be safe."

"Of course, he does. He worships you." Her words were bittersweet.

A pang of sadness hit Katrina. "Why don't you want me to marry your son?"

Sarah set her glass on the table. "It's not that. I just don't want you to hurt him, so I wish you'd wait. Did he tell you about his problem? The reason he saw a therapist after Rosie died?"

Katrina took a long drink to buy time. She recalled the morning after their first night together. He'd said he had some panic attacks after Rosalie died and saw a therapist for a while. "Yes, he told me."

"So, you *know*. That's a relief. You understand then."

Katrina might have felt a little more comfortable if the woman's words didn't have bite in them.

"Sarah, I'm a very honest person. I wouldn't do anything on purpose to hurt Aaron. I've loved him for a very long time. I know we don't know each other well in some ways, but we've been part of each other's lives for so long it really doesn't matter. Please don't worry."

Sarah's eyes seemed to think about smiling but didn't. "It's my job to worry, Katrina. Maybe someday you'll understand that. *When you're a mother.*"

The woman's words were sharp and her tone was foul. Katrina wanted the visit to end, so she rose from her rocker. "Would you like a quick tour before you go?"

Sarah hesitated, but agreed, so Katrina showed the interior of her home without many words because the woman's iciness discouraged speech.

Five minutes later, Karina delivered the woman to her front porch.

"Like I said before, you've done well for yourself." The combination of envy and admiration Sarah was wearing on her face wasn't a good look for her. "Thank you for the tour."

Katrina made herself smile because it was the thing to do. "You're welcome. Have a safe drive home." Once the woman's feet hit the drive, Katrina locked her front doors and went back to her garden.

Blood was bubbling under her skin. Breaths were coming faster than they should.

"Where are my gloves, Jake?" She and Jake scanned the ground where she was working prior to the grim interruption, but neither of them found the things. "Where are my fucking gloves?"

And then the waterworks started. Fuck.

"There they are." She snatched the gloves from the pile of weeds in the wheelbarrow and yanked them on. "Would've had all these pulled if *she* hadn't shown up."

On her knees, she wrenched handfuls of weeds out of the ground with less care than usual, not getting all the roots. And then her forearm got poked. "Damn it." Another bull thistle. This was punishment for not maintaining her garden. She grabbed the spade, shoved it under the tap root, and pulled the little fucker out.

And then she threw the blasted thing, thorns and all, as far away as her arm could send it.

And then she threw the spade.

Shaking with tears, she dropped. Jake whined when her head hit the grass. He rested his neck on her chest, blanketing her with his warm coat. He knew what she needed. He knew why her chest was heaving.

She swirled in sickening recognition of that feeling. That feeling of being accused when she'd done nothing. That feeling of being hated for doing nothing. For doing nothing other than wanting love. For wanting acceptance.

The woman was treating her like a villain. Like a witch.

Just like her father did.

It was 9:00 at night, much later than usual, so Katrina would be safe. She ensured the studio door was locked before she let it close behind her, and then she flicked on the lights and stripped down to her dance attire.

Sarah Keller would not haunt to her. Katrina would rise above Sarah or she'd cut Sarah out of her life; a reminder of her father was not welcome.

She connected her phone to the sound system and cranked up the sole piece of music that would let her emote and hamper the venom Sarah Keller had churned.

Night on Bald Mountain, Katrina's antivenom.

She lay on her back in the center of the wooden floor and let the power of the music penetrate her.

Katrina would not hurt because of Sarah.

Katrina was strong.

Katrina was exquisite.

The energy plucked her from the ground and sent her soaring. And while she extended and turned and articulated her body, tears flew from her, carrying toxins with them.

Four times through.

Until exhaustion forced her into the floor.

And when the music stilled, she absorbed the quiet.

Breathing easier.

More peaceful.

More confident.

She rolled over to look at the clock on the wall. It was nearly 10:00, so she needed to go. She gathered her things and hit the lights on her way out the door.

But as soon as she entered the hall, he was there.

"I want to know what I did wrong." Stevens, whose voice was lacking its usual edge, was standing next to her.

Unsure why, she tucked her left hand into the pocket of her hoodie. "You did nothing wrong." He was as gorgeous as ever, and he was standing too close.

He leaned his shoulder into the wall. "Then why did you disappear? You haven't been dancing. I've checked. And now you're here without telling me. Why?"

The gentle manner in which he'd spoken the words tugged her heartstrings, bringing to the surface a reality she'd attempted to ignore: she *wanted* him to play for her. The thought of never again dancing to Stevens' music made her ache. The musician and the dancer—that part of them had worked.

"I promise I won't mess up again. Please give me another chance." His eyes were as sincere as she'd once believed his words to be.

Her heart melted.

She forced herself to break eye contact and checked the time on her cell phone. "I'm sorry, but I can't. I just can't."

Taking care to keep her eyes on her phone, she left him.

AARON

Aaron's veins pumped so hot he felt faint as he sat on a dinette chair in his parents' kitchen and glared at his mother. "What the hell did you say to her?"

"Robert, please take Isaac outside." As usual, Dad did as she wished. She filled her glass with iced tea while she watched through the kitchen window, probably to be sure Isaac was far away in case she lost her temper. "All I did was ask her not to hurt you."

"You drove all the way to Charlotte and showed up without any warning to tell her not to hurt me. Who the hell does that?"

She slammed her glass on the counter, sloshing tea over her hand. "A concerned mother. That's who."

Aaron gestured at the glass. "You're lucky that didn't break. What the hell is wrong with you? You have no right to be upset with me. I have *every* right to be upset with you."

She rounded on him. "Aaron, you are moving too fast. And I'll be damned if I'm going to watch you destroy yourself. The impulsiveness of this decision you're making is scaring me to death. You. Don't. Know. Her."

He got up, determined to keep his temper. Pacing helped. Pacing always helped. "The only thing that would hurt me is losing her. And that is exactly what will happen if you scare her away."

"Oh." She rolled her eyes. "Nothing will scare her away. She's got it all, doesn't she? She's one of those women who gets everything she wants. And she wants you. And you're *falling* for it. What kind of woman just shows up on a doorstep and throws herself at a man and asks for a date and..."

The pacing wasn't helping. Punching something would help, but he hadn't punched a wall in two years. Damn it. He needed his punching bag. But he settled for crossing his arms to hide his fists.

"...then agrees to get engaged *and* married within the space of a month? Oh, and then says she wants a prenup and doesn't even plan to sell her house! Don't get me wrong, the prenup is the only thing that's holding me together at the moment. Otherwise, I'd think she's a bloodsucker in addition to a seductive little witch who—"

"That's enough! You have no right! What the hell is wrong with you?"

She crumpled into a chair, tears streaming down her face.

He wrenched back a chair and sat, taking long breaths in an attempt to calm himself. He pressed his hands flat into the tabletop. The pressure felt good.

Sarah's hair, eyes, shoulders...all looked defeated. "She said you told her about your problem."

His hands fisted again. "No."

"She says you did."

"But I *didn't*. You must have misunderstood."

She pulled a tissue from her pocket and blew her nose. "She needs to know, Aaron. If she doesn't accept you after she finds out then you will have saved yourself a load of heartache. A divorce would tear you apart. So would a relapse."

Sickness churned inside him. "Don't you *dare* tell her. She doesn't need to know. I've got it under control. I'm better now. But you aren't. You need to see Sheila like I told you to years ago. You need her just as much as I did."

She scowled. "I'm simply concerned for my son. A son who is marrying someone before he knows he can trust her. A son who needs to take more time."

Aaron couldn't stand to look at her anymore, so he got up and went to the back door. "I'll excuse your lapse in judgment because I know you have a problem that needs to be addressed.

This is your issue. Not mine. Not Katrina's. Go see Sheila and leave Katrina and me alone."

Out back, Robert was pushing Isaac, who was all smiles, in the swing. "How'd it go?"

"Badly." Aaron took over pushing and gestured for his dad to take a seat at the picnic table a few feet away. "You'd think she'd seek some help. Especially after your heart attack. Didn't she learn anything from nearly losing you?"

Robert chuckled. "Seems I learned to slow down and she learned to speed up. She's wound tight, that's for sure."

"But it's not healthy. *She'll* have a heart attack if she doesn't watch it." At the top of each swing toward him, Aaron pinched Isaac's shoulders just enough to make him giggle. The perfect medicine for a weary heart. "I told her to see Sheila."

Dad pulled a deep breath. "Yeah, she's resistant to that. Your mom doesn't believe anything is wrong with her."

"Or maybe she believes there is something wrong and doesn't want to hear a diagnosis."

"Sounds about right. But didn't she tell you?"

"Tell me what?"

"She did see Sheila. Once. A couple years ago when you were in treatment. And she got a diagnosis."

"This is news. Why didn't either of you tell me?"

Robert rubbed a hand over his head just like Aaron did when he was searching for words. Robert no longer had the hair that used to look like Aaron's, but he still had a gentle brow that expressed encouragement and joy more often than anything else.

"We didn't tell you because you were going through a lot. It didn't matter. Not at the time. But I have to agree that a return visit to Sheila might do her good."

"What was her diagnosis?"

"Different from yours. General anxiety I think. Or something like that anyway. Means she worries about everything. If you ask me, that Sheila was spot on."

Okay. Generalized anxiety made sense. And Aaron could see how that might prompt her to do what she'd done. "Do you think you can convince her to see Sheila again?"

Robert shrugged. "I can try. But if she doesn't want to help herself, there's not much I can do."

"Please try again."

"Alright, son."

Aaron continued pushing Isaac while Robert picked up sticks that had fallen out of the old elm. It wasn't easy for his dad to bend over these days. He was still as trim as ever, but his joints gave him a load trouble, as did his back.

Dad always said it was a good thing Isaac was born to remind him to take time to smell the honeysuckle. He'd spent too many years rushing. It took a heart attack and a grandson with special needs to drive home that lesson.

But his mom...

Isaac's birth—and everything related to it—intensified her negatives. She was the last to accept the fact that her grandson had Down syndrome. She was the longest to cry over Rose's death. She was unsupportive when Aaron decided to open more clinics; instead, she wished him to leave private practice and work for larger company. For security, she'd said. She was a naysayer and a killjoy.

He loved his mother, but her toxicity wasn't healthy. Not for her. Not for him. And certainly not for Katrina.

No. Aaron would not allow his mother to hurt Katrina—especially by outing his secret.

For the sake of his future family, Aaron had to keep his darkness where it belonged. In the past.

KATRINA

"I don't like the neckline." Katrina had her mother unzip the fifth dress, which didn't look right. "Ask if they have a halter dress."

Marina stepped out of the dressing room to talk with the sales associate while Katrina stepped into the next dress and pulled it up.

Yikes.

She stepped out and put it on the hanger.

"Good news." Marina closed the door after returning. "She said they do have a halter. She's getting it now."

The twinkle in her mother's eyes almost made Katrina feel like skipping. They'd never been girly girls—always having preferred dirt to dinner parties—so the excitement of this moment (finding a wedding dress together) caught them by surprise. If Katrina hadn't known better, she'd bet Marina would turn cartwheels across the dress shop. And if Sarah Keller hadn't dulled her spirits a couple of days ago, Katrina would be joining for a cartwheel or three.

Katrina smiled at her mom. "I've never come across a halter that didn't look good on me. Let's cross our fingers this one is it."

They crossed fingers and linked hands while they waited, which, quite honestly, was the most cheesy mother-daughter moment they'd ever shared. And it felt wonderful.

Katrina chuckled. "Your excitement is infecting me."

"Good. I'm so very happy for you, sweetie, and I want you to be happy."

The associate knocked, so Marina opened the door and grabbed the dress.

"Oh, this fabric is so light and feminine. Dreamy." Marina removed it from the hanger.

Katrina grasped the comfy fabric and then giggled. "It's just polyester and spandex, Mom." Yeah, they definitely weren't girly girls. But Katrina knew what she liked and an inexpensive dress was fine by her as long as she looked phenomenal.

She pulled the dress over her head and it slid into all the right places.

Marina bit her lip. "I think you've found it, sweetie."

The woman in the mirror took Katrina's breath away. The dress had found its home; it was comfy and form-fitting and flowed down into a skirt that draped her hips. And the hem was set at the perfect length to dance just above her knees.

"If you'd like, you can borrow my diamond stick earrings."

"Something borrowed." Katrina felt light and jittery, like a butterfly about to take flight for the first time. "Mom, I'm getting married. *In this dress.*"

"I know."

The two hugged tight and cried—a good girly cry, which was the only girly thing they'd always done together. Tears when they were happy. Tears when they were sad. Tears when they were in love. Wonderful, therapeutic, wet tears.

Katrina let go and wiped her eyes. "I think the stick earrings will be perfect. Thank you."

"Anything for you, sweetie." Marina blew her nose. "God, you're stunning. You know, Sarah will come around. You're my intelligent, accomplished daughter. A beauty inside and out. She'll see that in time."

The joy of the young butterfly sunk while Katrina appraised the woman in the mirror. Beautiful. That's what people always said. Yes, she liked to look her best. Yes, she desired to feel sexy. Sexiness fueled her sexuality, which was well-developed compared to her overall emotional health. But beautiful?

Until recently, her insides rarely felt beautiful. Her insides had always been too frightened to unknot. And believing oneself to be physically beautiful felt vain. She wasn't vain. She didn't live her life looking in a mirror like the simpletons might believe. She lived her life looking at others. At people like Isaac and Manuel. She saw their beauty, and it didn't live in angel eyes or tattoos.

She wanted Sarah Keller to look beyond the exterior and see the woman who wanted acceptance and security—no matter how pretty or unpretty she was. No matter how much she'd accomplished or not. She wanted Sarah to give the exact things that Aaron, as a little boy, did his best to give because he'd seen past the exterior. He saw the frightened little girl inside, and Katrina would always love him for that.

She prayed that Sarah was not one of the simpletons because, if Aaron were forced to choose between them, Katrina would make sure that she, herself, would be the chosen one.

"Well, here we are." Katrina addressed her students on their final day of class. "Before we review and before we take the exam, I want us to revisit something.

"During our first class, I asked you to think about Fredrick Douglass's quote, the one printed on your course pack. *It is easier to build strong children than to repair broken men.* What does this mean to you now?"

Jennifer was the first to raise her hand. "The thing that stands out most for me is safety. When the lady from Child Protective Services came in to teach us about shaken baby syndrome and the brain damage that can result from it. That's scary stuff. You can't fix that. We have to keep our children safe."

Several students nodded.

Elijah raised his hand. "I think about health and safety. Physical and emotional safety are extremely important, yes, but health is right up there, too. A child needs good sleep every night—to learn, to heal, to grow. Needs good nutrition, too, or else the brain won't be prepared to handle the stresses of life. Health and safety make them strong."

More students nodded.

"I'm not sure I totally agree with that quote." Manuel was doodling, as usual, and all eyes turned to him.

Katrina smiled inside. She was going to miss that man. "And why not?"

"The quote says it is easier to build strong children than to repair broken men, you know. And I don't think one is easier than the other at all. All depends on the situation, you know? It's hard to raise kids the right way. The way research says you should. Even educated parents with the best intentions can mess it up, you know? The best thing we can do is educate ourselves, try to use the things we know based in research, and give it our best shot."

Jane spoke up. "Yeah, parents mess up all the time. A big one is not knowing how to manage behavior. If more parents knew the stuff we learned in this class, I think the world would be a better place. And we'd have more strong kids. We'd have smarter kids. And fewer kids on medication to manage behavior."

Katrina smiled. "Any other thoughts?"

Some eyes looked into their textbooks and some still looked at her. Manuel was doodling. Nobody spoke.

"I'd like you to do one more participation assignment. On a sheet of paper, write down two of your favorite topics from this semester. Deliver your paper to my table and take the rest of the hour to review for the exam. I will take questions privately at my table. The exam will begin at 9:00."

Katrina took a seat and let them work.

Today was bittersweet. In eight short days, she'd be Aaron Keller's wife. This was her last time teaching as a single woman.

And that box of fears was trying to bust open.

She didn't want to leave this job. She didn't want to relocate her career. She loved it at GLCC. She'd get to stay for a little while, of course, but not forever. Not when she had her own baby. Babies were best supported by two parents—a team of any combination—but a team—and she was sure to be there for her kids. Every day. As much as possible.

As papers accumulated on her table, the hum of studying filled the room. She opened her attendance log, noted that everyone was present, and then ran through the papers to give credit for participation.

The favorite topics appeared to be: how to use time-out effectively (popular among the future day care providers), sleep, brain development, disabilities, adolescent behavior, depression and suicide, and—

She pulled out Manuel's sheet. His favorites were specific: trisomies and Gardner's theory of multiple intelligences.

Manuel was a quiet student, overall, having spoken only a handful of times this semester, but each time, he'd shared a gem. Such potential.

He was the broken man, wasn't he? He was the resilient one. He was the one that had to be strong.

Just like Katrina.

He wouldn't let fear stop him.

He wouldn't let his history destroy him.

He would rise above. He *was* rising above.

Just like Katrina.

So she would become Aaron Keller's wife, and she would

not let anything get in her way. Not herself. Not her boxes of fears or hopes.

And, most certainly, not Sarah Keller.

***

It was her last Thursday as a single woman and Katrina was pulling weeds. Again. But not in the perennial garden. No. Memories of last week's encounter with Bitch Mom lurked there, so she was avoiding that spot. Sorry perennials. For now, let the bull thistle grow where it may.

Instead, she was tucked between tomato plants, ripping roots from earth, while voices of killdeer and mourning doves floated by on the breeze. And then Jake's chest rumbled.

She froze.

Bitch Mom wouldn't be there again. Because *that* would be nuts.

Even though she didn't want to, she looked up to see what was bothering Jake and found Aaron's dad walking toward her. He was wearing a baby blue polo shirt, khaki shorts, a ball cap, and a smile as wide as the ocean. A welcome vision of what Aaron would look like in thirty years.

"It's alright, Jake." She got off her knees, tossed her gloves into the wheelbarrow, and walked to the edge of the garden where she met Mr. Keller on the grass. He opened his arms for a hug, so she stepped into his embrace. "I trust you're friend, not foe?"

His belly laugh jiggled her. "Sweet little lady, I'm definitely your friend."

He smelled amazing, like Aaron always did, and she held his hug much longer than she had held his wife's. She even gave an extra squeeze before she let go. "I must say this greeting is much warmer than the one I had last week. I needed that. Thank you.”

“Figured I deserve a tour. Sarah told me all about this place. Didn’t seem fair she got a tour and I didn’t.”

Katrina welcomed the wetness in her eyes. Something about this moment felt so *right*. “Absolutely.”

Jake accompanied them to the back porch where Mr. Keller took a few moments in the rocker while she prepared two icy glasses of minty lemonade.

“Here you are.” She handed him a glass. “How about we cover the grounds?”

“Sounds perfect, but first.” He took a moment to savor his first sip of her lemonade. “You know what? Sarah was right. Your lemonade is the best I’ve ever tasted.”

“Really?” Katrina was a little off balance as she led him down the steps. Probably due to the giddy disbelief that one of Aaron’s parents might like her. She took him around the south side of the house. “She said it was *that* good, huh?”

“Yup. She said it was the best.” He waved his hand toward the leafy wall. “What do we have here? A row of serviceberries?”

“Yes. I absolutely love them, especially when they’re in bloom.”

He reached out and stroked a leaf between his thumb and forefinger. “Ever make serviceberry pie?”

Her eyes widened. “Every year. Would you like me to bake one for you?”

“I’d be delighted.” He walked to the end of the row where some of her junipers, coneflowers, and black-eyed Susans lived. “Aaron told me you had a knack for taking care of things. You’ve got a little bit of everything here. Those were apple trees out back by your vegetable garden?”

"Yes. And pears. I also have blueberries and raspberries and rhubarb. I love playing in the dirt."

He chuckled and then took a long drink of lemonade. "I bet you grew this mint."

She winked. "Yup."

"The grounds are gorgeous. I'm curious what's in the house."

They made their way around front and he went up the steps where his son, not too long ago, gave her a rosebush—the one she was caring for in the pot because she still didn't know where she wanted to plant it.

"And you've got a porch swing." He shook his head. "If I didn't know better, I'd think I'm in a Normal Rockwell painting come to life. This swing is just calling me to take a seat and whittle some wood."

"Oh, do you enjoy whittling?"

"Not sure. Never had thought of whittling anything until this very moment."

They chuckled. He stepped over to the screen door and pressed the handle, which didn't budge.

"I keep the front doors locked. Let's finish the outdoor tour and we'll go in the back to see the house."

As the two strolled the property, they discussed trees and blooms and bees and bats. Yes, bats. Because she had three busy bat houses to keep the mosquito population under control.

And then she shared the history of her home. Built in 1900. The slab outside the kitchen door where they used to slaughter chickens. The fire that ravaged a portion of the second floor in 1970. And the elderly lady that lived in it before her—the lady who died in a chair by her stand at the road where she sold home-grown produce to the occasional passerby.

It was her neighbor, Jeff, who had discovered her body

sitting there with a basket of raspberries in her lap. She just sat there, still as peace, in a warm August rain. A dreadfully beautiful sight, he'd called it, but a wonderful ending for that wonderful lady. Doing what she loved—selling her produce.

Mr. Keller chuckled. "No wonder Aaron's so smitten with you." They were on the gravel drive, heading toward his truck. "I think you're the most engaging and independent woman I've ever met. Sarah was right. You've got it all. This is one spectacular piece of property. No wonder you don't want to let it go."

Katrina's heart sank. "Is that why you stopped by? To see if Sarah was right? To see if I've got it all? Because I don't have it all. I've had my share of heartache. She doesn't seem to like me much. Seems to think I want to hurt Aaron."

"Oh no." He pulled her into a hug—nice and tight. "Don't you worry one bit. That's not why I stopped by at all."

She let his peacefulness sink into her skin, but the tears happened anyway.

"I only meant that Sarah said many positive things about you. She really does think you have it all and I thought you should know that. It's a *good* thing." He released her and lifted her chin. "The fact that she's scared about your marriage has nothing to do with you. She's just a worrier. Too much of a worrier, so don't let her bother you. Not for one second." He wiped her cheeks. "I hope these are happy tears."

"Very happy." She gave him a little smile. "What you said kind of sounds like the thing a dad would say to a daughter. I'm not really sure how to act."

He chuckled. "Don't act. Feel. Just like you're doing now." With a smile that would light the dark side of the moon, he got in his truck and started the engine. "I think you're wise to keep this house. Isaac needs a place like this for summertime weekend getaways. You be sure to give him some country living. Teach him to get dirty and make friends with bees and bats. And he can help sell produce to passersby. Sounds like your neighbor might appreciate you having a sales partner." He winked.

She didn't have words, so she just smiled.

And he pulled away, leaving her frozen in a good way... because she'd just found the father she never had.

AARON

The day came. The day went.

For Aaron, the past month had been a frenzy of anticipation. Planning. Assuring. Reassuring. Planning more. Not only to help Katrina cope with the shock of marrying so soon, but to keep his mother in check.

So far, so good.

Of the three things he was anticipating most, two had gone off without difficulty. First, the ceremony in the woods in the same place where they'd shared their first kiss (only family in attendance), had been beyond what he'd hoped for. Katrina loved it. Score.

Second, the honeymoon in a little white cottage tucked among trees on the shore of Lake Huron (privacy and peace for his nature-loving wife) had been...educational. He tightened as memories of nakedness and crashing waves and orgasms—lots of kinky orgasms—moved through him. The woman was beyond what he'd hoped for.

But this third thing—what he was about to do—was the most anticipated of all.

He went into the former dining room off the foyer to see his wedding gift to her. Dark mahogany, the piano stood against the wall exactly where he'd asked his mother to have the delivery persons leave it while he and Katrina were honey-mooning.

He rushed upstairs to the hall closet and reached to the top shelf to get the package he'd tucked against the wall, saving it for *her*.

The day the package arrived had been one of his darkest. It was exactly two days after Rose's funeral, and Aaron was black with all the negativity a person could imagine—rage, fear, depression, etc. It was on this day that the intrusive thoughts started playing with the flimsy thread that held together his sanity.

He had spent the morning pacing the first floor of his home—and then the second floor—and then the basement—and then whichever floor was after that—while clutching Isaac to his chest. He couldn't let Isaac cry. Not that Isaac cried much. In fact, Isaac rarely cried, which was odd because babies were supposed to cry lots, weren't they? But Aaron wouldn't risk him crying because crying created stress, and Aaron couldn't handle any more. Especially when the thoughts of killing flashed in his mind.

Thoughts of stabbing Isaac.

Smothering Isaac.

Drowning Isaac.

Thoughts a father shouldn't think about his baby—the baby his dead wife would never hold again. And so Aaron paced. And paced. And held Isaac to keep him safe from the monster in Daddy's head. Letting go of Isaac's tiny two-month-old body meant Aaron might succumb to the deadly intrusive thoughts, so he would not—under any circumstances—set Isaac down. He loved Isaac too much to risk it.

The pacing carried Aaron (and Isaac) to the mailbox. Not that Aaron wanted to get the mail. He didn't give a fuck about the mail. But the pacing took him there nonetheless.

He didn't know why. And the small parcel he pulled out of the mailbox? It nearly caused him to drop Isaac on the pavement.

The parcel was addressed in Rose's handwriting. But not in the beautiful script of her healthy self. No. As if fate needed to deliver another wallop of sickening pain, the handwriting was decrepit. This package was from a dying Rose. It was an unwelcome reminder of how quickly she'd failed. An unwelcome reminder of how much he'd lost. An unwelcome reminder of how alone he was with a little boy he didn't understand. A little boy he couldn't put down for fear of losing control and killing him. Of killing the most precious thing Rose had ever given him.

Aaron stood at that mailbox, package in hand and Isaac in arms, and wept as he fought the urge to slip the package through the grate that covered the storm drain near his feet. The package bled into his hand, infusing him with more anguish, more resentment, and more of everything dark that had invaded his life since Isaac was born. He wanted to get rid of it. To forget it. To walk away from all the pain.

But he couldn't—he wouldn't—because the package wasn't addressed to him.

Now, three years later, the print on the package was a little faded, but Katrina would be able to read it.

Package in hand, he descended the stairs, hoping beyond everything that he chose right.

The shiny new bench was the perfect spot, so he placed the parcel on it, scooped Isaac into his arms, and dashed out to the garage where Katrina was following his orders and resting in the passenger's seat. Her eyes were closed.

"She doesn't even know we're standing here, Isaac. Maybe she fell asleep."

She smiled. "No. I'm awake in my imagination." She

opened her eyes and looked at them. "Hello, Isaac." She reached through the open window and stroked his cheek.

Isaac smiled.

As Aaron helped his new wife and Isaac's new mother out of the truck, she said, "I don't think I'll ever tire of your chivalry, Aaron. It makes me feel like a lady."

Aaron whispered in Isaac's ear. "Do you know who this lady is?"

Isaac looked at Aaron.

"This lady is your mommy." Aaron used his free hand to sign Mommy on his chin.

"I really am his mommy, aren't I?" Katrina's hands were trembling, so Aaron held Isaac until she had him secured against her body. She kissed his cheek. "I promise to be the best mommy. I love you."

Aaron wrapped his arms around his family and squeezed. "Are you ready to go inside and see your present?"

"But this is my present, isn't it? I don't need anything else."

He released them and took her hand. "Come."

Midway through the kitchen, she pulled Aaron to a stop. "Aaron, why is the formal dining set in the kitchen?"

"Very observant, as always." He shrugged. "I thought this would look better. I never used the formal dining room anyway. Kind of a wasted space. What do you think?"

"I love it."

He tugged her toward the former residence of the formal dining set.

When they arrived, she let go of his hand, set Isaac on the floor, and walked to the new addition, her eyes fixed on the dark finish. "I love this even more."

He wrapped his arms around her. "Someday, you'll play for us. I want to hear the melodies in your head. Your teacher makes house calls and is ready to start whenever you are."

She turned and buried her face in his chest, so he squeezed her. He wanted her as close as could be. Always.

"You remembered." Her voice was muffled in his chest. "But I had only mentioned it once during our first date. Only once. In passing. And you remembered." She looked into his eyes. "Thank you."

And he felt full. Like everything was righting itself after a storm.

She turned to the instrument and pulled back the bench on which the package laid. "What's this?" She picked it up.

"I'm not sure, but you should have it." Aaron felt more of his universe righting itself, as if the unreal were becoming real. "Read it."

Her eyes scanned print on the front. The package was addressed to *Mr. Aaron Keller's Second Wife*. In the return address, which was written on the back of the package, the sender had indicated it was sent by *Mr. Aaron Keller's First Wife*.

"Oh, god. This is from Rosalie?" Katrina's voice was full of the frightful wonder Aaron had felt in the years since the package arrived. Across the seal on the back of the parcel, under the return address, Rose had written:

Aaron, please do not open this.
Give it to Her after you are married.
Remember I love you. Always.

Katrina looked at Aaron. "When did you get this?"

"It came in the mail two days after the funeral. Turns out she had pre-arranged for her father to mail it on the day of the service. She never told him what it was, either, but I think I know what it is."

She looked at the package. "Um. Should I open it now?"

"That's up to you. It's yours."

She sat on the bench and closed her eyes with the package resting in her hands on her lap. She was a vision of peace, as if meditating, calling for guidance about how to proceed with the ghostly reality before them.

When she opened her eyes, she slid her finger under the corner of the kraft paper, and then pulled the wrapping to expose a box. Inside the box was a book, which she pulled out.

Aaron's lungs filled. "It is." He knelt on the floor at Katrina's knees, but at the same time he was far away in the distant end of a tunnel.

"What is it?"

It was a reminder of Rose's deeply caring nature. Always putting the maybe-baby—Isaac—first. She'd want Katrina to do the same.

He cleared his throat. "Her pregnancy journal."

"You've seen this before."

He looked into her eyes while she wiped tears from his cheek. "Nothing but the cover. She kept it private."

The weight of the moment pressed on him while Katrina traced the tree imprinted on the cover. "Aaron, do you mind if I hold off on reading this for now?"

He shook his head. "Take your time. It's yours."

PART SIX
CONFRONTATIONS
JULY THROUGH SEPTEMBER

SIX

AARON

On Friday afternoon, at the conclusion of Katrina's first week alone with Isaac while Aaron worked, Aaron found a slew of texts from her on his phone.

I'm going to write a book titled Lessons Learned Since I Became a Toddler's Mom.

Lesson One: Constant vigilance. Where's Isaac? What's Isaac up to? Is Isaac safe? Uh oh. Why is it so quiet?

Lesson Two: It IS OKAY to take a pee without placing Isaac in his crib each time.

Lesson Three: Never leave Isaac alone with a bowl of food.

Lesson Four: And place all food in plastic dishes.

Lesson Five: Knee pads are best kept in the kitchen.

Lesson Six: To avoid the daily spill...

Lesson Seven: There is no avoiding the daily spill, so use the knee pads.

Lesson Eight: Do not let Isaac escape the kitchen with a cup.

Lesson Nine: Holy shit. Cloth diapers are AMAZING for cleaning up liquids! Every kitchen should have them.

And every carpeted area in the house should have them too.

Lesson Ten: Don't forget to check the baseboards and walls and table/chair legs EVERY TIME because SOMETHING from the daily spill is going to be spattered on them. (Damn)

Lesson Eleven: And clean quickly or else the spatters will have dried. (Damn Damn) Note to self: Dried milk is a little bitch to clean.

A significant portion of Aaron knew she was joking, but the remainder was unsure. All seemed to be going well. Everyone was happy, in his opinion, but something deep inside nagged him to worry. As soon as he arrived home from work, Katrina called him from upstairs, so he dropped his things on the bench in the mudroom and went to the second floor.

She and Isaac were sitting on Isaac's bedroom floor, each wearing a pair of jean shorts and a red tank top. They were so damn cute.

Aaron scooped Isaac from the floor and settled into the rocker. "How was your day, buddy?"

As always, Aaron got a big smile from his son.

Katrina took something out of the bureau drawer—flashcards—and then knelt on the floor at Aaron's feet.

She tapped Isaac's knees to get his attention and then held up a card.

"Go." Isaac swept his pointed fingers off to the side, signing the word *go*.

It was impossible, but it was real.

"Very good, Isaac. Go." Katrina modeled the sign and then showed the next flashcard.

"Be," said Isaac, having read the word.

"Be," Katrina repeated. "I don't know a sign for that one. It's easy for him to articulate, so I put it in the pile. He got it after three days."

It was impossible, but it was real.

She showed the next card.

"Pee," Isaac said as he slapped his chest.

"Happy." Katrina demonstrated the proper sign for happy, which was difficult for Isaac. "We'll have to get used to his version of the signs. His fine motor difficulties get in the way. For example, he makes little guns with his fingers when trying to make the sign for play, which should look like the hang-loose sign." Katrina demonstrated the difference.

It was impossible, but it was real.

Aaron stared at his wife.

Isaac was only three years old—with Down syndrome. He wasn't supposed to be able to read until...middle school or something, right?

Aaron shook his head. "He doesn't always chew his food before swallowing. He throws his dishes. And yet you have him reading words?" His lungs filled again—in that comforting, elated way—as they'd been doing more and more of late. It was how gratitude felt. He smiled at his wife. "You're amazing."

"No. Isaac's amazing. He'll rise to the expectations we set. He'll always have some limits, but he's too young for us to know what they are so we need to treat him as if he doesn't have any. He's beginning to speak. This is not too young to work on reading. I show him the cards and signs before he takes a nap. When he wakes up, I go through the cards once more after I change his diaper. Our brains make memories while we sleep, so he's basically learning during naptime. And quickly, too."

Aaron set down Isaac, who ran across the room to his toy box.

Katrina crawled forward and placed herself between Aaron's legs, nuzzling her body into his abs.

Aaron stroked her hair. "You've been in our lives for eleven weeks and he's starting to read. I sometimes wonder if you're still a dream."

"Don't keep me on that pedestal. I'll get a nosebleed. I know some things. Get over it."

And there it was—that sharp tongue he loved so much. An erection made his appreciation clear.

"You like that, don't you?" She didn't hide the smile in her voice.

"You know your intelligence makes me want to..."

She got up and gave him her naughty grin. "To what?" she whispered. "Fuck me? Then you're a sapiosexual."

A sapio-what? He'd need to look that one up.

She winked. "We'll see what happens later." She took Isaac's hand and guided him out of the room. "Let's go finish making supper for Daddy."

KATRINA

Prayers and lullabies finished, Aaron closed Isaac's bedroom door. "You deserve a reward."

Katrina's belly curled. "Oh yeah? For what?"

"For teaching Isaac to recognize words. And for the delicious homemade tortillas."

Yeah, Katrina was ecstatic over how quickly Isaac was learning words. Every small achievement she and Isaac reached together fed her a cocktail of feel-good sensations. She loved being a mom—his mom—and this was an unexpected thing.

All her anxieties had been quelled by thoughts of *competence* and *commitment*. She'd told herself over and over that she was knowledgeable enough, honest enough, and faithful enough to be a good mother and wife. She'd approached marriage like a final exam—prepared by research and morals and a healthy drive to achieve the top grade—but the pure delight she felt when she and Isaac learned together proved theirs was a relationship that didn't need preparation. There had been no need for a trial period. And there was no examination to prove her worthy. She just *was*. She felt it deep inside. Being Isaac's mom was like experiencing a long forgotten something that brought back happy memories and feelings as she experienced it again. Their relationship was some sort of magic. It was meant to be.

"Come." Aaron led her by the hand to the backyard.

The sun descended behind trees that lined the western edge of their property. Between shadowy shrubs, the white privacy fence soaked in the orange light, setting it aglow. Katrina's bare feet padded over lush grass while warm light splashed her arms here and there and here again. Then Aaron's pants dropped to the ground.

And he wore nothing beneath.

"Um." Her heart fluttered as her man stood naked in the middle of an open yard underneath a cloudless sky—in daylight. "Ya lost something there."

He turned to face her.

Oh, fucking shit. His erection.

"I'm guessing your fear of potential public exhibition is conquered?"

He shrugged. "A reward for my lady."

Oh, fuck yes. Aaron had come a long way during their honeymoon. He no longer handled her like a china doll when they had sex. He'd found the rough and raw and real man inside himself. He'd found the man who could take sex—and fuck her—without losing the good guy who cared for her emotional needs. He didn't judge the animal inside her—the one who wanted to be licked and bitten and spanked. He didn't judge the woman who wanted to be manhandled in bed even though she'd fall to pieces if manhandled at any other time in any other way. He didn't judge her contradictions. In contrast, he seemed to *understand*.

Her entire life, she'd been protecting herself. Every day. Always locking doors and checking her back. Always suspicious of environment or motive. But during sex, she was liberated. Sex was a time to leave her head and experience her body with someone else. It was the ultimate dance. And as Aaron learned her drives and needs, something unlocked inside of him. She felt it. He also needed primal release for whatever reason, and, as such, they didn't make love. They fucked. Because during sex, she could *trust*.

Yes, it sounded odd, but it was true. Maybe it was because she'd only ever had sex with trustworthy men. She now saw that abstinence had been a wise decision for someone like her.

Abstinence ensured that the most sacred part of her—her sexual self—had been protected. Never mistreated. Never misunderstood. Never hurt. Her father had left that part of her alone and she'd done well taking care of it.

Aaron was how she wanted her man to be. He was both animal and protector. And while he gave her three orgasms under the open sky in their backyard, Katrina thanked the heavens for the dreams that brought them together.

Katrina stepped out of the shower, slipped on her favorite cotton tee and boxers, and walked into the master bedroom where Aaron was lying in bed, eyes closed, with a magazine collapsed on his chest.

She must have worn him out. "I loved my reward. Thank you."

He opened his eyes. "So did I. We'll have to do it again sometime." He patted the mattress to welcome her.

But she shook her head. "I'm not coming to bed yet. I'm heading downstairs to read some of the journal." She pulled the book out of her nightstand and walked around to give Aaron a goodnight kiss.

Jake joined her in the kitchen, where she poured herself a glass of wine, and followed her to her favorite spot—a reclining club chair in the piano room. She kicked back and pulled a lightweight blanket over her legs while Jake made himself comfortable on the floor.

The cover of the journal was made of cream-colored leather into which the silhouette of a tree had been embossed. Below the tree was an inscription:

Even if I knew that tomorrow the world would go to pieces,
  I would still plant my apple tree. —Martin Luther

"An odd cover for a pregnancy journal, don't you think, Jake?"

Jake looked at her for a moment.

She opened the book and found a folded piece of paper taped to the inside of the front cover. The paper was addressed to *Aaron's Second Wife* and gave the direction to read it first. Kind of surprised to find her hands shaking, Katrina detached the paper.

There was no need for a trembling heart. Rose was dead. There was nothing she could say that would hurt. Rose wouldn't mail a hateful thing. Why on earth would she?

Nerves still shaking her hands, Katrina opened the note.

I'm writing this before it's too late. I'm declining rapidly. It's clear I won't be raising my baby. I want you to know that, somehow, I'll find you for Aaron and Isaac. They'll need you. And you'll be perfect. I've begged fate to give me this one thing. If fate has a heart, she'll make this happen. Please read this journal, all of it, so you know. If you have a heart, which you must, you'll grant me this wish. My one desire. Please love my men like the mother and wife I'd always hoped to be.

Sincerely, Rosalie Ambrosia Keller

Oh, shit.

Katrina set the journal on the chair-side table, flipped the blanket to the floor, and then rushed to the kitchen to grab a tissue—no, a box. She blew her nose and wiped her eyes.

Box of tissues clutched in her arm, she made her way back to the piano room where she gulped the rest of her wine. She grabbed the journal, settled on the floor next to Jake, and pulled the blanket across the two of them.

She waited, eyes closed, until the wine kicked in.

Rose.

Unbelievable.

Something brought Katrina to Aaron. That was for sure.

But a *dead* woman?

It would explain the dreams.

Those dreams prompted the all-consuming drive to see Aaron. And now look at them. She *was* Aaron Keller's Second Wife.

Unbelievable.

The wine's warmth was giving her the green light to open the journal.

With Jake's cozy fur against her legs as a security blanket, she read.

April 16:

Aaahhh! I'm finally pregnant again!!! Woo Hoo!! Aaron is so happy and I am absolutely, 100%, over-the-moon, ecstatic!! I peed on the stick and the line showed up right away! We did not even have to wait for the results! Baby's due date should be sometime in January.

Katrina flipped through the pages to see if all the entries

were so short. Most were, but not all, and the majority of the pages in the journal were blank. It would be a quick read. She turned to page two.

April 30:
It has been two weeks since the pregnancy test and all is well so far. No bleeding. Whew! Aaron is a little concerned I am so excited. He does not want to believe this could be the pregnancy that sticks, but I know it will work this time. I can feel it. I keep telling him to have faith, but he is lukewarm. Happy, but guarded. I will cross my fingers for my glee to infect him soon!

June 3:
Ta da! The morning sickness has arrived, on sched-ule, so that is a good sign. I am at seven weeks and feeling mildly nauseous. As long as I eat something, I feel better. I am thankful for that. I am trying to take it easy as much as possible at work and at home. While I know this baby is the keeper, I do not want to put him (or her) at risk. Anyway, I am feeling super, super tired, so I figure the best thing for me is to rest as much as possible. I am still so excited!!!!!

Katrina stroked Jake's coat. "Gosh, Jake, her enthusiasm is

infectious. I'm almost smiling with her. It feels weird. Like I shouldn't find joy in her words." She ran her fingers over the page. "She sure was happy."

June 5:

We had our first prenatal appointment. Baby's heart is beating strongly! The doctor said all looked good. Aaron is starting to relax a bit. When we got home tonight, he spent a half hour gently rubbing my belly while we snuggled watching TV. He soooo wants to be a dad. The morning sickness continues and there is a new symptom with this pregnancy: headaches. I have been getting a lot of them lately. They are kind of continuous. The doctor said more frequent headaches are common during the first trimester and I could take some acetaminophen, but I would rather not take anything. I do not want anything to risk the health of this baby. I can tolerate the headaches, but I am not used to having so many. In two more weeks, this pregnancy will have lasted longer than the others!

Katrina knew what was coming...

June 20:
We Made It!!!

She smiled with Rose.

Officially at 9 weeks 3 days today!!! I am sicker than I have ever been and I am So Happy About It! This baby is going to make it!! I can still eat, but it is a chore. I have to rummage through the cupboards to find whatever does not make me gag. I can eat whatever that is. Earlier today, I ran to the store to buy jalapeño flavored potato chips because they were the only thing that sounded good. I swear those chips were the best thing I have ever eaten in my life!! I am so pregnant!! Aaron teased that he will support my cravings as long as he does not see me dipping dill pickles in mint-chip ice cream and salsa.

June 27:

I have an idea what I want for the baby's room. Blue skies on the walls because that is how I feel; all is blue skies with puffy white clouds. I am still sick, so Baby must be doing fine. I keep the morning sickness under control by eating frequently during the day; eating whatever does not make me gag. This week, I want lemons and steak. Lots of steak. Grilled. I am craving it medium-rare, but I will not let that touch my lips for Baby's sake. Well-done it is. Headaches are still here every day. I still will not take acetaminophen. Baby is too important and I do not want to risk anything. Aaron says I am being too protective and the acetaminophen will not hurt Baby. He is worried about me. I will keep the headaches to myself until they go away. I can handle them. I will tell him I took the acetaminophen. He will not know the difference. I will be tough for my precious baby.

"Uh oh, Jake." Katrina's whisper didn't rouse him. "She kept Aaron in the dark about the continued headaches. She didn't realize it was a symptom. And she—oh, God."

July 7:
We had a wonderful 4th of July. Aaron and I (and Baby) went to see the fireworks. Spectacular show, as always. Aaron took good care of me. He carried a heavy blanket for us to sit on and insisted I recline on him during the entire show. He likes to be close like that and so my numb derriere did not bother me as much as it would have had I not been resting against my handsome husband. His hands caressed my belly the entire time. I wonder if he even watched the fireworks. Maybe he was just enjoying time holding Baby and me. I am all smiles. He is going to be the best daddy. Thankfully, my morning sickness is not getting any worse, but it is still here, so Baby must be doing okay. I am a happy girl!

July 29:

15 weeks

I have not written in a while because we had a scare. I woke up from an afternoon nap on July 13, before the 13-week mark, and when I sat up, it felt like water was gushing out. I ran to the bathroom. Water was leaking and there was blood in it. They told me to go to the emergency room. My world turned upside down. I could not believe I was losing him (or her) too. I thank God Aaron was with me this time. It did not take them long to do the ultrasound, but the results took FOREVER. Aaron was stoic. I was a wreck. The good news is that the baby appears to be fine. The bad news is that I had a moderate-to-large sub-chorionic hemorrhage. They said I needed to stay off my feet for a week and ordered pelvic rest. The bleeding stopped within a day, but it felt like I had a boulder sitting in my pelvis. Very painful. They said I should not be feeling pain, but I did. To add insult to injury, the morning sickness got worse in the days following the hemorrhage. I do not know why. A week later, I started bleeding again. Not a lot, but enough for the doctor to order me to stay off my feet as much as possible for the next three weeks. My head hurts, my body aches, and I am constantly gagging. I feel rotten. Aaron is still stoic. He has thrown himself into chores and waits on me hand-and-foot, but he has distanced himself from *the baby. He has not touched my belly since the hemorrhage. I do not want to lose my baby, but, I must admit, I now have a feeling something is wrong.*

Katrina's stomach turned, so she closed the journal. It was getting ugly. And this was only the beginning. Heart heavy, she sent Jake to bed and went upstairs to check on Isaac, her little peanut, who was asleep in his crib. She pressed her hand against his back. His little breaths were a lullaby under her palm.

Her Isaac. Her gift...from Rose.

AARON

The guys were shooting hoops on the court outside the community center when they arrived. Aaron had bowed out of basketball for the past five weeks and the guys had no idea why. They were going to flip.

Katrina let herself out of the passenger's door, grabbed the diaper bag, and walked around to join him. "I'm a little nervous."

Aaron unbuckled Isaac. "I'm a little excited." As usual, she looked incredible in jean shorts and a white t-shirt. "They'll love you."

Isaac on his arm, Aaron walked his son and wife onto the court. Aaron loathed vanity, but he couldn't help himself today. He was as giddy as fuck and he was going to enjoy it.

When they reached the court, the guys stopped warming up. All eyes were on Aaron's family.

No. All eyes were on Katrina.

Aaron watched this new information register.

He watched their worlds stand still.

Eric's jaw dropped.

And then Aaron nodded, ridiculous smile and all.

Eric stepped forward and pulled Aaron into a handshake. "Good to see you, man. And who is this love-ly la-dy?" Eric's over-enunciation signaled approval as he held out his hand for Katrina's.

"This is Katrina. Katrina, this is Eric." Aaron gestured to his other friends who each stepped forward to shake her hand in turn. "And this is Gabe, Rob, Jason, and Terrell."

"Nice to meet you." Katrina smiled at all of the guys who smiled right back.

"Trust me. The pleasure is *all* ours." Eric winked at her.

The guys laughed and, all but Eric, broke away to resume shooting hoops.

"Thank you," Katrina replied as she took Isaac into her arms.

"We'll play for about ninety minutes." Aaron planted a kiss on her cheek and whispered in her ear, "Told you they'd love you."

She smiled and set Isaac down. The moment Isaac's feet hit the pavement, he took off running toward the playset next to the basketball court. Pride flooded Aaron as his wife followed their son and directed him through the gate in the fence separating the court from the playground.

"Damn." Eric's eyebrows lifted in appreciation. "You better put a ring on that."

Aaron popped his eyes for emphasis. "Already did." He jumped onto the court, stole the ball from Terrell, and made a shot.

"Oh, no you didn't." Eric took the ball and stopped play. He called out to the other guys, "He already put a ring on that!"

Aaron glanced at Katrina helping Isaac into the infant

swing. She wasn't looking at them, so maybe she hadn't heard Eric's announcement. Aaron held up his left hand.

The guys stared at him.

"You're married?" Eric's voice was even louder, and Katrina turned to look at them.

The guys turned to look at her.

She gave a cute little wave and blew the group a kiss.

Aaron's audience turned to face him again.

A few beats of silence.

Then cries of congratulatory disbelief converged on Aaron along with a series of pound-hugs and a number of hard slaps on the back of his head. The crew huddled with Eric as the mouthpiece. "When did all this happen, you lucky fucking bastard?"

"Over the past couple months." Aaron took the ball from Eric and made another shot.

The rest joined and the game commenced.

"Where'd you find her?" Eric asked.

Aaron shrugged. "She found me. Showed up on my doorstep on a Friday night in May."

"But she ain't a stray. Spill!"

Aaron grabbed the ball and toned it down. "Alright, alright. We've known each other since we were kids. Went to school together. She looked me up. We clicked. End of story."

"But dude," Eric said, "you're *married*. When the hell did that happen?"

"Enough." Terrell grabbed the ball from Aaron and turned to Eric. "Leave the man alone."

Terrell gave Aaron's shoulder a squeeze. "Wish you the best, man. Congrats. Now let's play."

Terrell's command threw them into a serious game of three-on-three and Aaron played like never before. Unable to resist stealing the occasional glance in Katrina's direction,

Aaron found that seeing his wife play with their son while he enjoyed a game with his buddies gave him a high he'd never experienced before. Life didn't get better than this. He was on point. Eric, Terrell, and Aaron crushed the other three.

Another round of congratulations came his way following the game. The guys even called out to Katrina to wish her a good night as they made their way to their cars.

But Eric hung back. "Why the hell didn't you tell me you were getting married?"

Aaron took a seat on the bench and leaned forward, resting his elbows on his knees. It had been a couple weeks since the honeymoon. He'd been back at work. He'd been adjusting to a new life. He'd been...happy.

For the first time ever, he'd been happy without the guys.

Katrina had become his world. With her, life was different. Enriched. Full.

But Eric had been Aaron's best friend through everything since they met on day one of graduate school. He'd been there through engagement to Rose, through marriage, through all those damned pregnancies and losses. He'd been Aaron's ear. Aaron's support.

And Aaron had left him behind.

Aaron looked at his friend. "Because it was between her and me."

Eric's face had the edge Aaron had long known. The first time he saw it was when Eric had learned his graduate-school sweetheart was fucking a classmate behind his back.

Aaron watched Eric watch Katrina, who was playing a game of tickle monster with Isaac in the grass near the playset. "We had a small ceremony on the Fourth of July. On her birthday. Only family attended. We spent the following week on our honeymoon. We've been adjusting to married life. She's living with me now. She has a badass German Shepherd named Jake. Isaac loves the dog."

Still watching her, Eric remained silent.

"Sorry, man, but she's the only woman I've ever known who became my best friend."

Face blank, Eric looked at Aaron.

Aaron waited for Eric's resilience to kick in.

A moment later, Eric raised his chin in playful superiority. "We'll see, Keller. The honeymoon lasts only so long and *then* we'll see who's your best friend." Eric held out his hand for a shake. "Congrats, man. She's hot."

Aaron pulled him into a pound-hug and waved for Katrina to join them. "Wait till you get to know her. You'll find she's beautiful. Plus, her wedding gift to me was a pair of half-season tickets to the Pistons. Great seats. I promised to take her to the first game, but you're invited to the second."

Eric smiled. "You are one lucky bastard. Hot wife. Season tickets. Sure as hell, I'll go. Thanks, man."

Aaron scooped Isaac into his arms because it was time for a more formal introduction. "Eric Mendez, this is my wife, Dr. Katrina Lopez-Keller."

"Doctor?" Eric's voice indicated approval.

Katrina smiled. "A doctor, not a physician. I have a Ph.D."

"In which field?"

"Psychology. And you're a physical therapist. You and Aaron have been friends since graduate school?"

"Yeah, and I was his best man when he married Rose. Congrats on your wedding. Aaron neglected to inform me he was getting married again." Eric moved closer to look Katrina deep in the eyes. "Yeah, man, I can see why you forgot to mention it. She's quite the distraction. You're forgiven."

Eric grabbed his basketball. "We'll have to double sometime. Things are working out with Ashley—the girl from the dog park." He turned toward his convertible.

Aaron took Katrina's hand and headed toward their truck.

"He's not a player, is he?" she asked as Aaron opened her door.

"Eric? No. He's a good guy. Keeps it real." Aaron buckled Isaac into his car seat and got in. "I guess you could say he's the closest thing I have to a brother. It hurt him to find out I got married without telling him."

"Why didn't you tell him?"

Aaron pulled out of the parking lot. "I didn't need his approval and our ceremony was intimate. It all happened so fast." Aaron shrugged. "I don't know. Didn't seem to matter at the time."

Katrina stroked his thigh, which felt great after the exercise. "I'm sensing it matters now?"

"Yeah, I should've told him. I didn't realize it until now, but I've been all wrapped up in us."

She squeezed Aaron's thigh. "Dangerous territory. I don't need many others in my life. Gen at work is about all I need." She paused. "Well, she's all I need besides my mother, brother, Jake, and now you. But I don't want you shutting out your friends because of me. If you do, all of you will end up resenting me."

"I could never resent you."

She withdrew her hand from his thigh. "Never say never, Aaron. It's a lesson I learned long ago."

Aaron drove home in silence as Katrina's uncomfortable nugget of wisdom wormed into his mind. His friends—all of them—found Katrina attractive. And she'd been a bit of a flirt with them.

His gut turned as a thought of Katrina hugging Terrell

attempted to spark a dark and deadly game with Aaron's confidence.

Aaron's heart pulsed harder.

No. Katrina would never do something like that. Never.

But the tightness growing in Aaron's throat didn't agree.

KATRINA

Summer trips to the dunes along Lake Michigan? Katrina loved them. Hilly greenery that carried her north when she and her mom visited the wineries or when she and Jake went camping? Beautiful. The drive to the little white cottage along Lake Huron? Pleasant. So she needed to make sure she wouldn't jab her eyes out the next time she made this commute. Something about driving to *work* awakened her to the grim reality that the stretch of interstate between GLCC and Aaron's home made for the most undesirable trek in Michigan.

"That drive sucked." She pulled into her usual parking spot on campus after the first of what would be many too-long commutes to work.

It was weird returning to work after living in fairy-tale-land for the past month. Today's schedule was short. She would have an assessment committee meeting at 9 a.m., after which she'd work on whatever came out of the discussion. Thankful she wasn't back full-time for a couple of weeks yet, she went into the building.

After gathering materials from her office, she went down the hall to the conference room at the end of her wing. As chairperson, she was the first to arrive, so she set out the agenda and data sheets. Then, her phone buzzed.

Welcome back, girl! Lunch at 11?

Gen's enthusiasm gave her a chuckle. It had been too long since they'd seen each other...since before the wedding. Gen was sure to be huge at this point, but that hadn't dulled—

"I thought I should arrive a little early to explain."

Katrina's heart thudded in reply to Stevens' voice. She set her phone on the table without replying to Gen and then looked up even though she didn't want to.

Damn. He was wearing her favorite black shirt.

Her heart drummed.

What the hell was he doing here?

She forced a smile. "Explain what?"

"Dr. Johnson retired unexpectedly in July." His voice was more professional than ever before, as if she were a new acquaintance. "Our department discussed his various responsibilities and faculty stepped up to take them over. I volunteered to represent the Science department on the assessment committee. I'm here for the meeting."

She racked her brain and vaguely recalled reading an email announcing Johnson's retirement. Crap. He'd retired, and she didn't do anything to acknowledge it.

Damn it, Katrina.

Maybe it wasn't too late to send a card.

This moment made two things very clear. One, she'd been too wrapped up in her own little world this summer. And two, being near Stevens still aroused her. And that wasn't supposed to happen. Because she was a *wife*.

She gave a sharp shrug. "Okay. Grab an agenda and a packet of data sheets."

Stevens grabbed the papers and took a seat at the middle of the table, a safe distance from her. She didn't want to look at him again, but she felt the pull. She heard him shuffling things about while she busied herself with paperwork.

Please people, arrive early.

The meeting was set to start in eight minutes, and she didn't want to be alone with him.

"You're wearing a ring."

She tried to restrain it, but a fleeting glance at him escaped her. His face was a pale shade of disbelief. She grabbed a neat stack of papers and moved them to another spot on the table even though she didn't need to. "That's because I'm married." She continued rearranging stacks of papers and forcing herself not to look into those pretty blue eyes that had promised not to mess up again.

Shit. She was shaking.

"May I ask your new name?" His voice was distant. "I don't want to offend you by using the wrong one."

She looked at him with her best poker face, which always failed at hiding her secrets. "My last name is Lopez-Keller, hyphenated."

Stevens shook his head. "Of course. The guy from the restaurant."

Of course, he remembered. She maintained the poker face.

"Congratulations, Doc-tor Lo-pez Kel-ler." His gaze seared hers.

Oh no.

An image of being with both Aaron and Stevens at the same time streaked through her head, infusing her with lust. She'd never been this responsive to Stevens before.

"Excuse me." Cell phone in hand, she flew past him without a glance and into the bathroom two doors down. She had four minutes to get a grip, so she ran her hands under cold water and pressed the chill into her neck.

What kind of woman was she, anyway? She loved Aaron. And she loved Isaac. She could *never* betray them. So what were these naughty sensations running through her?

The reflection in the mirror indicated nothing was amiss in

spite of the helter-skelter state of her insides. She just needed to get through the meeting and away from *him*.

She returned a text to Gen, agreeing to lunch, and then got on with it.

It was a full house when she returned to the conference room, so she dove in full throttle and led a productive session without looking at Stevens the entire time. The committee discussed college-wide assessment of writing, student growth, and fall semester opening days, which were two weeks away. As always, the assessment committee would be offering sessions for faculty professional development during opening days. This year, they would lead three sessions, one of which was the presentation on classroom assessment techniques that—

Oh no.

She needed a new partner.

She continued dodging Stevens' gaze when she announced with a knotted belly that she would need a new co-presenter for the presentation she had done with Dr. Johnson at the assessment conference back in May.

"I can present with you." Stevens' voice had an edge. "I have the paperwork. Dr. Johnson left it with the Science department. I've already reviewed it."

Blood drained from her head. "Well thank you, Dr. Stevens. That is certainly...convenient." Her eyes scanned other faces at the table, but no eyes were on her. "Did anybody else have interest in this presentation? If so, please volunteer now and we can work something out."

She kept scanning, but everyone was busy reviewing paperwork. Everyone but Stevens, whose eyes were smiling at her. Of course, nobody else would offer to help her out when such a willing volunteer was in their midst. And she wouldn't beg.

Damn.

She dismissed the committee.

She was weepy as she stacked her papers and placed them in their respective folders.

Stevens was still in his seat after everyone had left.

She shook her head, her eyes blurring a little. "What's this all about?"

Stevens stood up, gathered his paperwork, and walked toward the door. "I'm a good colleague, Dr. Lopez-Keller." His words were forceful. "You needed a new co-presenter and I'm stepping up. That's all. Don't go reading into things."

The damned racehorse was trotting in her chest again. Stevens was accusing her of reading into things? What about Greene's, when he massaged her shoulder in front of Aaron? And all the flirting. And the piano. And the moment of near abandon on the floor of the dance studio a couple of months ago. What about his hands kneading her ass? And his promise to do better this time?

Her belly flipped at her attraction.

Who was she kidding? She'd always loved his attention. Always. And he'd always known it. But she was out of bounds now.

Or maybe.

Maybe *she* was the one who couldn't be trusted?

The thought tore through her, reminding her of Isaac's angel eyes.

No. She could *never* hurt her family.

She'd find her grit. She would not let Stevens unhinge her.

"How's my girl today?" Gen asked when Katrina arrived at the table. Yup, Gen looked like she was about to pop.

Katrina shook her head. "A little nervous and now unsettled, but otherwise extremely happy." Unable to smile due to Stevens, Katrina held out her left hand.

Gen's eyes widened. "Shit, Katrina, you're married?"

Thankful Gen's voice hadn't carried too far, Katrina nodded. "It's official. I became Dr. Katrina Lopez-Keller on the Fourth of July."

Gen stared at her. "You're serious."

"Of course, I'm serious." Uncomfortable mixture of excitement and fear roiling inside her, Katrina went to the lunch counter.

Gen followed. "Katrina. You're moving insanely fast. Why the rush?"

Katrina grabbed a tray. "Insanely fast?" She grabbed a napkin. "I'm not insane." She grabbed too many utensils and put the second spoon back even though she'd touched it. "We've loved each other since childhood. We didn't rush. We just didn't delay the inevitable any longer." She got a turkey sandwich and cranberry juice and then returned to the table where she opened the package and took a bite before Gen had finished paying.

Gen lumbered over and lowered herself into the seat across from Katrina. "Okay. Well, I guess congratulations are in order." She busied herself with soup. "Wow."

Katrina continued to eat, but hardly noticed flavors. Insanely fast, huh? That's what everyone would think, wouldn't they? Whatever. Nobody mattered except Aaron, Isaac, and their families. And their families were happy about the marriage. Well, everyone was happy except Bitch Mom, but...whatever.

"So if you're extremely happy, as you say, why are you so edgy today?"

Katrina shook her head. "I have a problem."

Gen set her spoon on the table and folded her hands as if expecting the story to unfold.

"Stevens joined my committee. He's the new rep for the Science Department."

"Terrific." The sarcasm in Gen's voice tweaked the corner of Katrina's mouth into a tiny smile.

"Exactly. And it gets worse. During opening days, I'm doing that presentation on classroom assessment techniques. Dr. Johnson has always been my co-presenter, so who do you think volunteered to be my new co-presenter?"

Shaking her head, Gen giggled. "Only you."

Okay. It was getting easier to smile, so Katrina continued in her best imitation of Stevens' professional voice. "I'm a good colleague, Dr. Lopez-Keller. You needed a new co-presenter and I'm stepping up. Don't go reading into things."

It took a moment for Gen to recover from the water that had gone down the wrong pipe. "He actually said that? 'Don't go reading into things?' What kind of self-righteous dork would say that after all the blatant flirting he's done?"

"I know, right?" Katrina took a swallow of juice, torn between amusement and devastation that she still had sexual feelings for him. "I'm stuck doing the presentation with Stevens unless I figure a way out of it."

Still giggling, Gen shook her head. "Like I said, only you."

"What do I do?"

"If you can do the presentation alone, do it alone."

Katrina nodded. "That's what I'd like to do, but it wouldn't be a good move in terms of the presentation. We use audience participation at various points. If I don't have a co-presenter, the flow will be lost and the presentation will turn to shit unless I completely rework it. You know me. I don't do shitty work. And I don't have time to rework the presentation by opening days. I'm busy with Isaac when I'm home. And it would be obvious I'm trying to avoid him. It would be weird."

"Well, I would do it with you, but…" Gen pointed at her near-bursting belly. Her due date was a week away.

They finished lunch in silence, Katrina's mind wrestling her feelings the entire time.

"I can't come up with anything that won't make you look like a coward," Gen said. "I think the most professional way to handle this is to let it be. Stevens is well-respected for his work and his charisma will compliment yours. To be honest, I think you'd make a great team for the presentation."

Katrina bit her lip. She had to agree. Finding a way out of presenting with Stevens would reflect poorly on her. Stevens' work was well respected. And he had behaved professionally.

Until he did something that crossed professional lines and made her uncomfortable, she'd have to go with the flow…of the raging river she was about to ride. Because tonight, she needed to be a good wife and tell her husband the truth.

AARON

As soon as Aaron closed Isaac's door, Katrina jumped into his chest and wrapped her legs around his waist. "Fuck me." Her words, hot on his ear, surged through him.

"Gladly." He pinned her against the wall opposite Isaac's door, pulled down his shorts, and slid right in under her sundress. "Damn, babe, you're wet." She dropped her left leg to the floor and, in a manner only a dancer could pull off, extended her right leg over his bicep, giving him a nice tight fit. "How do you want it?"

"Just fuck me," she whispered.

And so, he railed her into the wall, the rhythm squeezing

him tight, pulling his blood down to the part of him that pulsed for her.

Her eyes closed as she called his name, so he went harder.

Harder.

Rocketing himself into her until he exploded.

Heart racing and legs trembling, he lifted and pulled her limp frame into his chest.

She wrapped her arms around his neck and held tight. "Thank you, Aaron." She pressed her lips to his...so gentle...as she lowered herself to the floor. "That was perfect."

He slid his thumb over her lush lower lip. "Agreed. For a quickie, anyway."

He followed her to their bathroom where, without a word, she changed into a tank top and panties. Then, without looking at him, she loaded her toothbrush.

Uncomfortable for some reason, he broke the silence. "Sorry, I never asked how work went today." After changing into a pair of boxer briefs, he grabbed his toothbrush and toothpaste. Her eyes were searching his in the mirror as they brushed, suggesting something was off. She was bothered.

When finished, they went into the bedroom.

She crawled into bed. "Wanna cuddle?" But her voice was tiny. Different.

He lay down and opened his right arm for her to nuzzle in at his side.

Her thigh lay across his pelvis like usual, but...something was definitely off.

"Did work go okay today?"

Her finger traced his pecs, so he massaged her thigh. "Well." Her voice was still tiny. "I have something to tell you and I'm a bit nervous to do so." She stopped tracing, propped herself on her elbow, and looked him in the eyes. "My committee meeting went well today. We're all set for opening days. We're doing three presentations that week. You know I'm doing one of them."

"Yeah, that one you did in May. At the conference when you visited me, right?"

She nodded. "I found out today that one of last year's committee members, Dr. Johnson, retired unexpectedly in July. Given I was preoccupied with us at the time, I didn't think much of it when I read the announcement on email."

"So you need to find another committee member. Is that a problem?"

She took a long breath, sat, and adjusted her top. "No. A replacement committee member found me before I realized I needed someone."

"Well then what's the problem?"

"Dr. Johnson was my co-presenter, the one who worked with me on that presentation I gave last May. Johnson was a chemistry teacher, a representative from the Science department, and the replacement needed to be from the same department. Like I said, someone has already stepped up and will be co-presenting with me during opening days. He's a biology teacher."

"Okay." Aaron opened his arm to welcome her back to cuddle, but she didn't lie down. Edginess was now taking root inside him. "Katrina, what's the problem?"

Her brow furrowed. "Do you remember that guy I told off during our first date? At Greene's?"

Oh, *hell* no. Aaron sat up, heart thumping. "Yeah, what was his name?"

"Cam Stevens, Campus Philanderer."

Her eyes were afraid. He mustn't lose his temper, but...*hell no*, Katrina. She needed to find someone else. He searched her eyes, which were searching his. He must *not* lose his temper around her.

"Say something." Her voice was a breath.

He couldn't lose his temper, so he lay down and opened his arm to welcome her back into his embrace.

She lowered herself to his side and hugged his chest. A moment later, she said, "Aaron, I hear your heart. It's pounding hard. Please say something."

He bit the inside of his cheek to keep his temper. "Isn't there someone else who can present with you? Why him?"

He would try to steal her.

He already had.

He would try again.

Aaron's right arm held her close while he stroked her thigh. He needed to be close.

"Are you mad?" Her voice was still too tiny for the strong woman she was.

"No," he lied, "but I don't trust him and I want you to find another presenter. And can you find a different Science representative while you're at it?" She traced his pec again, but it didn't feel good.

"I wish it were that easy. I've already discussed those options with Gen. Neither she nor I could come up with any way of replacing Stevens without me appearing immature or unprofessional."

"You met with him today?" Aaron couldn't keep the edge out of his voice now.

"Yes."

"And did he touch you? He grabbed your shoulder at the restaurant. I didn't like that."

"He didn't touch me. He was completely professional. He noticed my ring and I told him I was married. He remembered your name and put two-and-two together on his own. He gave me no reason to throw him off the committee or say no to co-presenting with me."

"And did he ever touch you before the restaurant?"

Katrina broke free and sat up. "Yes."

Her eyes were scared, but Aaron couldn't worry about that at the moment. The darkness was building inside him. "How many times has he touched you?"

She took a handful of her hair, tugged, and crushed her eyelids together. "Many."

Blood draining from his head, Aaron got out of bed. What the fuck was all this? He glared at his wife. "Have you touched *him*?"

"Well..." her tiny voice trailed off.

He couldn't look at her, so he took a seat in the club chair and stared at the wall. "Go on."

"Yes. We dated for a couple of months a few years ago, but I caught him cheating on me. So, I broke it off. He's kept flirting with me since."

"And you haven't reported him for harassment?" He continued to stare at the wall.

"Well, no, he never crossed a line."

His gaze snapped to hers. "He's crossed a line if he ever made you feel uncomfortable. If you're uncomfortable, it's harassment. Why didn't you report him?"

Tears welled in her eyes. "That's what I'm afraid to tell you."

Fuck. His heart was raging against his ribs, so he got up to pace the room. For the first time in two fucking years, he was feeling it. Full-blown panic.

Lightheaded, he forced himself to stop pacing and look at the woman. "Go ahead. Tell me."

"Well." Her eyes found his. "His flirting never made me uncomfortable. I always liked it. It turned me on. I didn't want it to stop."

She *had* to be kidding. He threw himself back into pacing.

"You want it to stop now, right? Report him." She got off the bed and put her arms around his waist, but he shrugged her off and walked away. "You *do* want it to stop now, don't you?"

She looked him in the eyes. "I swear to you I do not want him to touch me ever again." She looked at the floor. "But I can't promise I want his attentions to stop. They made me hot—"

"You are my WIFE!" Seeing red, he flew out of the room, down to the basement, and dropped to the dance floor for push-ups. He needed his muscles to burn. To get this shit out of his head before he lost it. He was on twenty-two when he heard her approach.

Twenty-three.

Twenty-four.

Twenty-five.

Twenty-six.

Twenty-seven.

Twenty-eight.

"I was going to say that his attentions made me hot for you." Her voice was thick with tears. "I couldn't get you out of my mind after seeing him today. You should have seen how jealous he was to find out I married you. Something about being with him today made me crazy to see you. Didn't you like that?"

He lost count. Even though he could do a hundred more, he rolled to his back and started crunches. He needed to burn this out of his head, damn it.

One.

Two.

Three.

Four.

Five.

He stopped. "How the fuck is this supposed to make me

feel better?" He was lying still, looking at the ceiling, his voice an unfamiliar blade. "You're telling me another man made you wet for me tonight. Yeah, I loved all of it except the fact that *I* didn't make you wet for me. STEVENS DID!"

Throttle her.

Oh no. It was starting.

Not again.

His heart flared.

Six.

Seven.

Eight.

Nine.

Ten.

Eleven.

"I figured you'd be upset, but I thought you should know. I thought a good wife would tell her husband about something like this. I thought I should be honest with you. I see why you're upset, but I ask you to see it from another perspective.

"Imagine that actress—damn—what's her name—that one you think is hot—coming in for physical therapy. You'd be bound to feel some sort of sexual attraction to her and I'd hope you'd be crazy to come home and bang my brains out instead of fantasizing about a tryst with her."

Throttle her.

Damn his head.

He needed to move, so he got up and went into the workshop to lift weights, leaving her behind.

She followed. "My point is that I'm not looking for an alternative. What I felt today energized me for you. I got married, Aaron. I didn't stop being a woman. I guess my body still responds if an attractive guy lets me know he finds me desirable. As long as that energy goes toward our sex life..."

His biceps were burning, but not enough to block out his

mind.

Throttle her.

Damn it.

"Aaron, I don't want him. I want you. It's always been you." Tears constricted her voice, but he couldn't look at her.

Throttle her, the whoring bitch.

An image of Katrina—dead, with skin white from cold—flashed in his mind.

He continued lifting, praying the burn would make his mind stop.

Until she left the room.

KATRINA

Katrina wiped her eyes. She hadn't wanted this. She hadn't asked for Stevens to remain an important part of her life. He just *was*. And she couldn't help that her body was still attracted to him in spite of her commitment to marriage and absolute love for Aaron. Her sex drive was natural, and she'd been honest with Aaron about everything.

Aaron would come around. Her honesty and their love would prevail. They had to.

Her reflection in the bathroom mirror told her Rudolph was in the house, so she blew her nose and threw the tissue in the trash. She grabbed a new box of tissues, carried it to her bedside table, and pulled Rosalie's journal out of the drawer.

The cover stared at her.

She settled herself in bed, sitting up with her back nestled into a pillow against the headboard, and flipped to the next journal entry.

August 5:

I had blood drawn for the quad-screen test today. I am glad that I am off work because the headaches are still here and my vision is off a bit. I am exhausted. Aaron waits on me hand-and-foot, thank goodness, because the morning sickness is still pretty bad.

How many entries were left, anyway?

She flipped through the remaining pages.

Ugh. Tear-stained spots. And Rose's handwriting was suffering. If Katrina weren't careful, there was a good chance some of her own tears would join Rose's on the pages. She blew her nose again.

August 11:

I got a call today. It was a nurse from my OB's office. My bloodwork indicates the baby has an 80% chance of having Trisomy 21 (Down syndrome) and a 20 percent chance of having Trisomy 18. They have scheduled an appointment for me to see a maternal-fetal specialist next week. They are keeping me off work until the appointment. Aaron was standing next to me while I took the call. I hung up the phone and fell into his arms. I cried for an hour. Aaron, on the other hand, did not show any emotion. He smiled and said it would all work out and he would love the baby no matter what.

August 20:

The specialist said he had never seen results of bloodwork so heavily in favor of Down syndrome before mine. He told us our options. I declined amniocentesis because of the hemorrhage. The baby's wrapping has already torn and there is no way I'm letting a needle in there. I don't want to lose this baby. The specialist praised our resolve and said that most women would go for the amniocentesis. (I like the specialist.) He wanted us to be aware, though, that we still have several weeks to abort if we change our minds. I am thankful Aaron agrees with me— we could NEVER kill our baby. We have a follow-up appointment in 4 weeks. I am written off work until that appointment.

September 18:

We saw the specialist again today. Baby's measurements support Down syndrome. Baby's head and femur measurements are small for gestational age. I cried on the table. He told us we are a special couple. If more people made our choice to follow through with pregnancy, there would be many more people with Down syndrome in our community. The specialist gave me a book to read. It is full of beautiful stories about children with Down syndrome. I have read half of the book during the past 6 hours.

I am still crying. To be honest, I am scared to death. I do not know anyone with Down syndrome. All I know is that I am looking at a lifetime of responsibility. Baby will not move out at age 18. Or will he? Oh yeah. I forgot to mention. It's a boy.

Katrina wiped her eyes, choking on the afterthought. "I forgot to mention. It's a boy." Rose grieved the death of her perfect Isaac, hadn't she? She could have gone into denial, but she grieved instead. Good for her.

September 19:
I am off work for the remainder of the pregnancy. (I forgot to mention that yesterday.) I finished reading the book this morning. I am still crying. Have been for weeks. The tension paired with these blasted headaches is debilitating. I'm glad I do not have to face work. I am so afraid. I am thankful for Aaron. I keep telling myself we can do anything together. We can even raise a baby with Down syndrome. We will be alright. Aaron is so strong. I ask him if he is scared at all and he says no. It will be our baby and that is all that matters to him. He is busy taking care of me and the house and going to work. I wish he could rest. Thankfully, our parents help me while he is gone. They take turns coming over and cooking for me during the day so I can rest as much as possible. God bless them all.

October 21:

I think I have finally cried myself out. At this point, if Isaac does not have Down syndrome, I think I'll be disappointed. I know all will be okay. Isaac will be okay, Down syndrome or not. Aaron is still strong. He has no worries these days, the way I used to have no worries.

November 30:

In hospital. Water broke. Not in labor. Isaac is at 32 weeks. Premature rupture of membranes (PROM). Specialist says Isaac will have extra challenges: premature delivery due to PROM on top of Down syndrome (well, most likely Down syndrome). Prematurity. They will induce labor once tests show his lungs are developed enough. My greatest wish is that he comes out breathing on his own. If he can breathe on his own, he will be okay. I am getting excited this pregnancy will be done soon. The headaches have continued throughout and have gotten a lot worse these past several weeks. And my vision is still screwy. Thank God I have been off work. I could not have handled the emotional rollercoaster, the pain, and work, too.

December 6:

Tests show Isaac's lungs are developed enough. They will induce labor today. I am excited. My precious baby is almost here.

And that was it. The rest of the pages were blank. Katrina closed the book and reexamined the quote on the cover: *Even if I knew that tomorrow the world would go to pieces, I would still plant my apple tree.* She slid her hand over the leather. "How intuitive were you, Rose? Your world did go to pieces, didn't it?"

"Did you finish it?" Aaron's voice was coming from the doorway.

"Yes." Katrina wished his voice relieved her, but she was a knot inside. She continued looking at the cover of the journal. "I thought she might say more."

"Where did she leave off?" He walked over and sat next to her on the edge of the bed.

She looked up and found him staring at the wall. "Before they induced labor. She said she was excited Isaac was about to be born."

Aaron was silent.

She slid Rose's note out of the journal and tapped Aaron's arm with it. "She wanted me to read this so I'd know what she went through, I guess."

He took the note without looking at her and whispered portions of it so she could hear. The strain in his voice tightened the knot inside her. "I want you to know that, somehow, I will find you for Aaron and our baby. They will need you. And you will be perfect. Please love my men like the mother and wife I had always hoped to be." Aaron exhaled. "She brought us together, didn't she? The dreams."

"She must have." The fact Aaron believed in the same

magic as she did loosened the knot a little.

He handed the note back to her and resumed looking at the wall. "She was in labor for fifteen hours, and then, when the time came, he was out in one push. Four pounds and breathing fine. She asked me if it looked like he had Down syndrome. I watched as the nurses worked with him and saw his neck. Too thick." His voice caught. "Before I could give her my answer, she went into a seizure.

"That seizure was the beginning of the end. We discovered a glioblastoma had been growing and growing. That explained the headaches and vision changes she'd been keeping secret. Inoperable. Treatments began too late. She declined so fast.

"And Isaac was in the NICU for five weeks while I ran around failing to be with either of them like I should have been. And I hated watching her suffer after she was so strong for him. She would have been the perfect mother. She *was* the perfect wife."

He turned to Katrina, his eyes full of tears. "And she was gone by the time Isaac was two months old. You have no idea how hard it was. All of it. It was hell." His voice was harsh. "You had once asked me how I avoided sex for three years. Well, sex didn't matter. Nothing mattered except Isaac.

"I'd lost everything that mattered except my little boy. And I promised her I would be the best dad I could be. But I would have given up my career. I would have given up my home. I would have given up all of my security to see her live so Isaac and I could have her. And here I am now, with a woman I thought topped even my precious Rosalie only to learn she isn't who I thought she was."

Katrina's head swirled. Her heart thumped her throat. The floor fell from beneath her.

She dropped the journal on the bed and slid next to her husband. She hugged his arm, but it was like stone and didn't ground her. Her swirling head loosened, threatening to tumble off her neck. She grasped at words and forced them out. "Aaron, I...I love you more than anything else in this world. You're my life now. I've only ever been open and honest with you. What did I do wrong?"

He stood without a glance at her. "He's going to want you even more now that you're taken. Be careful." And he left the room.

What?

That didn't answer her question.

She followed him, the knot inside twisting into spitting snakes. "You didn't answer me. I want to know. What did I do wrong? I told you the truth."

He halted at the top of the stairs but didn't turn around to face her. "You enjoy attentions from another man and you don't care that it hurts my feelings. That's what you did wrong." He stormed down the stairs.

The knot of snakes poisoned her blood, forcing her to follow her husband. "Wait a minute." No way in hell was he going to accuse her of not caring about his feelings. She was honest about Stevens *because* she cared. She was not a lying cheat.

She followed him through the kitchen and into the garage. How dare he ignore her? "I did nothing wrong. I told you the truth because I *do* care about your feelings!"

Aaron's eyes were hard. "No, you told me the truth to ease your conscience! You didn't do it for me. You did it for you!" He yanked the shop vacuum over to the truck, threw open the truck doors, pulled out the carpets, and threw them to the garage floor. Then he flicked on the vacuum.

She flicked it off. "Yes, I did it for me! Keeping a secret from my husband is not healthy for me. And it's not healthy for YOU!"

His face was red. "And it's healthy for me to hear my wife wants attention from OTHER MEN? Where did you get your psych degree anyway? Mail order?" And then he muttered, "My mom was right about you all along." He flicked on the vacuum.

Oh, *NO* he didn't. She flicked it off.

He threw down the vacuum hose and attempted to remove Isaac's car seat for whatever reason.

"What do you want me to say, Aaron? You want me to keep secrets? You want me to shut off my feelings? You want me to *lie*? Is that what you want in marriage? Because if you do, you married the *wrong girl*!

"I love feeling sexy and you know damn well you love me to be sexy! Yes, being near Stevens turned me on. FOR YOU! And I came home, crazy to have sex. WITH YOU! And I even told you the truth about it! And here you are, accusing me of being, what? Stupid? Unfaithful?"

Her blood pushed her further. "Yeah, so maybe my response to Stevens is naughty. Maybe it's a little perverse, but I'm not perfect! Cut me some slack! I'm human! I told you to take me off that pedestal!" She flicked on the vacuum and headed toward the kitchen door, letting more fly at the top of her lungs. "POOR AARON, MARRIED TO A 36-YEAR-OLD HOTTIE WHO WANTS HIM TO FUCK HER BRAINS OUT! POOR AARON, HIS WIFE TELLS HIM THE TRUTH!"

The truck door was slammed so hard it interrupted the shrill hum of the vacuum, so she spun around. Aaron was stalking toward her, anger pulsing beneath his skin. Raw power in the most beautiful package of man she'd ever seen.

She grasped the nearest support, the Road Runner behind her, and released her anger to embrace the electric current that was charging down her middle in spite of herself.

He pinned her against the car, his pelvis pressing into her just right. His mouth brushed her lips, and then he placed his lips next to her ear. "Tell me who you want, Katrina."

His words were a command and a plea.

His emotion intoxicated her.

Her heart pounded for him. She pulled his ear to her mouth and bit it. "You."

"Hello, Dr. Lopez-Keller."

Katrina had been afraid of this. Their presentation had gone well last week, professional synergy at its best, and Stevens was liable to think their chemistry would draw her to him. She finished packing, placing her Abnormal Psychology textbook and syllabi in her bag. When she looked up, he was leaning against the doorframe, sexy as ever.

"They have you teaching in the science wing this semester? Interesting." He approached the teacher's table and placed his things next to hers. Too close, but not uncomfortably close.

She slung her bag over her shoulder, wishing she didn't have to deal with this. "I've taught this class in this room for the past three years. It's a bit large due to the lab tables and I don't care for the sink." She gestured to the sink next to his things. "But it works. It's a nice change of setting."

She grabbed her iced tea and headed for the door, but she stopped in the doorframe to address him once more. "Cam, they slotted me into this room when the social science wing was under construction a few years ago. It's worked out fine. Given you've never taught in this classroom right after me, I never felt the need to request a location change. Please ensure I don't need to request one now."

As she stepped out of the classroom, she heard his voice.

"Don't do this."

She was frozen in the hallway, torn between walking away and walking back in. She needed to shut this down. For Aaron. For her marriage. But for some reason unknown to her, she didn't want to push him away.

She went back into the classroom, along with several students, and walked up to him at the front of the room where he was turning on the projector. "Don't do what?"

"Don't shut me out," he whispered. "I know I've lost. You deserve better than me, I know, but I'm not the asshole you think I am. You're a beautiful dancer and I want to play for you. Let my art accompany your art. Please give me that much. As your friend. Make it so I don't lose you completely."

The classroom was nearly full. "Now isn't the time." And she left him to his students.

Just under four months ago, she was going to give him another chance. She let him *believe* he would have another. And she felt the weight of guilt.

But why?

This question turned over and over in her mind as she walked to her office.

She hadn't told Stevens the truth about her marriage because...

She unlocked her office door and plopped on her chair.

The weight in her chest got a little lighter.

She'd been thinking about it all wrong.

Her physical attraction—her lustful, sex-deprived self— had blinded her to the fact that she'd let Stevens inside her emotional walls long ago.

That was it.

Every time she pushed him away, he'd responded respect- fully. Patiently.

He'd given her distance when she needed it. A hundred

percent.

But he *never gave up*.

He'd been kind. Helpful. Attentive. And in doing so, he'd proven something important. He hadn't been a monster to keep out. He'd been someone to keep close. His art. His support. His always being there. In their own messed up way, she and Stevens had become *friends*. Yet she hadn't seen it. No. Instead, she assumed the worst about him, and, by extension, she'd created a horrible image of Stevens in Aaron's mind. Which meant...

Aaron's current emotional state was her fault.

Stevens truly loved her. She'd known it for years but never admitted it to herself until now. And part of her loved him back, but that part of her was *platonic*.

Unaware, she'd naturally separated her physical cravings from her ability to love him as a friend. The moment of abandon on the dance floor was a misstep on their path, which was why she couldn't follow through with it. Cheap sex wasn't the way their friendship was supposed to play out. *This* was why she'd kept the marriage a secret. She hadn't wanted to hurt her friend when she thought everything between them was about sex.

Her newfound clarity lifted the weight even more. He was asking for something simple and true. Friendship.

Her biases and mistrust and fear had destroyed her chances of friendship as a little girl. And they'd tainted her perception of Stevens—Cam. Just as she'd done as kid, she'd looked for his faults and pushed him away. And his fault—infidelity—had been huge. Gigantic. But her judgment of him...

Her judgment had been driven by fear.

Yes, Cam made a mistake—for which he'd apologized—but she was still holding it against him. She'd badmouthed him to others. She'd treated him coldly. Harshly. And he never once did the same in return. No. Instead, Cam's words and actions had given and asked forgiveness a hundred times and more. Of the two of them, *she* was the one who needed to give and receive forgiveness.

She opened her email and composed the message she knew she must send.

```
From: Katrina Lopez
To: Camden Stevens
Date: Tuesday, September 12 at 2:28 PM
Subject: forgiveness?
--
Hello Cam. Please forgive me. I've
been rude, distant, and dishonest. You
don't deserve that. Yes, you made a
mistake in regard to me a long time
ago, but that doesn't give me the
right to hurt you back. I forgive you
and I hope you'll forgive me. Yes, we
are friends. But I love Aaron and his
little boy with all my heart. Maybe
someday you'll meet Isaac and then
you'll understand even better why I
need to say no to your offer to play
for a private dance. I'm learning to
trust and I choose to believe you
won't hurt me again. Thank you for
being my friend. Sincerely, Katrina.
--
Katrina Lopez, Ph.D., Associate
Professor of Psychology, Assessment
Committee Chairperson
GLCC
```

She unpacked her bag, put the materials on her bookshelf, and pulled out what she needed for tomorrow's General Psychology class. When she returned to her computer, Cam's reply was there.

```
From: Camden Stevens
To: Katrina Lopez
Date: Tuesday, September 12 at 2:33 PM
Subject: forgiveness?
--

Katrina, Understood. All forgiven. I'd
like to meet Isaac. Got class. Talk
another time. Your friend, Cam.
--

Camden Stevens, Ph.D.
Professor of Biology
Great Lakes Community College
```

Everything lifted inside. Welcoming this friendship felt right. She needed to trust it. She needed to trust, period. No more fear. No regret. Only possibilities and hopes and believing everything works out as it should. And maybe some-day, if she kept trusting and overcoming the hurts—because life would always deliver hurts—she'd rip out the footings of her emotional walls for good.

AARON

"Gosh, Aaron, it's been a long while."

"Yeah," Aaron's voice cracked, "seems I need to talk again." He couldn't believe he was back here. He'd thought he was free.

"And I see you brought a support person. Hello, Sarah."

Sheila gestured to the couch, welcoming Sarah to sit next to her son, and then turned on the desk lamp and turned off the overhead lights. Sheila's notes must've reminded her that he found the soft light calming. "What would you like to talk about?"

He stared at the nameplate on her desk:

Sheila Thompson, Ph.D., Clinical Psychologist

Sheila didn't look a day older than the last time he saw her over two years ago. She was a striking woman, nearly as tall as Aaron, with rich dark skin and no-nonsense ebony eyes he felt compelled to obey.

"Yeah, um." He glanced at Sarah. Her eyes were red, but she wasn't crying. Instead, she was rigid with negativity. He felt it rolling off her. He shook his cloudy head. "I'm not sleeping well again. Thoughts have come back. Bad thoughts. And I need to get rid of them."

Sheila waited.

Sarah waited.

Aaron hadn't told Sarah anything because he wanted Sheila to buffer the conversation for him. He couldn't handle his mother's negativity on top of everything else, but he needed her to know why he was having a relapse because if things got worse...

Also, part of him hoped his openness during this session would convince his mom to get the help she needed.

He swallowed past the lump in his throat. "A couple months ago, I got married to the woman of my dreams. Katrina. I've known her since I was five. She's amazing. And then something happened that snapped me. I just want to get back to where I was when I was happy. Before the thing." His head replayed the image of Stevens touching Katrina in the restaurant. Then his mother's warnings, cold and scratchy, sounded in his brain.

But both women remained silent and still. Waiting.

"She works with this guy I can't trust. He has a history of flirting with her. She told me she likes his attention, but that she never has, and never will, have sex with him. My head doesn't trust her now. My head keeps telling me to throttle her." His insides squeezed at the sound of those words coming from his mouth. And this was why he needed to come. Sheila didn't wince at the fact Aaron's head was telling him to strangle his wife.

"And have you told Katrina about these thoughts?"

"No. She doesn't even know I have OCD. I only told her I have some anxiety. She doesn't know how messed up I was. Or how messed up I am, apparently."

Sarah leaned forward, about to say something, but Sheila put up a hand and stopped her.

"And why not?" Sheila asked. "Why haven't you told her?"

The black emptiness he'd been carrying inside grew darker at the thought of telling Katrina. The truth would drive her away and losing her would break him.

His shrug felt pathetic. "She's dealt with so much in her life. Abusive father. PTSD. I don't want her to worry about me. I want to be strong for her."

Sheila wrote a note. "What does Katrina do for a living?"

Aaron sniffed. "She's a clinical psychologist who teaches college."

"And you want to be strong for *her*?" Her voice was as no-nonsense as her eyes. "Sounds like you need to let her be strong for *you*. Close your eyes and begin with your right foot. And Sarah, you might as well do the same. It'll feel good."

Aaron did as he was told and participated in the progressive muscle relaxation exercise.

When finished, his body was tranquil.

"How do you feel?" Sheila asked.

"Like some darkness has left me."

"Alright. Now tell me all the symptoms you're experiencing. Is there anything beyond the thoughts of throttling her?"

Aaron slid his hands down his thighs, applying deep pressure. "Yeah. Images of her cold, dead eyes flash through my mind. I've been alleviating my anxiety by cuddling her. That helps, but she doesn't know anything about it."

"That's a lovely compulsion. Cuddling."

"But cuddling out of fear doesn't feel good."

Sheila put on her readers and took some notes. "How frequent are the symptoms?"

"I get them every time I see her, like first thing in the morning and when I get home from work, so two to three times a day."

She continued writing and so he ventured another glance at his mother.

Sarah was looking up at a delicate mobile hung from the ceiling, placed in just the right spot for someone to lose their thoughts in its dance. Seagulls gently twirling.

"Penny for your thoughts," Sheila asked, holding out a penny she grabbed from the jar on her desk labeled *Coppers*. She offered the penny to Sarah.

Sarah didn't take the penny, so Sheila laid it on her desk. But Sarah did take a breath as if about to speak, so Aaron waited.

His mother had come reluctantly because her concern about Aaron's emotional agitation outweighed her desire to avoid talking with a psychologist. She'd made that much clear to him during their ride to the office. She'd said nothing else.

And she remained silent now.

Aaron got up and took the penny, as well as the sheet of paper Sheila was holding out for him. "Nice mobile."

Sheila smiled. "I got that last year at a craft show. Each wooden seagull is hand-crafted and hand-painted, each quite detailed if you look closely. I've found it to be a soothing addition to my office space. I'm glad you like it."

Aaron looked at the notes she'd written on the paper. "So, my homework is to do progressive muscle relaxation exercises morning and night and to work on identifying the trigger for my thoughts." He scoffed. "I know the trigger."

She smiled. "You think you do anyway. You're going to tell me it's that gentleman Katrina works with, right?"

He nodded. "Everything was fine until that issue came up. I went for two years without a single intrusive thought. I was happy." He grabbed his hair in frustration. "She was perfect, but it all went to hell."

"She sounds like quite a woman, but you know nothing is perfect. Everything has flaws, even that mobile." She pointed at the seagulls. "One of them has a chipped beak. It's been hanging in here for a year, but I didn't notice until a client pointed it out to me last week.

"Think, Aaron. You don't have the trigger all figured out yet. It's not as obvious as you believe it to be. The gentleman she works with is not entirely the answer."

"No, he's not." Sarah, crumpled and worn, looked her son in the eyes. Something warm was there in his mother's gaze. It was a warmth he hadn't seen since Rose died. Tears slid down her cheeks. "Katrina is just about perfect, Aaron." She took the tissue Sheila held out for her. "You already have the answer, love, and I'll tell you why.

"What I'm about to say *cannot* leave this office. Ever." Sarah's eyes flashed warning at Sheila, as if Sheila would break confidentiality, and then she looked down at her own hands wringing in her lap.

"I cheated on your father." Sarah's voice was quiet. "Before I had you. It was only a kiss. But it *was* a kiss and it was tied to feelings. And, to me, that was cheating.

"We'd been married a year. I was feeling insecure. I did it. It was wrong. And I've regretted it ever since. I *love* your father, Aaron. I always have. But the problem is..." She sobbed. "I never *told* him. And y-you have Katrina, a woman who *told* you. She told me she was honest. She-she told me she'd never hurt you on purpose. And I didn't believe her. I didn't trust her. But no!"

Sarah's face contorted into self-disgust. "I kept a secret from your father all these years because *I* didn't have the courage to do what Katrina has done for you! My god, Aaron, that woman may not be perfect, but she is! For you! She is!"

Pity. That's what Aaron felt as his mother, small and child-like, mumbled self-critical remarks to herself between sobs. Her entire married life had been spent feeling guilty and dishonest? No wonder she had generalized anxiety diso—

That was it.

Anxiety. Guilt. Hurt. Katrina's honesty about Stevens was protecting Aaron from exactly those things.

And in being honest, she'd been protecting *herself.*

Of course.

Katrina wouldn't live with negative feelings inside. She'd tried to tell him that her honesty was healthy, but he hadn't believed her. Instead, his OCD made him lose faith in his wife.

"I'd like to see you again in two weeks."

Sheila's voice gave Aaron's heart a start. He doubted the intrusive thoughts would leave any time soon, but he felt buoyant again. He felt like he got his wife back, and he couldn't wait to see her.

Sheila continued, "If the symptoms get any worse, please call and we can arrange an appointment before then. And I believe it would be wise to tell your wife what is going on. I'm sure she loves you and would want to know, especially considering she's a psychologist."

He gave Dr. Thompson a half-smile. "Thank you. I'll think about it."

"And Sarah?" Sheila touched Sarah's arm to draw her attention away from the hands wringing in her lap. "I have an opening next week if you'd like to talk to me again."

Sarah's bloodshot eyes looked up at Sheila and, without a sound, Sarah said yes.

"So how was work today?" Aaron attempted to keep his voice free of concern and waited for Katrina's response, which he knew would be as matter-of-fact as ever.

"I didn't see him. You know I only see him on Tuesdays, Thursdays, and committee days. Today is none of those. And, beyond that, he and I are only friends. That's all we ever were. It's all we'll ever be."

This had become her mantra, and he never tired of the reassurance.

Aaron continued pushing Isaac's jogging stroller down the trail. It was a mid-September evening, an hour before sunset, and his family, including Jake, was enjoying a cool breeze and rays of sun shining through the canopy of rustling cottonwoods. He breathed in the crisp scent of autumn.

The moment was nearly perfect. He had his beautiful wife and his beautiful son and this beautiful evening. If only the thoughts would leave him alone. He tried to block them, but they skipped through his head, taunting him to play their disturbing game. He hadn't told Sheila the truth. The thoughts happened more than two to three times a day. They messed with him all the time.

"Isaac, do you see something?" Katrina swatted Aaron's rear, a welcome jolt. "Stop, Aaron."

Aaron obeyed.

She knelt next to Isaac in the stroller and pointed at something on the ground near a bench on the side of the trail. "Isaac, I think I see something shiny. Do you see it, too?"

Aaron watched Isaac watch Katrina's face.

"Look where I'm pointing, peanut." Katrina used her free hand to turn Isaac's head in the appropriate direction. "Do you see it Aaron?" She looked into Aaron's eyes.

Oh, man, he loved her eyes. He held her gaze and found his smile. She deserved his smile. She was true and kind and all he ever wanted. He knew he could trust her. He knew in his heart. If only his head would stop playing graphic horror scenes of her demise, he'd once again be the happiest man on the planet.

He bent to look at the place where she was pointing and nodded to acknowledge that he also saw something shining on the ground near the bench.

"Let's check it out." Her voice bounced with enthusiasm, so Aaron smiled a little more.

She unbuckled Isaac and removed him from the stroller. Holding their son's little hand, she led him over to investigate. Aaron followed and parked the stroller next to the bench.

Isaac approached the shiny object—a present, the size of a small pencil box, wrapped in bright blue foil and shiny silver ribbon. He grabbed it and threw it into the ferns that lined the trail.

"Isaac, don't throw." Aaron tried not to smile at the misbehavior.

"I'll get it." Katrina stepped into the ferns. "You two take a seat."

Aaron scooped Isaac off the ground, settled him on his lap, and watched his wife bend over to grab the package.

Her long, dark hair blew in the breeze as she stood up and studied the wrapping. "It says, 'To Aaron.'" Her large eyes played with his.

His smile wasn't genuine even though he was trying. He held out his hand as she bounced into the seat next to him to hand him the package.

Aaron read the gift tag aloud. "To Aaron. From God. Happy Birthday!" The chuckle that escaped felt good. "From God, huh?"

She beamed. "Definitely from God."

"Maybe it's that new tie I've been praying for."

Katrina's eyes claimed ignorance.

His curiosity fueled more of a smile as he pulled back a portion of the wrapping. He positioned the package for Isaac. "Pull the wrapping, Isaac."

Isaac patted the wrapping and smiled.

"That's close enough." Aaron continued unwrapping the box, allowing the little boy inside to venture out for the first time in weeks. "Wow. A pink pencil box. Just what I've always wanted." He looked to the sky. "Thank you, God."

Katrina laughed. "You're such a dork. Open it."

This box couldn't hold anything that topped season tickets to the Detroit Pistons. He snapped open the lid and pulled back several layers of pink and blue tissue paper.

Tears leaked from his eyes.

The lump in his throat made it hard to swallow.

He looked at her in a world that stood still.

She was smiling, silent tears running down her cheeks. "He or she should be due in June."

Isaac played with the tissue paper as Aaron looked closely at the plastic stick taped to the bottom of the pencil box. Two pink lines, clear as day. He wiped his eyes. "When did you take the test?"

"This morning. My period was due in two days and I was so excited to see if I might be pregnant that I didn't wait. The two pink lines showed up immediately. I wanted to surprise you for your birthday. Surprised?"

He felt her excitement trying to force itself inside him. He set down the box, secured Isaac in his stroller, and pulled her to standing. Then he hugged her. Hard. "Surprised. Happily surprised." He kissed her head.

His tears fell into her hair. She was making sure Isaac wouldn't be alone.

But his damn head.

"I have to tell you something." The words had escaped without his consent, causing his heart to pound.

The beautiful woman who was carrying his beautiful baby needed to know the truth about him.

Her wet eyes looked up at him. "What is it?"

"I have OCD." Saying the words sent Aaron off-balance, so he stepped back to keep himself upright.

She stepped back, eyes wide. "I didn't see that coming, but okay."

He couldn't look at her, so he took a seat and cradled his head in his hands. "After Rose died, I developed morbid obsessions. My head kept telling me I'd kill Isaac. I had visions of drowning him. Cutting him. Smothering him. I believed I might do something horrific, so I threw out all sharp objects and used butter knives to cut everything, including steak.

"I was afraid I'd kill him if I had anything sharp within reach. I gave him sponge baths for months because I didn't trust myself to give him a regular bath. And I removed all soft objects from my home, including my own pillow. No pillows. No plush toys. I didn't want temptation to smother him. That's where my panic attacks came from." Throat tight, Aaron looked up at her blank face.

"Go on," she said, her voice calmer than expected.

He swallowed through the tightness. "After a few months of living in fear, I realized my behavior was irrational. I went to a clinical psychologist. She diagnosed me with OCD and taught me to trust myself again."

Katrina looked at Isaac for a long moment and then returned her gaze to Aaron. "Is that all?"

He looked at the ground. "My head keeps telling me to throttle you."

"Since when?" Again, her voice was calm.

"Since you told me about Campus Philanderer."

Her breath caught, and then she did the unthinkable.

Facing Aaron, she straddled his legs on the bench and sat on his lap, placing her upper body within a foot of his. When he looked up, he found tears streaming down her cheeks.

She took his hands in her warm grasp and placed them on her neck. "Squeeze hard."

His thumbs trembled against her throat.

Her skin pulsed against his fingers. Delicate. It would only take a few moments, wouldn't it? He'd break her without even trying.

Heart pounding, he gagged on the thought.

"I said *squeeze*." She commanded the words in his favorite way, which released his tears.

He tore his hands away, grasped the bench, and swallowed. "I could never do that to you." His breath shuddered. "I could never do that to anyone."

She sniffed and smiled. "Exactly. And do you know why?"

He slid his hands onto her thighs and stroked them. The act felt like home. "Maybe, but I want you to tell me."

She lifted his chin, so he looked into her eyes, earnest and in love. "You could never do it because you're not a *psychopath*."

He blinked away his tears. Her words were so direct. So obvious. So ridiculously simple. It all was ridiculously simple, wasn't it?

"Your thoughts frighten you, which makes all the difference. You're not a monster. We need to get you past the fear. I'll help you learn to dismiss your intrusive thoughts. But let's start with this. You will never lose me to Cam Stevens or anyone. And you won't lose me to cancer. Fate wouldn't do that to you twice. Isaac won't be alone." She rubbed her pelvis. "And you can trust that I love you. *Forever*."

Aaron sniffed and wiped his eyes. "Yeah, I guess I need to thank you for my birthday present. It's a pretty good one. Relief and a pregnancy all in one day. Shit."

She smiled. "I'm glad."

Then he saw it. His mind captured an image destined for the piano room wall. Katrina's face, tilted and smiling, framed by gorgeous locks blowing in the breeze. Understanding, caring eyes would be the focal point.

Their children would see him *draw*.

He pulled her tight to his chest and nestled his nose in her hair. "I'm amazed you could keep the pregnancy to yourself all day."

"Well, I was having a little trouble resisting the urge to call you and spill the beans, so I used an outlet to stop myself. I started a journal when I was at work."

Aaron shook his head. "Another journal? I don't like how the last one ended."

"I'm not sure I agree. I think the ending led to a pretty

wonderful beginning." She pulled out of his embrace, winked at him, and turned her attention to Isaac. "You're going to be a big brother, Isaac. Can you sign brother?" She got up and showed Isaac the sign for brother.

Isaac watched her hands and smiled. She kissed him on the cheek and took Aaron's hand.

Her grasp felt safe, a sensation that claimed his heart. His core. And he knew.

Beautiful Dr. Katrina Lopez-Keller was his. Forever.

Katrina's Journal

September 18:

Hello Journal! I have some big news! I pulled it off. I surprised Aaron on his 36th birthday. And now that he knows, I can tell you. Ready for it?

I'M PREGNANT!

I wrapped the positive pregnancy test in a pretty package. I'd asked my wonderful father-in-law to leave it for us to find at our special spot in the woods—the place where we exchanged our vows on July 4 of this year—but, surprise of all surprises, my slow-to-warm-up mother-in-law asked to do it instead! (I think she might like me a little bit.) Aaron was totally surprised. And it was such a beautiful evening, too. Perfect! Well...almost perfect...

He's still struggling to be happy. My honesty about Cam devastated him. Turns out Aaron has a grim mental disorder that he's been keeping secret. After he disclosed that much, he explained that his mother has a serious anxiety disorder. Thankfully, she's agreed to go to therapy. Gotta love it. All this time I was feeling rejected, but the real issue lived within her.

Anyway...I finally found the perfect spot for the rose bush

Aaron bought me in the spring. I've taken good care of it in the pot all summer and it should survive.

It turns out my new home—Aaron's home—has an empty space in a garden bed near the back of the property. The space was reserved for an apple tree that Rosalie had planned to plant in the spring following Isaac's birth. After she died, Aaron left the space alone. He was kind of busy, you know, learning to parent a baby all by himself. Anyway, he's nearly finished building a gorgeous cedar arbor in that very spot. His rose bush and some others will join the arbor in the perfect location for a rose garden.

So, why didn't we plant an apple tree in honor of Rose? Well, we felt that Rose's Garden should have roses! Besides, her apple tree is thriving in the house with Mommy and Daddy. He shares his fruit everywhere he goes—making people happy through his beautiful eyes and angel's smile.

And baby makes four.

The End

AFTERWORD

I'm weird. Many authors tell about how they always wanted to write a novel (ever since they were old enough to hold a crayon) and wrote story after story after story until their dream came true, but this was not the case for me. You see, I never once desired, or planned, to write a novel.

Rosalie's Apple Tree is one of those stories that came from a mystical place that chose me to tell it. It did not come from me —it came *through* me.

I have a demanding career and a full-time family; I have no time to be a writer. But that didn't stop this story from falling into my head one winter day when I was a 40-year-old without any thought of writing for an audience.

On that dreary December day, *Rosalie's Apple Tree* started writing itself. I recall it clearly. I was playing on the living room floor with my young children when two characters started having a conversation in my head. The characters' voices were so determined that I told my kids I had to get to a computer to write a story that was telling itself in my mind. When my husband came home and found me at the computer (when I wasn't supposed to be working), he asked what I was doing. I said, "Apparently, I'm writing a story."

I had no idea what kind of story it would be, but I wrote for five hours that night. A year later, the first draft of *Rosalie's Apple Tree* was complete.

Given that I'd never planned to write a novel, having one come out of me over the course of a year was odd. The story was stubborn—it wouldn't shut up. It insisted I continue writing even when I wanted it, or needed it, to leave me alone. It kept coming when it was inconvenient. It kept coming when I was tired. It kept coming when I was stressed from my responsibilities as a psychologist, wife, and mother. It kept coming and coming...until I wrote it all.

And the dreams. Yes, the dreams. Prior to the story falling into my head, I'd been having regular (sensual) dreams about a particular someone from my past. There was no triggering event to cause the dreams. There was no sense in having the dreams. My husband knew all about them (no, they weren't about him), and we were both dumbfounded as to why they kept occurring so regularly. These dreams came to me for years, and, eventually, integrated themselves into the story. And when the story was finished, the dreams stopped.

But not for always.

Given that I hadn't had any training in writing fiction prior to writing *Rosalie's Apple Tree*, it was important for me to learn the craft and dive into the editing process. So I threw myself into self-study in the years following completion of that first draft. During those years, I revised the manuscript extensively —many times.

Eventually, I believed myself to be ready to query literary agents, and so I did. At that point, I realized my self-confidence was not where it needed to be. I had doubt, lots of doubt, and I often wanted to give up the whole idea. But every time I decided to give up on *Rosalie's Apple Tree, the dreams came back.*

It was clear to me that this story *wanted* to be told, so it became my mission to ensure that it achieved publication. After all, a story that comes out of nowhere and insists on being written must be intended for someone; only the reader will know if it was intended for them.

If you're a reader for whom this story was intended, I'm thrilled you and this book found each other. I consider myself blessed to have been chosen to bring this story to you. And I thank you, deeply, for reading it.

Acknowledgments

My team is small but precious.

My husband. Look what you've done. Haven't you tired of encouraging me? For over 30 years, you've supported my artistic endeavors without fail, and this book is the greatest one, by far. You have read and read and read my writing and never hold back severe critiques. You never fear telling me what needs reworking and what needs to go. Meanwhile, you take care of our life while I'm busy making this dream happen. Your guidance is spot on. I will never be able to thank you enough for what you've done to support me as a writer, an artist, a mother, or woman. I'm so proud to say that this book baby is mine and, guess what, babe...it's your baby, too!

My kids. You told me to keep going, and so I did. It's so hard dividing time between family, work, and a writing life, but you wouldn't let me quit. You made sure I saw this dream come true while you worked on growing up. This book would not exist without your understanding and encouragement. I'll always treasure the gift that is each one of you.

Marlene. The most voracious reader I know. You believed in my writing when I didn't, and I kept going because of it. I hope this book has made you proud. I'm blessed to have your support.

Lily. You have helped me persevere in the face of self-doubt. Your endless support, comforting words, wisdom, patience, and insight have helped make me an author. And your belief in this story gave me the courage to publish it in its entirety.

My friends. Your message to me was the same: persevere, believe, and publish. Thank you, my dear friends. I did it!

My beta readers. You provided valuable feedback that helped me find where my story began, where my story lost itself, and where to make make it stronger. You also believed in my poetic prose and helped me remember that my writing is something special (as part of me).

So many poets and writers, past and present, who continually inspire me to write better next time.

And finally, all the beautiful souls who have supported my poetry and prose on social media, particularly Instagram. Your positive comments, encouragement, and excitement when I post something mean the world to me. Your positivity makes my world brighter. Please keep spreading those good vibes to all the artists and writers and people. The world needs them!

Ann Garcia has a Ph.D. in psychology and is the biological mother of a child who has Down syndrome. Her poetry and fiction, which are highly introspective and evocative, primarily explore nature, self, and love. She draws inspiration from waters and woodlands within the Great Lakes region of the USA and her life as a wife/artist/mother/scientist.

Ann is the author of *Fantastical for Real* (prose poetry) and *Love Me Like October* (poetry and photography). She is a contributor in publications by Humana Obscura, Sunday Mornings At The River, and The First Line Poets Project, among others. Her poetic writing style flows into her fiction. *Rosalie's Apple Tree* is her first novel.

Ann is an active artist on Instagram where she shares her photography, poetry, and her newfound creative outlets, watercolor and digital art. Find her on Instagram @solaceinraindrops or in the nearest garden where she's bound to be taking photos of blooms, bees, or slime mold while holding off two corgis and trying not to hear her kids yelling, "Mom!"

anngarciabooks.com

riverblossoms.com

Reader's Group Questions for Rosalie's Apple Tree

by Ann Garcia

INTRODUCTION

Two lists of discussion questions are presented here. The first list, which does not reveal aspects of the plot, presents basic questions easily explored by readers at any point in their journey through this novel. The second list provides in-depth, though-provoking questions and is best reserved for readers who have finished reading *Rosalie's Apple Tree*.

BASIC QUESTIONS:

1. Did this story engage you immediately, or did it take you a while to "get into" it? Why?
2. What was your favorite part of the book? Your least favorite?
3. Who was your favorite character? Your least favorite?
4. Which scene has stuck with you the most?

5. Which aspects of the story did you find most interesting? Which aspects of the story did not hold your interest?

6. Were you surprised by complications or twists in the storyline? If so, which ones?

7. Why do you think the author chose to tell the story from both Aaron's and Katrina's viewpoints?

8. Do you want to read another book by this author? Why or why not?

9. Is the ending satisfying? If so, why? If not, how would you change it?

10. If you could ask the author any question, what would you ask?

IN-DEPTH QUESTIONS AND TOPICS:

1. What was your inner experience while reading *Rosalie's Apple Tree*? How did the story affect your emotions? Did this story change you in any way? Has it broadened your perspective?

2. Did Katrina's preference for a solitary life frustrate you, or could you relate to it? What are your thoughts about the social-emotional balance in Katrina's life in the beginning of the story compared to the end? In the end, do you feel that the author left Katrina in a healthy social-emotional space? Why or why not?

3. Did Aaron's drive for a family frustrate you or could you relate to it? What are your thoughts about Aaron's psychological status in the beginning of the story compared to the end? In the

end, do you feel that the author left Aaron in a healthy psychological space? Why or why not?

4. Why does Katrina behave as she does? Discuss some of her behaviors that would put you outside your comfort zone and why. Discuss some of her behaviors that seem foolish to you and why. Is there anything about Katrina that you admire? Is there anything about her that you dislike?

5. Answer the same questions from #4 for Aaron's character.

6. If you were in Katrina's shoes, how would you have handled that first introduction to Isaac? Compared to her, do you feel you would have been more open or more closed in terms of accepting Isaac?

7. If you were in Rosalie's shoes, how would you have handled the news about expecting a child with Down syndrome?

8. Did you learn something about Down syndrome while reading this novel? If so, what did you learn?

9. Are there any secondary storylines that you would like the author to expand in the future? If so, discuss why you're interested in them.

10. The author chose not to close the bedroom door on the reader, so *Rosalie's Apple Tree* contains explicit sex scenes. How did the sex scenes contribute to story development? How did the sex scenes contribute to character development?

11. How did you feel about the dreams? Did you appreciate how the author presented them in the text or would you have integrated them differently? Or would you have preferred them to be left out of the story?

12. One of the author's goals was to write respectfully and sensitively about the challenging topics included in the story (i.e., mental illness, domestic abuse, cancer/death, pregnancy loss, Down syndrome). Do you feel that she succeeded? Why or why not?

13. Did certain parts of the book make you uncomfortable? If so, why did you feel that way? Did this discomfort lead you to new understandings about life that you hadn't thought about before?

14. How does the book's title, *Rosalie's Apple Tree*, work in relation to the book's contents? If you could give this book a title, would you change it? If so, what would your title be?

15. What themes did the author explore? Which symbols did the author use to reinforce main ideas? And, specifically, what does *Rosalie's Apple Tree* represent?

16. How does the cover art reflect themes in the book? If you don't think it does, what would you depict on the cover if you were the cover designer?

17. Did any passages strike you as insightful or profound? Discuss.

18. Did you enjoy the author's writing style? Name some other authors who have a similar writing style. Name some other books that have a similar feel to *Rosalie's Apple Tree*.